Touched by Evil

Growing Up as a Serial Killer

Henry R. Hermann

ISBN 978-1-961017-33-7 (Paperback)
ISBN 978-1-961017-34-4 (Ebook)

Inquiries and Book Orders should be addressed to:

Leavitt Peak Press
17901 Pioneer Blvd Ste L #298, Artesia, California 90701
Phone #: 2092191548

Acknowledgment: The author would like to thank artist Bradford Shaw Hermann for creating the front cover of this book, using DALL·E 2 at Openai.com.

Chapter 1

Conception Failures

I believe we'd agree that life is often unfair. Ralph and Jennifer Housler found this out early in life. They had promised themselves the world when they graduated from Warren Eastern High School on the west end of Canal Boulevard in New Orleans.

After getting married in their late teens, they both had held various odd jobs off-and-on that never brought in much of an income. Instead of finding their way to fame and fortune, their lives went through some rough times, and they didn't really know how to make things better. It was as though they were under some kind of voodoo curse.

Ralph, had completed a couple of years at Delgado Trades School and an additional year of college at the University of New Orleans, but he lacked direction and disliked studying. Some would say he was a bit lazy.

Consequently, his grades were terrible, and his attendance fees were causing serious financial problems, resulting in tension between him and Jennifer. He took a break from his schooling one summer and went to work full time to help pay off college debts, and he never returned to get his degree.

Why should he, he thought? Times were getting better because of the additional income, and he had begun to see a faint light for a better life at the end of the long, dark tunnel they had become adjusted to. However, times got worse with the years. As with Jennifer, he hopped from one job to another, always looking for greener pastures, and they never were able to put money aside for a rainy day. And, of course, his progressively increasing drinking problem and piss-poor attitude about life didn't help matters.

They often wondered what had happened to the great life they had planned for themselves? The crowning blow was a devastating hurricane in which everything they had was destroyed. Nothing was insured, and it didn't look like they'd ever get out of the hole they were in. They, in fact, were becoming destitute, and the emotional burden negatively affected every aspect of their daily lives.

Because of their moving from job to job, they never developed a decent health plan. They never felt they needed one. They were young and healthy and felt invulnerable to the outside world. It was difficult for them to understand that one never knows what life has in store for them.

Right about the time he began to think that life sucks, Ralph landed a job at a used car lot which occasionally brought in some decent money, but it wasn't long before he was injured on the job and had to enter a period of recuperation. Ralph's medical treatment and the money required to get him through his convalescent period had to come mostly out of his very shallow pockets.

With Ralph not bringing in any money, their life was facing a crisis when, out of the blue, Jennifer made the decision of her life.

"I want to have a child, Ralph." Ralph momentarily went into shock.

Although he and Jennifer at one time had talked about having children, he knew there was no way in hell they could have and raise a child with his lack of income, especially with the bills that remained unpaid. What she was proposing was sheer madness.

In addition, his disposition about life in general had become quite soured by their continuing unfortunate circumstances. Jennifer, however, felt having a child may bring them back together again, make life worth living, so to speak. Ralph rightly concluded that they were set in their ways now, and he was pretty sure he couldn't tolerate a child, no matter how good he or she may be.

Nevertheless, under pressure from a determined Jennifer, Ralph reluctantly consented to at least listen to what she had to say. To be honest, his decision was based on the lesser of two evils. It was either start a family and make an attempt to tolerate a pain-in-the-ass child or listen to Jennifer's never-ending bitching, which he was sure would never cease until she got her way. He wasn't sure which of the two evils was least tolerable.

Their love-making, the little they had, had been lacking any degree of passion for quite some time, but they now had a goal. At least, Jennifer had one. After a year of trying without getting pregnant, both Ralph and Jennifer wondered where the source of the problem was. *Was it due to the stress of their lifestyle,* they wondered, *or could something be physically wrong with one of them?* Although Ralph occasionally seemed to express some very faint signs of empathy for Jennifer, he actually felt this may be the end to her desire to have a child, and for him, this was good.

However, he wasn't aware that the force behind Jennifer's desire was the only thing keeping her going. Take this away, and she had no desire to even live.

She was determined that this would change their lives, no matter what Ralph thought. Following further failures, Jennifer felt it was time to seek professional assistance, in spite of the increasing financial problems they were having.

To avoid additional strife, Ralph, once again reluctantly went along with her decision. He was getting tired of her bull shit, though. He had other, more important things to do. What these other things were seemed to be deeply locked away in his brain.

After approaching gynecologist Dr. Harry Stockwell with the problem, Jennifer went through all the required tests to determine why a pregnancy had never occurred. Ralph reluctantly did the same with the few tests he was required to do, but not without complaining. As it turned out, both she and Ralph were found to be responsible for their failure to get pregnant. She didn't produce viable eggs, although her uterus appeared to be in reasonably good condition, and Ralph's sperm count was extremely low. Ralph took it hard, not because it appeared they couldn't have a child, but because he felt his manly libido had been threatened.

"Don't worry, hon," Jennifer said, misdiagnosing Ralph's concern. "We'll find a way." Ralph, on the other hand, didn't see an end to her bull shit. She, in her mind, didn't realize he really didn't give a damn.

After advice from Dr. Stockwell, a regulated protocol was followed to find out why the Houslers weren't functioning in a healthy reproductive way. For Jennifer, there was the stress of progesterone suppositories, along with the ingestion of doxycycline antibodies and methylprenisolone pills. She had to undergo physical exams, PAP smears, further uterine cavity evaluations, and other laboratory tests in preparation for baseline ultrasound and estradiol/utilizing hormone blood tests, more injections, further testing, and God knows what else. She was feeling used and abused. Ralph's examination was simply a sperm count evaluation.

While they both were experiencing stress from all the testing and the thought of even more exams, their main concern was actually the cost of everything. They had already spent what appeared to them to be a fortune on tests and attempts to get pregnant. Their bills were mounting to a point at which Ralph thought they would forever be in debt. He was afraid to think of the hours of overtime he'd have to work in order to continue paying their bills. *Where was it all going to end?*

When the Houslers approached Dr. Stockwell about the possibility of obtaining financial assistance, he told them that he would like to help them, but there was no way he or his evaluation team could foot the bill for what they needed to get Jennifer pregnant. Upon making his statement, he noticed Jennifer's immediate disappointment, and he wondered if he had been too harsh with the evaluation. As tears appeared in the corners of Jennifer's eyes, he decided to recommend the Brockman Fertility Clinic.

Jennifer directed a serious stare at him and asked, "What is that."

"It's a new facility on Canal Boulevard," he said. "The people who run it are fertility specialists, and in addition to doing routine fertility procedures and abortions, they carry out research on difficult pregnancies, and they have a large sperm and egg bank. Occasionally, they obtain grants to test new fertilization procedures.

"From what they tell me, it's possible to do almost anything with DNA and fertilization these days. They may have a technique that would work for you. Would you consider talking with them to see if they can help?"

"Of course, we would, Dr. Stockwell," Jennifer said. "Would you call them for us?"

"Yes, I can do that."

"Thank you." Judging by what he said and how he said it, Jennifer realized this was their last opportunity. Ralph remained quiet, apparently in a stupor over having to go along with Jennifer again.

Chapter 2

A Proposition

Dr. Cornwall, the consulting physician at the Brockman Fertility Clinic, had been temporarily hired by the clinic on a part-time basis, to intercede between clients and their staff. Other than this, the way the clinic functioned was a little mysterious.

Dr. Steven Morrison, the clinic's director, had never been seen and could only be reached by phone. However, there was no reason to talk to the director. Dr. Cornwall's function in the company included carefully listening to each client's dilemma and introducing them to the staff that would serve them.

After reading Ralph and Jennifer's reports on failing reproductive issues, he immediately concluded that their situation left them with no options but to receive the clinic's assistance. He commenced to offer them a new proposal that would be difficult to reject, even under the circumstances that he was about to elaborate upon.

"Maybe there is a way the clinic can help you. As you know, your original doctor, Dr. Stockwell I believe, has attempted almost every known method with you to make pregnancy a reality, and nothing has worked. Embryo transplantation is the only other alternative available to you. Do you know anything about this type of fertilization."

"No, not really. What is it?"

"It's simply a method which involves carrying out the fertilization process in labware and then transferring the embryo to the uterine wall to carry out its prenatal development."

"Is it safe?"

"Yes, it is, but there are no guarantees.

"Yes, that's what Dr. Stockwell said. But that's not the only problem we have, doctor."

Before Jennifer went further, Dr. Cornwall said, "I know you are concerned with the financial aspects of further procedures, along with the period of going through pregnancy and the birthing process."

Both Ralph and Jennifer acknowledged Dr. Cornwall's statement by shaking their heads affirmatively. "Frankly, I'm surprised we got this far," Ralph said. "To spend more money on additional procedures is just out of the question." Jennifer rightly thought this was Ralph's way of copping out, but she remained determined.

"What would you say if I told you there is an experimental embryo transplantation procedure that may work for you and simultaneously eliminate your financial burden?"

The Houslers glanced at one another with puzzled looks and returned a stare at Dr. Cornwall, giving him their undivided attention.

Ralph suddenly broke the silence before giving Dr. Cornwall a chance to speak further. "Please don't take this the wrong way, doc, but this sounds too good to be true . . . . However, . . . if this procedure does what you say it will do, I think we'd both agree to learn more about it." A spark of both surprise and enthusiasm appeared in Jennifer's eyes and voice, showing that she agreed wholeheartedly with Ralph. *Maybe he cares after all.*

Dr. Cornwall continued. "There is a research program being set up at this very moment to use a new technique that has shown tremendous promise in the field of embryo transplantation."

After a brief description of the procedure, he let it be known that he wasn't in a position to divulge further details of the technique at this time. Actually, he really didn't know the details himself, but he assured them that the technique had already helped couples in other countries that had failed to conceive under all other methods currently being used.

"The specialists currently researching this technique have been looking for just a few couples who are having difficulty with pregnancy. From what I understand, the technique is so promising that it may revolutionize the way many people conceive."

Ralph and Jennifer remained silent, staring at Dr. Cornwall and waiting for anything that could explain such a procedure that had all the earmarks of something that could change their lives.

"Couples chosen for this procedure will, of course, be given more information about it by the committee, and they will receive special benefits," said Dr. Cornwall. "In fact, it comes with a very appealing monetary package. Would you be interested in hearing about it

"Yes, of course." Ralph replied. He finally was hearing something he was interested in.

"Basically, the sponsors of the research will provide money to raise the child and put him or her through school. In addition, they are willing to eliminate the bills that have already accumulated for you over these last few years."

Dr. Cornwall had to admit to himself that the research he was describing had the earmarks of some of the procedures the Nazis carried out at their concentration camps during World War II. But he was being paid a handsome commission to entice people to take part in the research, and he never questioned the process. He assumed it was legal.

Once he was finished with his evaluation and spiel, he let them know that further business for them would be handled completely by the fertility clinic's full-time staff.

After hearing about all the benefits, Ralph immediately was skeptical. "Is this a safe procedure, Dr. Cornwall, a technique that you can't elaborate further upon and with financial aid we normally can only dream about? It sounds fishy to me. How do you know the technique would produce a healthy and intelligent baby?" he asked. "I don't want Jennifer to be a guinea pig for an experiment that is going to cause her harm and end in a nightmare that will haunt both of us for the rest of our lives." At that moment, he actually showed signs of caring. Yet, he was selfishly considering the chores he'd have to do if Jennifer was harmed by what they were about to do.

Dr. Cornwall could clearly see that they were on the verge of saying no to his proposition before he had a chance to cover its benefits in more detail. Since he was about to lose them as clients, he decided to skip some of the preliminaries and expound on the benefits to help them understand the advantages of acceptance.

Again regurgitating information supplied to him, he said, "Well, I will say this. I can assure you that the fertility clinic sponsoring this research project has one of the highest reputations in the business, and there will be no more harm done to Jennifer in this procedure than in any other procedure. However, we can't promise the sky and the moon. You're not guaranteed perfection, no matter what spermatozoa and eggs are used, not even if they're your own. Things happen.

"However," he said before Ralph asked any additional questions, "you have a better chance of getting an intelligent and healthy baby through this procedure than with a natural birth. The genetic lines of egg and sperm providers have been thoroughly studied. Also, if anything should go wrong with the technique that would cause problems for Jennifer, they would step in and abort the pregnancy and try again. They check the conditions in the uterus and amniotic cavity more than any other institution would. This is a service you would never get at other clinics.

"As with all pregnancies, we can only hope for the best. Your pregnancy, like all others with sperm and egg donors, will be based on what the donors are like."

At this point, Ralph was impressed, but he still wasn't comfortable with the limited information they had, and he was certain that Jennifer felt as he did. "Can you tell us any more?"

Dr. Cornwall went on. "Yes, of course. The female donor is very intelligent, healthy, and of good anatomical stock. You will be given information on many of the egg donor's characteristics, like physical attributes and her medical, obstetrical, gynecological, social, and educational histories."

"Based on the information supplied to me," Dr. Cornwall said, "the male that we have selected was the subject of great importance to geneticists, and his DNA has been thoroughly examined. With the combination of his sperm and the egg of our donor, the team at the fertility clinic feels the cross will carry the best features of both mother and father."

Dr. Cornwall continued. "One of the beauties of this program, other than the substantial monetary assistance provided, is that the team of doctors who will collaborate in carrying out the procedure are all highly respected in their fields. They all collaborate in choosing the best egg donor they can find."

Convinced that the team responsible for carrying out the procedure was exceptional, Ralph asked, "Can you elaborate further on this monetary assistance?" For him, it was still about the money.

"Yes, of course. I apologize. I got sidetracked for a moment. One of the prime benefits to you, in addition to having a son or daughter, is that you won't have to worry about food, clothing, medical bills, and many other things that other parents must spend their money on for their children and for themselves. All his or her schooling will be paid for, including when he or she reaches college age. In essence, all your bills for raising your child will be taken care of, and you will probably be able to put money aside."

Ralph still couldn't believe what he was hearing. "Please go on."

"There's also the financial burden you currently have to consider. This will also be paid, so the stress of raising your child won't adversely have a bearing on his or her life. You see, the welfare of the child is of extreme importance to the researchers.

"Your part in the technique would be to carry the fetus through pregnancy and care for the baby throughout its young life, just as any responsible parents would do. Also, you must agree to periodic medical and psychological examinations, but that will also benefit you and your child. Want to hear more?"

"More?" Ralph asked. "Yes, please go on."

"You'll also be given a house in a very respectable neighborhood to live in until the child leaves to establish his or her own career, rent free. Any money that you make from undergoing this technique and from your regular job can be put into a retirement fund for both of you to use when you reach a later stage of your life. Unless you have sufficient money already coming in to put into the process that you must go through to become pregnant and simultaneously save for your future, this appears to be the deal of a lifetime.

"I understand your concern," he said. "You may be thinking that this all sounds too good to be true. However, researchers occasionally find a breakthrough in fertilization procedures that shows special promise. They obtain substantial amounts of money to test the procedures, often through private supporters, granting agencies, or companies that own the rights to certain products used in the procedure, and this is apparently the basis of this opportunity.

"Personally, with your medical and monetary history, I wouldn't pass it up. Not many people get a chance like this, so it's something you two should seriously talk over. It appears that you are in the right place at the right time. But think hard on it, because if you don't accept it, someone else will, and the opportunity will be gone."

Dr. Cornwall was unaware that the main reason a house would be provided was because their son or daughter would be under careful scrutiny during his or her entire life in that house. It would be provided with timing devices, microphones, cameras, and mirrors through which they could constantly observe their experimental child.

After all, it was an experiment that would enhance both the director's and the clinic's image, and secondarily, it was a way of assisting a couple to fulfill dreams that were otherwise impossible. In a way, it would be a reciprocal agreement, although the Houslers wouldn't know about the reciprocal arrangements or the behind-the-scenes devices.

"There's one last point I must make," Dr. Cornwall said. "The fertility clinic has put a deadline of a week on accepting this offer. If, by that time, you do not accept it, the offer will be preseented to another potential recipient."

Chapter 3

Competing for the New Procedure

Because of the mysteriousness of the offer, they had almost decided to reject Dr. Cornwall's proposal, that was until they carefully rehashed their current position in the lower echelons of society, the omnipresent financial problems they faced and above all, Jennifer's determination to have a child.

Upon reevaluating their experience with the numerous doctors and procedures, one thing noticed by Jennifer immediately was that she and Ralph were actually getting along better than they had been in a long time. They were communicating. She was certain that their focus on having a child was bringing them closer, and this made her feel their relationship was going to be stronger when the baby came. It was the right thing to do.

"I want to have this child, Ralph. I need a family and a child to raise. What else can we do? We've been through hell with all this testing, and until this procedure was offered to us, we had no choice in the matter. As it stands, it's either accept the conditions of the experimental technique or forget about becoming pregnant and suffer through years of overtime to pay our mounting bills." Ralph said nothing. He had to admit, Jennifer was right, but in his mind, it was her who had brought on at least part of their dilemma.

"Please, Ralph, think of what we'd be passing up. We're already in tremendous debt, and there's no way we can pay for the tests and procedures that are ahead of us. We really can't even consider adoption until our current bills are paid, and that won't be at any time soon. And we're not getting any younger." She obviously was already sold on the procedure. It was now all about getting Ralph to make up his mind.

In the meantime, Dr. Cornwall, his employer, and the team of reproductive specialists involved with obtaining an embryo recipient didn't wait for Ralph and Jennifer to make up their minds. They began screening other potential recipients for the cross.

§

What couple they chose really didn't matter. The director had two goals in mind in setting up the clinic: one centered on the secretive experimental nature of the conception process, for which he would no doubt receive world-wide acclaim; the other was more of a personal nature, to generate a sizeable income for him and two partners mostly by carrying out routine gynecological procedures and storing their considerable profits in a secret offshore account. Upon their retirement, they would have a more-than-adequate amount of money with which to live out their remaining years in absolute comfort.

Chapter 4

A Precious Baby Boy

Unlike most of the other candidates, Ralph and Jennifer finally decided it was too good to pass up. Dr. Cornwall made an appointment for them to start their testing at the fertility clinic on the following Monday. Ralph went along but didn't have his heart in it. It was going to be Jennifer's baby, anyway. Even with what had appeared to be a sincere interest in what was about to happen, he remained unenthusiastic about even having a child at this stage of his life.

Jennifer endured more tests than she ever thought possible. She was happy Ralph was at her side. All the pills, injections, and suppositories required to get her uterus in prime condition to accept the embryo were given at the prescribed times and in a special sequence.

"Ralph," she said, "I want to thank you for sticking by me. I know it's no fun for you. I love you."

"Don't worry about it, Jen. If things go well from here on, it will solve many of our problems, and we'll look back on it as a long-passed memory." He didn't mention the baby or love. For him, it was still all about the money.

Jennifer looked at him, uncertain of what was really on his mind. He completely evaded the emotions poured out by her. If her suspicions were correct, she feared the child would be raised and fed by her only. *Would there even be a father image for the child?* In contrast to her believing the process of having a baby was cementing their relationship, she was beginning to think that he never expected to put much time into being a father. She only hoped her thoughts were incorrect.

On a Friday during her third month of pregnancy, she hemorrhaged and lost the embryo. Besides the negative emotional state that the abortion had put her in and the apparent subsiding interest Ralph seemed to have, Jennifer was suddenly convinced that she would never have a child.

On Jennifer's second attempt to get pregnant, it wasn't until the final month of pregnancy that she began experiencing additional swelling, and, at first, it appeared she could lose the fetus. To everyone's delight, she carried her child to full term, and she had what appeared to be a handsome baby boy that weighed six pounds, ten ounces.

When tiny Lance Housler was finally presented to Jennifer, it was a very special emotional event. Everyone at the clinic beamed and spoke of his beauty. Jennifer and even Ralph appeared beside themselves with pride and joy. Their dreams were finally coming true. They had a son, and he was the most beautiful child they had ever seen. It now all seemed worth the hardships they had to endure. Their luck had changed, and it was going to be a good future. Ralph could finally relax.

Making a quick appraisal of Lance's parents and their reaction to the new addition, the observation team at the fertility clinic concluded that the feeling of love expressed by Jennifer was absolutely genuine in every way but that love was lacking in Ralph. When Jennifer conversed with someone, it was "Lance did this," and, "Lance did that." On the other hand, Ralph said very little, and when he did comment, it was generally in an anecdotal fashion.

There was no doubt about Jennifer's happiness. In her eyes, little Lance was a blessing and a sincere pleasure to have around. Precisely what it meant to Ralph during the first couple of months of Lance's post-natal existence was uncertain, but he was clearly relieved at the lack of stress around their home, mostly due to Jennifer's contentment.

And that was only part of their dream come true. Along with Lance, the beautiful house, and the financial assistance they received from the fertility clinic totally transformed their lives. It was almost surreal.

Even though Lance didn't sleep through the night bothered them a little, Jennifer seemed to quickly adjust to their new life and accepted the fact that Lance was one of those babies who would keep them up at odd hours. He occasionally woke up screaming, and Jennifer would spend time holding and singing to him until he settled down.

"I wonder what he could be dreaming about that scares him so," she said to Ralph, "when he really doesn't have any memories to dream about."

Ralph simply commented, "Who the hell knows?"

He never got up during the night, even from the start. If he awoke first, he would jostle Jennifer to do the honors, and he'd roll over and attempt to go back to sleep, pissed off that he was awakened in the first place.

The little toleration he had abated as time went on. His subsequent role in taking care of night-time business was to yell to Jennifer, "Would you shut him up so I can get some god damn sleep."

Other than for his nocturnal needs, Jennifer loved being with Lance from the time they got home from the hospital. She played little games with him, tickling his cute little legs and feet while he kicked and made his precious baby noises.

She read to him whenever she could, but Lance seemed to prefer kicking those little roller toys at the foot of his crib and waving his arms at the encircling mobile that hung over him. Jennifer couldn't complain about Lance's demands for attention because he was often quite content to be by himself in his little baby world.

The Houslers, in fact, had never seen a baby who appeared to prefer being alone, except at feeding time. Only then did he demand immediate attention. This didn't bother Mom Housler, though, because she understood it was just a matter of forming a routine. After she fed Lance, he always returned to being the angel child that everyone thought he was.

He learned rapidly to imitate the gestures and baby sounds that Jennifer demonstrated before him, and he came up with ones of his own. Unlike many babies that she had seen, Lance looked directly at the person in front of him, sometimes making faces at them that appeared almost like snarls. He'd wrench his darling little mouth into all sorts of shapes that she'd never seen before. She was aware that these and other unusual gestures demonstrated by babies were part of their cute individual personalities. If an adult had made the same faces, it would be something to worry about. He was adorable.

"Babies, as everyone knows" she said to a neighbor, "are not in control of all of their precious facial expressions at this early stage." She had evidently been reading Dr. Spock or a comparable how-to-raise-babies book.

"Neither are they in control of their body and limb movements." Lance was prone to flapping his arms and feet, and there were times when he increased the complexity of his movements by simultaneously kicking and flapping. They appeared to be powerful kicks for a child his age. As Ralph told his colleagues on one occasion, "He's a strong little bastard."

You sometimes had to watch out for his flailing extremities when you got close to him. A neighbor bent down close to Lance one day to admire his innocent sporadic movements, and little Lance's legs were moving up and down so fast, it looked as though he was riding a bicycle.

"Isn't he cute," she said, and when she bent down to tickle his leg, Lance kicked her in the nose, causing her to bleed profusely. It was a hard kick and a solid connection, and she was in obvious pain. In spite of Lance's smile and apparent excitement, she immediately lost interest in him, and even though the Houslers rationalized with her that it was an accident, they never got a visit from her again.

Chapter 6

The Baby Sitter

Ralph was now relatively happy, or to put it another way, as happy as he could be with what he felt was a possessed baby. He went to work most of the time with what superficially resembled a smile on his face. He had a new lease on life, now that he didn't have to worry about paying bills. Going to work had a new meaning; it gave him an excuse to get out of the house.

He was happy that any money he made was now being invested so he and Jennifer would have that nest egg they had always dreamed about. It wasn't a perfect world for him, but it was much better than it had been, and Jennifer was off his back about this baby she wanted.

To Jennifer's disappointment, Ralph wasn't the type of man who pitched in on the housework and taking care of babies. He was gone all day, and when he returned from work, he usually poured himself a stiff drink and began demanding that Jennifer wait on him hand and foot. He also insisted that his meals be ready at specific times, and he threw a fit if he couldn't eat immediately after finishing his drink.

If Lance needed attention, Ralph called Jennifer. If Lance cried too much, Ralph got up and went outside to get away from him until Jennifer got him quiet again. "Shut him the hell up," he would say as he left.

Jennifer was an overly patient and tolerant woman who was happy to stay with Lance day and night for the first few months, but by that time, even she began to feel claustrophobic and wanted

Ralph to take her out. Now that they had been relieved of their debt and actually found it possible to save a little money, she felt it was time to relax and enjoy themselves a little, maybe even periodically take a few moments to repair their defective marriage.

Ralph complained, of course, not wanting to upset his routine of coming home, having the drink or two he now seemed to require in order to survive, and vegetate in front of the boob tube. In spite of Ralph's bitching, Jennifer was relentless in her attempts to pry him away from his monotonous existence. To him, however, he saw her actions as a return of her bitching. He thought he had solved that problem.

One evening, as Jennifer worked on Ralph to get her way, they discussed the pros and cons of babysitting, and neither of them felt perfectly at ease about leaving Lance with someone else, so they put their pleasures off for a while longer. It was Ralph who made the decision. Jennifer wasn't certain that it was Lance's welfare that kept Ralph from taking her out, but what he said made sense, and she went along with his decision for the time being.

Jennifer had to admit that while their relationship wasn't good, it was periodically better than it had been before Lance came along. Actually, though, with Ralph's current attitude, Jennifer was amazed that she and Ralph were getting along at all. Since Lance was born, they had begun working out their major problems together. Although there were times when Ralph became especially difficult to deal with, it was far better than their former life had been, at which time he would constantly bitch and complain about everything she did or was supposed to do.

Jennifer knew that Ralph had an increasingly serious drinking problem back then, but she had always attributed it to the pressures he felt from his job and their constant shortage of funds. She didn't actually blame him at that time, but he certainly had made life difficult for her.

She now looked to a brighter future. She really couldn't complain about Lance's behavior. She had gotten the son she always wanted, and that, alone, made her thankful. Life for her was sweeter than it had been in a while. She understood that Ralph got upset with a screaming baby at times, but he seemed to settle down once Lance became quiet.

As time went on, co-existence between the three of them became increasingly strained. Ralph was growing more intolerant of Lance's crying, and Jennifer continued to feel the pressure of not having time away from her daily chores. She wasn't blaming Lance. As with any parent, she once again just needed a break.

When Lance was eight months old, Jennifer began talking again about going out, and Ralph gave in to what he described to his friends as "her constant bitching." Jennifer made arrangements to have Lance watched by Patricia Clayton, a neighborhood teenager who often did babysitting jobs to make a few bucks.

At fifteen, Patricia knew almost all the kids in the neighborhood, and she came highly recommended. Jennifer was told that she was an honor student who was serious about life, and she already had plans to go to college as a psychology major when she graduated from high school.

She seemed to enjoy watching children and their vast array of what she called "interesting behaviors," but her real interest was in studying the criminal mind, especially if it dealt with deviant behaviors. She told Jennifer that with a background in that field, she could take a job with the FBI or a forensic team to investigate homicides. It was Ralph's opinion that Patricia was watching too much TV.

§

Jennifer's first night away from Lance made her apprehensive, but she and Ralph went ahead and attended one of the Frank Statton rock concerts that were so popular around the nation. They had their cell phone with them, so if anything happened, they knew Patricia would give them a call, not that they would hear the phone ring over the screams and shouts of a rock concert audience. With all the bases covered, they got into the concert with the rest of the crowd and, like most of the audience, left with scratchy throats and ringing ears.

Since they had arranged to be home by midnight and it was only eleven o'clock when they got out, Ralph decided to stop at a twenty-four-hour neighborhood restaurant for coffee and a piece of pie, in spite of Jennifer's desire to go home and have a snack there. She still felt apprehensive about being away from her baby, but Ralph insisted they take a little more time off to relax. That's when they got a call.

Chapter 7

The Accident

When the cell phone rang, it startled Jennifer. They never expected a call and initially hadn't realized it was even their phone that was ringing.

Jennifer frantically dug it out of her purse, pressed the phone icon, held the phone to her right ear, and said, "Hello?"

Patricia was on the other end, screaming about something. All of a sudden, Jennifer's expression changed. She pressed the earpiece closer to her head, stuck a finger into her left ear to eliminate extraneous noise, and became confused, not really understanding what was going on at their house.

"What's wrong Jennifer? Tell me what the hell's wrong." Ralph didn't like surprises.

In a highly emotional state, Jennifer answered, "I don't know, Ralph. I can't make out what Patricia's saying."

Ralph grabbed the phone from Jennifer and yelled into it, "What's wrong, Patricia? Calm down, and tell us what's wrong."

Patricia settled down a little and, through broken, sob-enhanced sentences, told Ralph that, "Something has happened. While I was getting ready to feed Lance, I had cut up some pieces of celery to let him suck on, and I laid the knife down on the table where I thought it was out of Lance's reach.

"I got a little bowl to put the celery pieces in. I returned to where Lance was sitting in his chair and was putting the bowl down on the platform in front of him when Lance picked the knife up and swung it at me. When he did, he caught my hand just behind my thumb with the blade, and the knife cut deeply into my flesh. I think it hit the bone."

Ralph was thinking all the while, *what the hell did she have to tell me all that bull shit for. Why didn't she just say she cut her god damned hand. I don't need to know her whole god damned life history.*

He continued. "Are you alright?"

Jennifer kept trying to get Ralph to tell her what was wrong, but he held his right hand up to shush her. She evidently had more to tell him.

Patricia was still frantically screaming and again began to speak in sentences that were half unintelligible. He could make out enough to understand that she didn't know what to do, that the wound wouldn't stop bleeding. Blood was everywhere.

"What about Lance? Is he okay?" It seemed that Patricia forgot to mention Lance, and Ralph wondered if she had taken the knife away from him or that maybe he did something to himself. "Where is the knife now?"

"I took the knife away from Lance immediately. He's okay. Please tell me what to do about my hand."

Attempting to stay calm, Ralph said, "Here's what you need to do. Take a towel and hold it to the cut, and push down on it to stop the bleeding. Keep it there until we get home, and we'll handle the situation. We'll be there in about ten minutes." Not waiting for her response, he pressed the off button on the phone and turned to Jennifer. "Let's go Jenn."

When Jennifer heard the words knife, cut, and bleeding, she became more frantic, thinking that Ralph was talking about an accident that had happened to her son.

Tell me what's going on Ralph. What's happened to Lance?"

"Nothing's happened to Lance, Jennifer. God damn, would you calm down. It's Patricia that's hurt. It appears that she got careless with a knife and left it close to Lance. Somehow, Lance got hold of it and cut Patricia. You know how babies wave their arms all around the god damned place when they're holding things.

"That's all I know. But it sounds like the cut is bad, and we'll probably have to take her to the god damn emergency unit at the hospital to get her stitched up. She's had trouble stopping the blood, so the knife probably hit an artery.

Jennifer understood Ralph wasn't happy with the situation. It was in both his expression and manner of speech.

"This really pisses the shit out of me," he said. "We hear screaming all fucking day and night from Lance, and when we try to take a little time off, we get a call and have to listen to god damn screaming over the phone from a terrified god damned teenage bitch. I just can't take this shit."

Even though Jennifer was used to Ralph's poor attitude about life, she was surprised at his outburst. He had a short fuse. On the other hand, it was obvious he was more worried about his peace of mind and comfort than he was about Lance and Patricia.

On their way home, she thought about the detriments of having time for just the two of them and getting a baby sitter to watch Lance. Maybe they had done the wrong thing. Maybe they should have waited until Lance was a little older.

When they arrived at the house, Patricia was a little calmer than she had been on the phone, but she still had a frantic look in her eyes. She had gotten most of the blood stopped, and when Ralph attempted to examine the injury and unstick the towel that was now glued to her hand with dried blood, blood recommenced oozing out of one corner of the wound. While he wrapped the cut with a makeshift pressure bandage, Jennifer packed Lance up so they could all go to the hospital together.

On the way, Patricia apologized for the problem. "Something like this has never happened to me before. I'm usually very careful about what I put down near a baby. I'm sorry I put that knife close to Lance, but I thought it was far enough away that I wouldn't have to worry about it. I'm glad he wasn't hurt too.

"I don't really know what happened. When I turned around, Lance was coming down with the knife. If I didn't know better, I would have sworn he was doing it on purpose, but he's a baby. He doesn't even know what a knife is. But when I looked at him, he smiled when it was over. It was scary."

Ralph kept thinking that he wished she would just shut the hell up. It was as though she wouldn't stop talking, a constant verbal barrage of bull shit, and he couldn't wait for it all to be over.

The attending physician put eight stitches in Patricia's hand, gave her a tetanus shot, and wrote her a prescription for antibiotics. Ralph, in the meantime, went for a walk. If they had been near a bar, he would have gone in for a drink or two, anything to kill the discomfort of dealing with what he considered incompetence.

As a nurse finished dressing the wound with a bandage that covered most of Patricia's hand, one looking at it would imagine that her entire hand had been mutilated. The sling she was given held her arm up and close to her body.

While they were waiting for this to be done, Jennifer phoned Patricia's mother and told her about the accident. When her mother calmed down a little, Jennifer managed to squeeze in the fact that it was a cut on her hand and that it was being taken care of as they spoke.

"Patricia will be alright," she said. "You don't have to come to the hospital because we're bringing her home immediately.

Mr. and Mrs. Clayton were standing at the front steps when they arrived. They ran to Patricia and hugged her, noticing the gigantic bandage. Her mother, quite upset over the ordeal, said, "Baby, my God, what did he do to you?"

That was all Ralph needed to hear. He began to fume inside, thinking: *Where does she get off saying, "What did he do to you?" It was your daughter's god damn fault. Get your shit straight, bitch.*

Patricia told them about the experience, that she got eight stitches and assured them that the size of the bandage was beyond appropriate for the cut she got.

Her mother asked, "How are you feeling, baby?"

Patricia, now calm and with a light smile at the attention she was getting, said, "I'm okay."

Jennifer relayed to Mrs. Clayton what the doctor had told them, and after she offered a sincere apology, they left.

On their way home, Jennifer said, "You know, Ralph, it was actually Patricia's fault that this happened. She never should have put that knife down by Lance. He could have seriously hurt himself with it. We're lucky it was just her hand that got cut. Let's not do this again for a while."

Ralph agreed. Maybe this was a good thing, he thought. He wouldn't have to listen to her nagging about going out again.

He was now mumbling something to himself about the evening's events, and when Jennifer finished talking, he began shouting again. "I'll tell you what this is, Jenn. It's a pain in the freaking ass. That damn Patricia should have put the damn knife in the sink. She must have had her head up her ass.

"That little bitch caused us to have a miserable evening, and I had to pay her money for it. And it will probably cost us a bunch more. Who knows how much?"

After a brief pause, he said, "You're going to have to just watch Lance yourself. I can't do it. I have a job, and I work hard all day, and when I get home, I don't need all this shit. My job is at the car dealership, and your job is taking care of Lance. You're the one who wanted a god damn kid anyway."

In immediate shock, Jennifer didn't say another word to Ralph the entire evening. She cleaned Lance and put him into his crib, tears coming down her cheeks.

As she looked at Lance, she sobbed and wondered what had happened. This little boy who was supposed to brighten their lives and make their problems go away was innocent enough, but things were returning to the way they had been before, maybe even worse. And now poor Lance had to listen to shouting and cuss words, both of which no doubt upset him and may scar him for life.

Ralph was becoming his old self again. She always had thought it was their financial situation that was causing him to be the way he was. Yet, those problems were behind them. She concluded that the problem stemmed from whatever caused Ralph to leave his comfort zone, and this time it apparently was Lance. She wondered how she was going to cope with it all.

Chapter 8

The Psychologist

Unbeknownst to them, everything that had occurred in the Housler's home that evening had been recorded by the fertility clinic. All observers became very concerned with the events of the evening. While they wanted to intervene immediately after Lance had slashed Patricia's hand, they thought it would appear odd that they should show up on that particular evening to help this teenage girl in distress, so they remained at their observation post and continued to stare at the closed-circuit television screen, waiting for further developments. They decided that if anything else happened or if it appeared that Patricia was losing too much blood, they would have to intervene and pretend they were just paying a routine social visit.

They audited the telephone conversation, as well, and felt a lot better when Ralph handled the situation like he did. They weren't happy about his attitude, however.

Dr. Stewart (Stu) Bridges, the psychologist in charge at the fertility clinic, remarked, "This is not good. I can understand why he would be upset, but this is ridiculous. A side of Ralph is surfacing that we didn't know about. It appears that our boy, Lance, is not going to have the happy environment we had planned for him to grow up in."

Since Lance was born, arrangements between the Houslers and the fertility clinic were handled initially by Stu. Dr. Morrison, the mysterious laboratory director who no one had even seen, had preferred to stay out of the picture during the fertilization, prenatal, and natal periods, although it was carried out under his direction, and he continued to remain a mystery to the entire staff.

During the weeks prior to the accident, the Houslers learned through Stu that it was actually Dr. Morrison who had been responsible for setting up the research program to test the new technique that had helped them start their family. Knowing this made Jennifer interested in meeting and talking with him, if for no other reason but to just thank him.

When Stu called Jennifer the morning after the accident, she told him that she was glad he called, that she was thinking of getting in touch with the director. When Stu told her that the director was often away on business and not accustomed to visiting with clients, she opened up her thoughts to him.

During the conversation, she related to him what had happened the evening before, and he made an attempt to encourage her to put the event behind her. "After all," he said, "it was an accident, and it may help everyone to be a little more careful about what they lay down in the presence of a baby."

As they spoke, Stu tried to have Jennifer comment about her present life with a new baby. Although she commented on some of the good things that happened between Lance and her, she was reluctant to bring up any negative aspects of her life. When he was convinced he had exhausted the possibilities of learning more about her life with Lance, he turned to the subject of her relationship with Ralph.

"How are you and Ralph doing these days?" he asked, "other than having to deal with that evening's events?"

Jennifer remarked that they were doing just fine, except for what happened to the baby sitter. "We couldn't be happier with Lance. He's a doll, and we can't thank everyone enough for him. You'll have to come over some time and pay him a visit. We'd love to have you."

"I think I'd like that, Mrs. Housler. I do plan to check on you periodically to make sure you have everything you need. But I would like to consider visiting on occasion simply as a friend, just to see how you, Mr. Housler, and Lance are doing."

"I want to thank you for all your help. Please call me Jennifer, and call my husband Ralph. There's no need for formality. We'd love to have you come over as often as you care to."

Stu took advantage of the offer and made arrangements to visit the Houslers the following day, at a time when Jennifer thought Lance would be awake. It was also at a time that he knew Ralph would be there. He didn't want to miss an opportunity to also talk with him about life in general.

Stu had advanced degrees in biology and psychology, and he had specialized in child psychology prior to making a commitment to work for the clinic. To the Houslers, Stu's true identity was kept hidden, and he portrayed himself simply as a caring representative of the clinic who occasionally would come by to see if they needed anything, a caring delegate, if you will. As a psychologist, he was hoping to become a welcomed friend, a position that would allow him to observe Lance in person long enough to notice any unusual behavior.

When he arrived, Jennifer offered him iced tea. Sitting in front of the TV, Ralph shook Stu's outstretched hand with his typical dishrag grasp but didn't seem to offer any conversation along with it. Stu said all the routine things a person tends to say about the weather, and, not getting any response, he asked, "How are you doing, Ralph?" When Ralph responded with an unenthusiastic, "Okay," Stu didn't push the issue and went over to Lance.

"Hi, Lance. How are you? He's really a very cute little boy, Jennifer." Stu moved his hand toward Lance, and Lance grabbed it without the indecisiveness you would expect from a baby his age. "And he's very strong too." *Ralph could learn from him*, he thought.

Jennifer smiled.

As they talked about all sorts of things, Jennifer couldn't help but thank him and his company again for the things they had done. "We'll never forget it," she said.

Stu immediately questioned if Jennifer actually believed she was speaking for both she and Ralph. He acknowledged her appreciation and let her know that they meant a lot to them. "It is our pleasure to help you in any way we can. Here are my office and cell phone numbers. If ever you need me, call, any time."

They chatted for a while longer, Jennifer commenting mostly about their new outlook on life and how things had been since Lance came into the world. When Stu's tea had almost disappeared, Jennifer filled it up again and offered him some cake.

He politely refused, excusing himself and saying, "I have been putting on a few pounds lately and have to get serious about losing some weight."

After two hours at the Housler's, Stu made excuses about why he had to go. His real reason for leaving was that he had observed both young Lance and Ralph first hand, and now he wanted to jot down what he was thinking before he forgot it. His hidden recorder would fill in the blanks.

Before he left, he mentioned that he would be periodically checking on them to see what they could do to help. "Of course, I'll always call before the visit," he added.

All in all, Stu felt that it was a good two hours spent. If at all possible, they were going to be friends. He hoped Lance wouldn't disappoint him.

Chapter 9

Learning Right from Wrong

Stu paid the Houslers numerous visits after that, and he noticed a definite negative change in Ralph. He was growing more distant in his relationship with Lance, not that he was ever really close to him. When they watched the family on the lab screen, they noticed that Ralph seemed to be more into himself lately, and he very seldom seemed to have an interest in his son, except to yell at him when Lance sought his attention or caused him discomfort in some way.

Stu spent time playing with Lance whenever he paid them a visit, and Jennifer remarked about how cute they were together. He was there when Lance improved his crawling abilities and stood for the first time. He also shared his first walk from Jennifer to him, which came soon after learning to crawl. Lance, in fact, was earlier in learning to walk and expressing a lot of other aspects of behavior than most babies his age.

On one of Stu's visits, Jennifer mentioned that she was thinking of getting a dog, "something Lance could grow up with." Looking for approval, she asked, "What do you think of this, Stu?"

Stu had to think long and hard about this one. He knew that Jennifer had occasionally invited neighborhood children to play with Lance, and she took him to their house whenever they were invited. They also went to the park where he could play with other children. The problem was that Lance didn't seem to play very well with others. He dominated them and occasionally hit them. They typically ended up crying and wanting their mothers to take them home. Lance didn't appear to feel any remorse for what he had done. To the contrary, he seemed to be happy with the outcome.

It wasn't long before Jennifer stopped getting invitations to bring Lance to visit the neighborhood children, and the neighborhood mothers stopped bringing their children to the Houslers. This left Lance without playmates, and Stu was concerned.

"Well, I don't see anything wrong with a pet, as long as it isn't something that would hurt Lance. Maybe a small to medium sized dog for now, something that has a good disposition. Since he doesn't have a brother or sister, it may be good for him to have a companion." In addition, Stu thought, it may keep him away from Ralph.

Stu once remarked to others on the team, "I don't see anything in particular wrong with Lance, but he's rather strange in wanting to be alone all the time. I've noticed that when he plays with kids his age, his attention is on just about anything but his playmates. And God help a kid if he takes something from Lance. Lance has no qualms about picking up a toy and knocking the living hell out of him with it."

One of the team members remarked, "But don't you think that's normal for kids to be possessive about their toys?"

"Yes, it is normal, but Lance takes it a step further. He clobbers the poor kid, and he does it with a vengeance, like he really wants to hurt him and teach him to never do it again. Maybe it's partly because he's so strong and knows he can dominate those around him, but it's a little different from what you'd expect from most children. I believe these are signs of a darker personality emerging. Let's watch him very closely as he gets older.

"Needless to say, he doesn't have many friends his age, unless the other kid is so subordinate that he just doesn't do anything to antagonize Lance. Lance is definitely a dominant individual at this stage of development, and he's likely to retain this dominance throughout life.

"We must attempt to let the Houslers understand that Lance needs some structure in his life. He needs to grow up learning right from wrong, obeying their wishes, and doing chores around the house, and he doesn't need to be spoiled. If he is, this dominance behavior may get out of hand. I don't quite know how to tell them this without letting his parents' know what our position in this experiment actually is, but it has to be done.

"The Houslers had gone through hell to get Lance, and he is the most important thing in their life." This wasn't quite right, he thought. He knew this was true for Jennifer, but he was sure Ralph had different thoughts about the situation.

Because of Ralph's shitty outlook on life, there was no way Lance would get through life without being abused by his father and spoiled rotten by Jennifer. To keep Lance happy, she had already given him everything he needed, plus much more. Toys were everywhere. It was hard to walk through the house without stumbling on something. And if anyone tried to play with one of his toys too long, he put up a fuss. Also, Jennifer was a little casual in correcting him when he needed it.

Ralph, on the other hand, was overbearing in correcting Lance. Actually, it wasn't so much that he corrected him as it was to simply stop Lance from doing certain things that annoyed him.

He mostly yelled at Lance, and he was also beginning to yell at Jennifer to get some of the toys up. Once, the team even witnessed Ralph purposely smashing one of Lance's toys with his foot when he stumbled on it.

Stu was almost certain that Ralph did this particular act in plain view so Lance could see it. Lance, in return, picked up the broken toy, and with tears in his eyes, showed contempt for his father with a devilish stare and a protruding, pulsating lower lip. When he did this, Ralph just laughed at him. Lance then made motions like he was going to throw the toy at him.

On one occasion when he picked up a toy and hit Ralph in the leg with it, Ralph knocked him halfway across the room. Lance's screaming brought Jennifer who wanted to know, "What happened?"

Ralph said, "Lance just fell. You need to get some of those toys picked up before we do the same."

The team now realized even more that Lance needed something like a pet that would occupy his time and keep him away from his father. As Stu pointed out, "It's obvious that Ralph isn't going to be the father Lance needs, and Jennifer has other things to do besides watch Lance twenty-four hours a day. Lance also needs someone who will correct him when necessary and help him to form certain values in his life."

In spite of what he said, Stu had no choice but to ignore the current situation and any other problems that arose in Lance's life. He and everyone at the clinic had to work as a team and abide by the director's original plan, and that was to not interfere with Lance's life. Regardless of what Stu thought, it was hands off in straightening out any behavioral or psychological malfunctions.

Stu had to admit, it was a good experiment to see how someone's personality would develop under stringent conditions, but in a way it was inhumane to watch Lance being the subject of abuse. "One can only imagine having a similar child with good parents. Would the same child be more apt to develop a pleasing personality?"

Over time, matters in the Housler house didn't get any better. As Lance got a little older, Jennifer once again attempted to read to him in the mornings and evenings, but he often got bored almost immediately and wanted to get down to play. After this happened on several occasions, Jennifer concluded that he didn't have the attention span or a desire to learn what was in the books she had chosen, and she'd let him play.

Chapter 10

Penny, the Dog

Stu surprised Jennifer one morning with the cute dog she wanted so Lance would have a pet during his young years. Its name was Penny. It was a sheltie, and Lance took to it immediately. It wasn't a baby dog. It was an estimated eight or nine months old at the shelter, but its disposition was flawless, and it was house broken. Everybody at the shelter was happy to hear Penny was going to a good home. Stu had his doubts.

"Thank you very much, Stu. You have been wonderful, and we appreciate you."

"It's my pleasure, Jennifer. I hope Lance enjoys her."

"I'm sure he will."

Lance went through a period of observing his new pet, then his behavior changed to include more contact with her. He could pull on her long fur, grab her legs, hide and jump out at her. You name it, and he did it to Penny. It was the first time he had seen Lance with a smile on his face. Stu acknowledged that Penny seemed to have a positive affect on Lance, but he was beginning to treat her with some degree of abuse.

The dog repeatedly took whatever Lance dished out, no matter what agony Lance seemed to concoct on her behalf. Every now and then, Penny would tire of him and meander off to a quieter spot, only to be harassed again when Lance found her.

Once in a while, Lance would get tired of harassing her, and he would put his head down on her and fall asleep. Penny would lie there, apparently content, until Lance woke up. At such times, it was as if Lance and Penny were the best of friends, in spite of his occasional outbursts. Since both Jennifer and Ralph were not witness to his more dominating behavior at this time, they were convinced that getting Penny was the best thing they could have done.

In an altruistic way, Jennifer saw the benefit of having Penny because of what it did for Lance. On the other hand, Ralph saw a benefit in the break he got from Lance. There was no doubt about it. Lance's attention was now mostly on this new animal. However, Ralph made it plain that he didn't like dogs, and he got pissed whenever Penny wanted to interact with him.

It was when Lance was one and a half that he was moving around pretty well and getting stronger that he played a little rougher with Penny. On one particular day, Lance had been repeatedly hitting Penny with his toys, and the dog couldn't take it anymore.

Lance had been relentless in his pursuit, chasing after her all around the house, repeatedly attempting to pick her up, and kicking her whenever he noticed his mother wasn't paying attention to them. When Penny finally had enough, she showed her teeth in defiance and snapped at him.

Jennifer, of course, wasn't looking at the two at the time. If she had been watching, she probably would have chastised Penny for snapping at her angel. When it happened, Lance jumped back and stared at Penny. There were no tears or even an attempt to cry. When Penny showed her teeth, he reciprocated by mimicking her.

With his little hand rolled into a fist, he swung at her, hitting her across the nose. When his small knuckles connected with Penny's bony nose, Penny yelped, and Lance flinched at the pain in his hand. When he cried, Jennifer ran to Lance and picked him up.

"What did that bad dog do to my little angel? You two are always getting into scraps. What am I going to do with you? Why don't you play with your toys?"

Lance looked at his mother, showed his teeth, apparently practicing what Penny had taught him, and he hit her on the side of the nose with his good hand.

Jennifer wrenched her head back, experiencing the burning sensation. With a look of surprise at the strength of her son, she couldn't comprehend his reason for doing what he did. Tears formed in her eyes from the burning as she said, "Lance, baby, why did you hit mommy?"

Ralph looked up and said, "What's wrong?"

"Lance just socked me in the nose, and it was a hard blow. I don't understand why he did it."

"Well, you know how those damn kids are. They don't really know they're hurting you when they do things like that."

As she listened to Ralph, wondering if this was really true, Lance looked directly at her, put his arm up and rolled his fingers into another fist as though he was warning her that he was going to do it again. Jennifer grabbed his hand and said, "Lance, be careful. You're going to hurt mommy again."

Thinking that Lance may be tired and needed a nap, she put him into his small bed and gave him a bottle. He threw the bottle out onto the floor and began to scream. She picked him up and started to rock with him, and he squirmed to get back to the floor. He apparently wanted to be alone.

In the laboratory, Stu watched Lance closely and took notes. He had a sincere interest in his behavior, maybe more of an interest than he had for any of his former subjects in his years as a psychologist. Of course, he never had a chance to observe a subject twenty-four hours a day before. This was a psychologist's dream-come-true.

But it was actually more than that. Lance was an extremely interesting subject. Stu had seen all the behavior before, the independence, the temper tantrums, the lack of control by parents who either didn't want to hurt their angel children or didn't want to be bothered with them, and the occasional bursts of sadistic behavior by the child toward other living things in his environment.

There seemed to be a pattern forming, but he wasn't sure where it would lead. Lance was really too young for Stu to determine if he was just a spoiled child or if there was a more deeply seated flaw in his personality. Although there were very evident signs of inappropriate behavior being displayed, he didn't want to come out and say anything officially at this time. It would take a few more years to develop a definite personality. He asked himself, *would Lance's behavior change when he became old enough to realize that being aggressive would cause more animosity to form in those around him.*

He did mention to the others at the clinic that Lance had a malicious streak, and they agreed. They also agreed that Ralph was at least partially to blame.

Stu continued with that thought. "I have noticed that when I'm there, Lance sometimes seems resentful that I'm visiting. It's like he doesn't want to be bothered with someone else sharing his attention."

With a sign of seriousness in his expression, Stu said, "Keep your eyes and ears open. I have a feeling things are going to get worse."

Since the time Penny snapped at Lance, it appeared he had lost interest in her, except when he threw toys at her or clobbered her with one of them. And when Penny appeared to require his attention, he would push her away or attempt to hit her with something. Then he would get up and go to another spot in the room. He had no compassion for the dog he was supposed to love.

Stu took all these features in as a sign that Lance had acquired a behavior pattern similar to what his adopted father had demonstrated. He was most definitely independent, dominant, and intolerant.

Stu had to admit that in spite of Lance's egocentricities, someone that didn't know him might say he almost fit into what modern society called the norm. He was smart, learning things faster than most kids his age. He was aware of his environment, seeming to have an understanding of his surroundings that other children in his age group lacked. But there were questions, many questions, that pertained to Lance's deep-seated and sometimes frightening behavior that remained unanswered.

Chapter 11

Jiggers, the Cat

In spite of Ralph's constant complaining about Lance and life in general, Jennifer recognized that even he had what she would call his tender moments, times when it appeared he actually gave a damn about the two of them. When he was in one of his rare good moods, he sometimes even offered to take them somewhere.

It didn't really matter where they went. Jennifer was thrilled to get out of the house. At two, Lance was extremely curious about anything in his surroundings, but he seemed to be happiest when Jennifer and Ralph took him somewhere special.

Going somewhere also meant that Lance would get presents of some sort, but if they didn't get him something new and unusual, he'd let them know that they'd better or he'd make their lives miserable. Ralph would immediately grow tired of his whining, loose his patience, and begin to ignore him.

Lance enjoyed going to the zoo more than anything else. Maybe it was because he spent this time with both parents. It was one of the few times the Houslers truly functioned together as a family.

He sometimes looked at the animals for long periods, raised his little arm and wiggled his cute little fingers in their direction as if to say, "Hi, guys, it's your friend, Lance, here to see you again." Jennifer admired his innocence at these times.

Sometimes, when he looked at the snakes, he laid his head on the glass and stared at them for long periods, waiting for them to move. Jennifer thought the zoo brought out the best in him.

Momentarily inspired by his son's ability to focus on animals, Ralph said, "Maybe he's going to be a vet. He seems to like animals more than anything else."

Jennifer didn't say what she was thinking. She saw a paradox between the way Lance passionately looked at these animals and the way he treated Penny. He seemed to barely tolerate her nowadays, and when there was some interaction between the two of them, it was Lance doing something to hurt the dog. In many ways, his behavior mirrored Ralph's.

As he got older, his attacks on Penny became more malicious, and Jennifer contemplated giving her away. She had gotten a cat, thinking that maybe Lance would enjoy a change in pets, and this did seem to interest him for a while.

He hit Jiggers on occasion, but it wasn't as bad as the things he did to Penny. That was how their relationship remained until Jiggers scratched Lance in an attempt to get some peace from his persistent harassment.

When it happened, Jennifer became frantic. Lance was screaming as he looked up at his parents with three long, bleeding streaks across his face, one of which was close to his left eye. Jennifer immediately picked Lance up and rushed him to the bathroom sink, all the while shouting, "My baby, Jesus," and "My God, baby, what happened?"

In the meantime, Ralph was yelling at Jiggers and attempting to catch him. What he would have done to Jiggers had he caught him remained locked away in Ralph's brain. He terminated his chase with throwing a shoe at him and saying, "You son-of-a-bitch, one of these days I'm going to get your ass, and when I do, it's not going to be a pretty picture."

Lance continued his crying as Jennifer used a wash cloth and cold water to remove the blood from his face. When she used perox-ide to cleanse the area and stop the bleeding, it foamed up and scared Lance, making him cry even more. Once the blood was gone and the foam was removed, the wound didn't look half as bad as she thought it was, and Lance's crying subsided.

Ralph left the living room, cursing under his breath, and entered the bathroom to examine the extent of the scratches. Once he saw that they weren't too bad, he yelled, "I'll tell you what, Jenn, if that cat hurts Lance again, I'm going to kill that son-of-a-bitch."

Jennifer felt Ralph's remarks contrasted dramatically with his general attitude toward Lance. When had he given a damn about his son, anyway? On the other hand, the choice of words he used for Jiggers was entirely appropriate to describe his attitude toward their pets.

'Kill' was a word that Lance was not familiar with before Ralph's outrage, but he would eventually get to know it very well. At this early age, however, the sound of it and its vague meaning became imprinted in his memory to be something to contemplate at a later date.

Once Jennifer got the bleeding under control, she put some antibiotic salve on the scratches and commented about how she hoped it didn't leave scars. Meanwhile, Jiggers was in hiding and wasn't about to come out to face Ralph, no matter how pleasant his beckoning was becoming.

After the scratching episode, Lance seemed to shy away from Jiggers. Jiggers now occupied the same position on Lance's shit list that Penny held, maybe at an even higher level.

Weeks after the event, they found Jiggers in the dish washer, and months later, in the clothes drier. Fortunately, Lance wasn't big enough to turn the machines on. They didn't know about some of the other events, such as Lance throwing Jiggers into the toilet or later attempting to run him over with his tricycle. If Lance had been a bigger child, God only knows what he would have done to him.

When these types of events occurred, Jennifer scolded him and punished him by not giving him the candy he always demanded, but when he didn't get her gifts, he made her life miserable, and she eventually gave in to him. When Ralph got home and Jennifer told him what had happened, he ignored it, just as he had on other occasions. It was obvious that he didn't like the animals either or didn't want to be bothered with the problem.

Penny and Jiggers learned to get along just fine with one another. It was as though they found trust and contentment only in each other. Whenever possible, they both got as far away from Lance as they could to take a nap next to one another, and they remained there until Lance once again interfered with their rare tranquility.

With Lance getting older and more independent, Jennifer decided to put him into a day care center during part of Ralph's working hours to give herself a rest.

Ralph's comment was, "As long as you control him while I'm home, I don't care what the hell you do with him while I'm gone. That's your problem."

Lance didn't seem to mind his new environment, and it hurt Jennifer a little when he didn't put up some kind of fuss when they parted.

Jennifer said to Ralph, "I wish Lance would show more affection toward me."

Ralph responded as usual with, "Lance is probably going through a phase."

Lance was overly aggressive towards all the kids at the center in his age group, and he didn't tolerate intentions from anyone to direct his behavior in any way. When one of the boys attempted to take one of his toys, he picked up a plastic truck and clobbered the kid with it, not once but three times. He may have hit him more, but the teacher, Mrs. Colby, caught him before he could do it again. When she scolded him, she moved to the top of the shit list with Penny and Jiggers.

On another occasion, Mrs. Colby found Lance attempting to look at a little girl's privates. As she scolded him again, Lance bit her on the leg. It was a hard bite, leaving deep depressions in her skin, but it didn't break the surface. Nevertheless, she stared at Lance in disbelief and scolded him again.

It wasn't long before she quit her job and was replaced by a younger girl, Rachael. Whether her quitting had anything to do with Lance, they never knew, but she hadn't been a congenial person toward him after the bite.

Lance seemed to like Rachael. She was tolerant of him to a point, but when she scolded him on occasion, she used a bit of diplomacy. Consequently, Lance didn't seem to mind it when she told him why he shouldn't do certain things, but he didn't show any signs of remorse for doing them either. He just took the scolding and went about his business.

Both Jennifer and Ralph took pleasure in having Lance spend part of his time at the day care center. For Ralph, it was more of a pleasure to occasionally come home during the day for a bite to eat, followed by a drink or two, and not have Lance in his presence. For Jennifer, it was not only a relief from Lance but she got to see Ralph when he wasn't on edge.

However, Ralph was nevertheless growing more intolerant of Lance, although he saw him for only a portion of the day. Even Jennifer was getting a little upset with him on occasion. He was becoming a hand full, and they were losing the little control they had over him. They weren't sure they could survive a three-year-old after what they had faced in the terrible twos, and Jennifer thought she may need additional help with him.

When she talked with Stu, she asked if she could get them to recommend someone to help watch Lance at home. Stu said, "Sure. I don't see why not. Is he getting to be too much for you?" Stu knew more about Lance's changing behavior than Jennifer realized, but he wanted to hear what she had to say.

"Well," Jennifer said, "there are times when I have very little or no control over him, and he does things to us and to the pets that I don't think are normal. Ralph just says it's a phase he's going through, but it sometimes appears that he knows exactly what he's doing."

Jennifer hesitated a little before continuing, apparently wondering if she should tell Stu any more about Lance's behavior. Then she said, "I should also mention the nightmares. Lance has been waking up just about every night, screaming, and when I ask him what he's afraid of, he just says, 'They're watching me,' and 'They're going to hurt me.' When I ask who is going to do all this to him, he just says he doesn't know. Where is all this coming from? What am I doing wrong, Stu?"

Chapter 14

New Help for Lance

Stu knew about the nightmares. They had heard them repeatedly at the laboratory, and they wondered what was causing them, as well. They thought of the abuse by Ralph, but Lance was saying, "They're watching me," and "They're going to hurt me." *Who were they?*

Stu took advantage of the opportunity to throw in a bit of advice, although he thought it was a little late to alter the situation. Much of Lance's behavior pattern was already set. But, what the hell? Late is probably better than never. He took a chance, hoping he wouldn't hurt her feelings.

Trying to gather his thoughts, he said, "Well, Jennifer, in the little time I've spent with Lance, I've seen him change some over time, and it just seems like he may need a little more structure in his life.

"I believe you are a wonderful mother, but I think Lance has a very strong constitution, and while he needs your love, he also needs to be shown that you and Ralph are in command. In short, he needs to abide by some rules."

"Well, I try Stu, but I don't seem to be able to control him, and Ralph hasn't been much help lately."

When she began to cry, Stu didn't really know how to go on without hurting her more. He was reluctant to bring up one of his main concerns, that Ralph's behavior was seriously affecting Lance, fearing that this would create a deeper resentment in her toward Ralph and ruin the little trust that remained.

"Maybe you're right, Jennifer. Maybe we should get someone to help you with Lance. That would give you and Ralph a break. Maybe you're too close to the problem, as is the case with many parent-child relationships. I'll look for someone and get the help you need."

Stu thought getting someone else in Lance's life was a good idea for a number of reasons. It would allow Jennifer to have more freedom and get someone in there that could handle Lance a little better. In addition, they could establish better values in his mind. It would also keep Ralph away from Lance, helping to cool Ralph's temper down, and keep Lance from learning to replicate Ralph's intolerant behavior.

In a more helpful way, it would also allow them to watch Lance and Ralph a little closer. Sometimes, laboratory observations weren't enough. There were times in Lance's life when he wasn't observed at all, and this wasn't acceptable for their studies.

The team brought in Dr. Coleen Malvey, a young psychologist who would be working with Stu. Stu became the Senior Psychologist and Behavioral Director at the fertility clinic, and Coleen was in charge of establishing a close relationship with Lance and discussing it with Stu on a daily basis. She would spend about four hours a day with Lance, five days a week, depending on their needs.

To the Housler's, Coleen functioned as a part-time nanny. It would be Coleen that took Lance on some of his nearby outings, and when the Houslers wanted to spend time with Lance, Coleen would usually go along with them. With her training primarily in aberrant behavior in children, she jumped at the chance to work with Lance.

Within an hour of observing Lance, Coleen related to Stu, "I agree with you, Stu. Lance has a serious malicious streak and a narcissistic personality. I've seen it many times in other children, but it manifests itself much quicker in him. At this stage, it could develop either into more serious, problematic behavior, or it could dissipate, depending, in part, on how Lance is handled. I have a sneaking suspicion that there's a chance that some of his behavior may be genetically determined, but as you told me earlier, influence from his father most likely will influence how he turns out."

"Why do you feel these features are important, Coleen?" Stu asked.

"Because it's known that genetic imbalances, when combined with certain negative behavioral circumstances, can trigger negative responses in both children and even in adults. In the latter case, their behavior is generally set when they are younger, and it is difficult to treat, and, therefore, the problem must be attended to when the individual is young."

Although Stu understood the concept, hearing this from Coleen reinforced his thoughts which didn't please him in any way. "We have some limited history on the egg and sperm donors," he said, "and we have done some preliminary studies on his peculiar DNA, but we really don't know much about Lance's genetic make-up."

He wasn't aware of the origin of the sperm, and he wasn't sure of what mutations could have occurred in the production of parental gametes. And maybe there was some degree of incompatibility in the genes contributed by the two parents.

With Coleen's input, Lance appeared to be doing alright for a period, and then he slipped back into his old, more sadistic behavioral routine. At five, he showed the same intolerances that he had at three, but he seemed to have developed a more cunning approach for what he did to the animals and objects he didn't like.

He broke many of his toys, and on a couple of occasions, he cut both Penny and Jiggers with the sharp edge of a broken glass he had gotten hold of. Upon seeing the blood on the floor and Lance playing in it as though it was a pool of water, Jennifer became frantic, thinking it belonged to him.

"My God, baby, what have they done to you?" When she found out the truth, she was overjoyed that Lance didn't meet with mal-treatment from their pets.

Chapter 15

The Demise of Jiggers

Through these early years of Lance's life, Jennifer could see highly significant changes in Ralph's behavior. He was now complaining about his job again. He had, in fact, even stated a few times that, "I'm thinking of quitting." He wasn't the happy man he was when they first experienced the early bliss of young love.

In spite of Ralph's occasional comments about Lance "being in a mood" and "having a spell," he was growing progressively more intolerant of him, and he screamed at him during apparent episodes of correction. Once in a while, he even used his belt to lay huge welts on Lance's tender skin or he picked Lance up and shook him uncontrollably. After that, his hitting of Lance subsided somewhat, but the shaking was, in many ways, a worse emotional experience for the child, which could have resulted in brain shearing.

Ralph had found that having a stiff drink in the evening, after he had gotten home from work, was not only desired but absolutely necessary to take the edge off his tension. To him, drinking was a life saver, and it therefore became a mandatory part of his daily ritual. It allowed him some degree of chilling out so he could forget his miserable day at work and cope a little better with an evening of crying, tantrums, and pet abuse. Over time, though, one drink led to more, and Ralph commenced going down to Kelly's Bar for a few stiff ones even before going home.

Jennifer wasn't happy about Ralph's new approach to problem solving, although his being absent from home gave her some relief from his bad behavior. Yet, she felt the additional pressure of his negative approach to life, in addition to having to deal with Lance day in and day out.

There was still day care, and she had Coleen, thank God, but she was there only part of the day. And at the top of her list, she couldn't help but think that in spite of their having childcare and getting their finances in order, their marriage was again on extremely shaky grounds.

At six years old, Lance entered public school. On the first day of class, he cried and said, "I want to stay home."

After being introduced to his teachers and carefully coaxed to remain at school, he adjusted to his surroundings and appeared to be fine. However, it wasn't long before his teacher realized he was going to be a problem.

He didn't get along with his playmates, often hitting them if they even showed signs of wanting to share his time. The only student he admired in his class in the beginning was a girl that he wanted to be closer to. She was cute, with long curly brown hair and dark brown eyes, and she had an outgoing personality, even at her young age.

She apparently was also attracted to him until he pulled his privates out in her presence and scared her away. Because of her reaction, he never liked her again.

He often played with himself, both at home and at school. His mother didn't know he did this until he spent a night in bed with them. She woke to unusual movement and caught him playing with his penis.

"What are you doing, Lance?" She scolded him and said, "It isn't healthy to do that." He never did it again in her presence.

School was a different story. He often played with himself in the presence of others, especially when he was around the girls. If he got their attention and they began to make fun of him, he lost interest and didn't exhibit to them anymore.

He was not a serious student by any stretch of the imagination. When he wasn't stroking his genitals, he was playing games at his desk, drawing morbid pictures, or simply day dreaming. When he was caught drawing on several occasions, he refused to stop or do what the teacher demanded of him, and he ended up being sent to the principal's office. Jennifer had to go to school and talk to the school psychologist about this, but nothing further was ever done about it, even though she told the principal she would work on improving his behavior.

Because of his playfulness and constant day dreaming, his grades weren't good. When teachers confronted him about his lack of focus, he just said, "I was watching the birds out the window."

By the end of the year, he was sent to the next grade, but with reservations. He had not learned much in kindergarten, and the teacher expected him to have trouble in the next class where reading, writing, and arithmetic were the subjects to conquer.

During these early school years, Lance became more sadistic toward his pets and learned to hide much of his inner feelings toward them. Much of his behavior was unknown to the clinic because Coleen's stay at the Housler home was of a short duration, and most of Lance's day was spent at school. Her time with him was split into a couple of hours in the morning, getting ready for school, and an hour or two after school let out. These were the times that were most trying for Jennifer.

When Lance was seven, Jennifer attempted to console him on one particular occasion because she envisioned him upset with the disappearance of Jiggers, when, in truth, Lance had burried her in the garden after hitting her with a brick he found in the back yard.

The beating he gave Jiggers was much more than a corrective measure. Lance had held her down and hit her hard with the first blow, and Jiggers immediately went silent except for a few final life-lingering jerks. Lance continued smashing the brick to her head until her brains oozed out through the separating pieces of shattered skull and broken skin, and he seemed happy about the ordeal.

He also took some of Jiggers' teeth by pounding on his face until all of his jaw bones were shattered. With this event, the back yard had become his new playground, and he always accomplished assorted feats of cruelty during periods when he was certain he'd be alone.

The cat-killing was a recorded event because the team had a candid TV camera installed in the back yard at an earlier time while the Houslers were on a weekend outing with Lance. They had gone to a campsite outside of town so they could take Lance to swim, providing adequate time for the workman to complete the installation before they returned.

When Jennifer tried to console Lance by talking her sweet baby talk to him about how Jiggers may have just gone away for a few days but probably would come back, Lance just smiled. Even though Jennifer was sincerely upset that Jiggers was gone, she actually had a good feeling that Lance was concerned with the missing animal. This, she thought, was an exhibit of compassion and a step in the right direction.

After a few days had passed, the Houslers noticed a strange smell in the back yard, and Ralph found Jiggers under a two-inch pile of fresh dirt. When he realized what had happened, he screamed at Lance and began questioning him. Lance denied any connection with events that led to Jigger's demise, even when Ralph shook him so hard he couldn't talk. After he severely chastised Lance, Ralph put him in one of the bedroom closets and told him to stay there until he realized what he had done and could tell the truth about it.

Not believing that her son had actually done such a malicious thing to one of their pets, Jennifer wondered if Ralph had killed Jiggers and put him there himself, even though this didn't make any sense, or did it? Ralph was becoming a strange man.

Ralph hated the pets, and he had talked about killing Jiggers on occasion. In his present state of mind, she wouldn't put it past him. On the other hand, he probably would have taken it away, unless he was too lazy to do it or wanted to pin the blame on Lance. As horrible as it seemed, this was plausible. Whatever the reason, though, Jiggers was still dead and Lance was still in the closet.

Chapter 16

Closet Time

Actually, Ralph subsequently found the closet quite exceptional as a tool of correction. He not only could look forward to some peace and quiet when Lance was in his solitary confinement, but he noticed that Lance behaved much better once he was let out. So Ralph used the closet as often as he could, whether Jennifer agreed with his methods of correction or not.

When Ralph first started using the closet, Lance threw a temper fit, and Ralph took him out and beat the living hell out of him. When Lance finally curled into the fetal position on the floor and became silent, even when the belt straps laid immediate welts on his skin, Ralph picked him up and returned him to the closet, telling him he'd get more of the same if he acted up again.

Strangely, the Houslers, according to Jennifer, still had their good moments. Whenever they would go on a weekend outing, everyone seemed to enjoy it. Of course, Coleen was usually along to handle Lance, and Ralph's bad behavior was generally controlled more in her presence.

Whenever they planned a weekend trip and asked Coleen to go, she always reciprocated, trading one or more of her days during the week in order to satisfy their needs. Jennifer attempted to interact with Coleen and Lance, but Ralph usually walked off to be alone, or he drank until it was obvious he didn't feel any pain.

Lance's first grade report showed that his day-dreaming was still a very serious problem. His teachers found him completely disinterested in his subjects, collectively recommending that he repeat first grade. They also requested an audience with Lance's parents.

Jennifer arrived at his school at the recommended time and visited each of his teachers. They consecutively told her that, "Lance is no particular problem in class except for his day dreaming, which we are afraid has become worse." He sat in the back of the room and occasionally played with himself, but he hadn't gotten caught during the entire school year.

When they asked where Mr. Housler was, Jennifer lied and said, "He is working and couldn't get off." Actually, she had asked Ralph to come with her and he refused. He could have taken the time off, but he didn't want to be bothered. "You wanted a god damn kid, so you can take care or these things," was generally how he looked at it.

Jennifer asked each teacher, "Is it absolutely necessary to keep Lance back a grade?"

Each told her, "It would be best for him because he is poorly prepared to go on. It will be extremely difficult for him to cope with new material when he hasn't learned what has already been presented to him. He needs to be more attentive."

Jennifer finally asked, "What should I do?

She was given a variety of recommendations and told, "It all boils down to having you watch to see that he does his homework, and we want you to encourage him to pay attention in school. Also, a tutor would be helpful. This will encourage him to think more about his studies and get him to listen better in class."

Lance's tutor turned out to be Coleen. Knowing that his attention span was very short, she and Jennifer did whatever they could to improve his attitude about school, and they honestly believed it was doing some good.

Chapter 17

Results of Chronic Abuse

By the time Lance was eight, he had experienced the isolation and silence of the closet numerous times. Ralph was not much more than a drunk by that time. He still held a job at the place he had worked when Lance first came along, but he had been demoted twice and had no ambition to get ahead.

He was leading a miserable life, physically and mentally abusing both Jennifer and Lance in the process. No one knew the reason for his attitude. He refused to talk about it. On one occasion, he came home from work, as usual, by way of Kelly's Bar, and he found Lance playing with matches while Jennifer was lying down, crying. He beat the hell out of both of them and then sat down to another drink, grumbling under his breath, while they licked their wounds. Jennifer got a broken rib, a black eye, and bruised jaw out of it, and Lance suffered a broken ear drum, along with facial and body bruises.

Jennifer kept Lance out of school for two weeks, telling school personnel that Lance was sick. She got a doctor's excuse and told him that Lance had a fight at school with an older student. She conveniently covered her bruises with make-up. Lance was a witness to the lies his mother had told in order to avoid any outside criticism, learning from both parents that it paid to lie during certain circumstances.

On another occasion, Lance was caught hiding behind the sofa and playing with himself, and Ralph beat him with his belt until his genitals and back were almost bleeding. He had to stay out of school for a week because his genitals had swollen to such an extent that he had trouble walking. Much of that time was also spent in the closet.

Most of Lance's closet time was during periods after Coleen left their house in the evening. Ralph was careful not to use his method of correction in her presence, but both Stu and Coleen knew about it because of Lance's bruises and their hidden cameras.

Jennifer was now beside herself with fear for Lance. Her most immediate concern was that she was afraid of how far Ralph would go with his abuse toward him, and all the progress they had made with him would have been for naught. Actually, she didn't seem to have a clue that what Ralph had done to Lance already had permanently altered his personality and behavior and would cause him to experience a very difficult future.

She didn't know if she would survive his brutality either. There was no love left between them, and she didn't see much of it toward or from Lance. Life had somehow slipped into the gutter.

Coleen said to Stu, "We were right about Lance. By being chronically abused, he has developed a serious sadistic streak, and I am afraid it has taken its toll on him."

At this point, she was afraid there wasn't much they could do to change things unless they would step in and take over, and this wasn't going to happen. She was doing everything she could to help Lance through his traumatic life, but he was succumbing to his father's torturous treatment.

Stu remarked for the umpteenth time, "I understand how you feel, but remember, Coleen, the team has said that it wants to strictly enforce a no-hands-on approach to dealing with Lance. According to some of the team, we have interfered with the Houslers too much already. It's important that we continue to take notes and record videos, but we're not supposed to alter his behavior.

"It's frustrating for both of us, but as was pointed out at the last meeting, this is an experiment and the director, wherever he may be, insists it will remain that way. Without a hands-off policy, the experiment no longer is viable.

"But Stu," said Coleen, "everyone on the team is concerned about Lance's fate, and what Ralph is doing to Lance is not ethical by any means. I'm also concerned about Jennifer. What she has been through is a downright shame."

"Yes, I totally agree," Stu responded, "and I'm beginning to wonder more about Ralph's family background. I'll bet if we look into it, we'll find some indication of abuse. I'm certain we'd also find abuse by him toward Jennifer at an earlier time in their married life. They conveniently left this out when listing all their family traits during the acceptance period for embryo recipients. He's got some very serious problems."

"I see where the director is coming from Stu. However, I don't like it. You've made some good points, and I think we should at least look into Ralph's earlier life, the lives of his parents, and possibly even deeper into his genealogy." Jennifer was now seeing a psychiatrist, a Dr. Theodore Pelleck, who was highly recommended by Stu on one of his visits to the Houslers. Stu felt the sadness in Jennifer and wanted to help her, but he also understood the rules.

Dr. Pelleck was informed that he was to report all observations to the Fertility Clinic and that he was to go light on attempts toward solving any of their family problems. To help Jennifer over her difficult times was alright, but further corrective measures were to be avoided.

Subsequently, she had poured her heart out to Dr. Pelleck about her unhappy situation. She now realized how serious her marital problems were, and she also elaborated on her total lack of control over Lance. It was obvious that she believed many of her problems were her fault when she said, "Maybe this was all a bad idea. I apparently am not a fit parent. I can't face the pressure, and I don't know how to deal with the problems that have been coming up."

Dr. Pelleck told Jennifer to see him twice a week, and he would help her with her stressful life. He also advised her to tell him if she or Lance was the subject of further abuse by Ralph.

While it was not possible for the team to interfere with the Houslers, he could, as he understood it, offer advice as a psychiatrist to Jennifer. He may even be able to arrange for medication for Ralph so he wouldn't represent a constant threat to them. Exactly what he could do for her beyond that, he had no clue.

He wanted to talk to Ralph, which he thought would come with time. However, to drag him in without his permission would only cause problems, and Ralph was not about to talk to a shrink of his own accord at this time.

During Lance's eighth year, he grew further apart from both parents, and he got into trouble with the law on several occasions. Jennifer had given him more freedom to play outside with some of the boys that lived nearby. Little did she know, Lance and the other boys left the vicinity of the house and went to some of the neighborhood businesses.

He was caught on more than one occasion stealing things from a variety of stores, things that he really didn't need. He also stole money from his parents, and his mother confronted him about it. He lied, even though he was aware that she knew he had done it. As she cried, it almost appeared to her that Lance felt some degree of remorse for what he'd done. But he never confessed.

Chapter 18

Kelly's Bar

Jennifer no longer told Ralph about most of the things Lance did. She didn't want to provoke him into doing something to Lance that they would both regret. But she told Dr. Pelleck during her biweekly sessions. She had to tell someone, and she needed Dr. Pelleck's input.

Another reason she kept it from Ralph was because every time she brought Lance up to him, he took his despondency out on her before he decided to take care of Lance. This meant receiving both mental and physical abuse, and she couldn't take much more of it.

Ralph was now showing up at work a little on the buzzed side. He wasn't doing his job properly, and since his pay depended on the number of sales he made, he wasn't bringing home much money. The money he did bring home he squandered on himself, and Jennifer had to buy all the things they needed as a family, plus those required by Lance, from the money provided by the Fertility Clinic.

Very little of the money was saved as they had originally planned. It went through his body in liquid form, all of it. He had long lost any self-esteem, and he took his grief out on anybody who was in his way. That included not only Jennifer and Lance but his potential customers and fellow salesmen, as well.

When his boss, John Conti, took him aside to talk with him about it, Ralph showed contempt even toward him. John finally said, "Ralph, you and I have known each other for quite a while. We grew up in this business together.

"I never said anything when you and Jennifer were having trouble a few years back, and I wasn't going to bring it up now. But I've never seen you like this before, and I don't like what I see. I'm afraid that if you continue drinking and treating everyone like an ass hole, we're going to have to let you go. I don't want to do that, but our business is suffering because of your piss-poor attitude."

With glazed eyes and in complete silence, Ralph hung his head and made an effort to listen to John. He then broke down and told him about his miserable life, about Lance and Jennifer. It was obvious that he had lost all control of his life, and John felt empathy for him.

"I understand your grief, Ralph," he said, "but you're going to have to try to do better at your job."

"I will," Ralph said, and he apologized to John for the things he'd done and for losing it during their conversation.

For a while, it seemed as though Ralph was doing better. Of course, it was partially because he wasn't going home very much. He was hanging out at Elaine's apartment. Elaine was a chronically lonesome woman he'd met at Kelly's Bar a year earlier, and they had a thing going ever since.

Elaine felt compassion for Ralph and took him in whenever he couldn't face what he referred to as "the nagging bitch and the little son-of-a-bitch from hell." Ralph was now with her most of the time.

Jennifer knew about Ralph and Elaine. At first, it seemed to be a hard blow to her self-respect as a woman, but with time she ignored it and took relief in the hiatus of cruelty that Ralph seemed to enjoy at their expense.

In spite of what was going on between his mother and father, Lance's grades in school improved. Evidently, Coleen and Jennifer were making some headway toward rehabilitation. Either he was paying attention a little better in school, or it could have been because he repeated the class he had the year before. At any rate, he moved to second grade, but again with some reservation.

Jennifer, again sitting before Lance's teachers, was told, "He still day dreams, although there seems to be some improvement in that category. The main problem is his lack of concern for learning, and he occasionally is caught playing in class. And, of course, there's the time he was caught fondling himself and exposing his genitals to classmates."

Jennifer remembered very well when that happened. She had been called in and had to face the parents of several students about Lance's promiscuous behavior. She forced Lance to apologize to both the students and their parents, and it appeared that he had learned his lesson. They didn't catch him when he did it again the following day.

Lance grew worse behaviorally at home with Ralph gone most of the time. At nine, he was a holy terror. He wasn't just doing his mischievous deeds at a casual pace. He was actually looking for things to do. It was as though he was trying to take revenge on anything he could to rectify all those nightmares he was having and the trauma caused by closet time. He was especially hard on the backyard wildlife and neighborhood pets.

On one occasion, Jennifer found several toads lined up in the garden, through which Lance had shoved wooden spikes. Some were wiggling their last signs of life. At another time, she found lizards stuck with pins to the fence post, all of them on their back and flailing their legs in an attempt to escape their peril.

When Jennifer asked Lance why he had done those things, he said, "I was just playing."

"But honey," she said, "you shouldn't kill things just because you're playing. Those animals didn't hurt you, did they?"

Lance said, "No," and Jennifer looked at her son and wondered what was going on in his mind. He didn't comment any further, and he never mentioned what he had done to some of the neighbor's dogs and cats.

Since Jennifer wasn't getting much sleep because she was running into Lance's room every night, attempting to quiet him after his sudden awakenings and screams, she decided to let Lance sleep in her bed. She thought maybe that would calm him. It wasn't like anyone else was sleeping with her.

Actually, it did calm Lance to be sleeping with his mother, and when he put his hands on her breasts, she didn't mind. In a way, it was a form of attention that she enjoyed and had been starved from, and she would even move like a purring kitten to encourage their closeness, no matter what form it was taking.

The only thing that Jennifer couldn't get used to during the night was Lance's bed wetting, so she laid a rubber sheet beneath both of them. It wasn't unusual for her to get up in the middle of the night, dripping wet from Lance's urine.

She learned to shower and lay towels atop the wet bed until they awoke in the morning. If she woke Lance, he would act like a little bastard, and if she put fresh sheets on the bed, they may be wet again by the time they arose in the morning.

Lance still had his nightmares, but at least she was there to calm him, and it did seem that he had less of them than when he was sleeping alone. She didn't know what else to do, and she was hoping this was a phase that would pass with time.

Lance's behavior during the daylight hours was exactly opposite to what Jennifer experienced at night. Even at this young age, he was ornery and hateful. As she did her daily wash to rid the sheets and night clothes of their pungent urine load, he spent much of his time chasing Penny and breaking his toys.

She thanked God again for Coleen. Without her, life would be unbearable. Coleen seemed to have better control of Lance. She talked to him in a congenial manner, and he sometimes reciprocated. But this wasn't always the case. He showed contempt for her, too, but she seemed better able to handle what he dished out.

Jennifer also thanked God for Dr. Pelleck. While Coleen was primarily for Lance's welfare, she depended on Dr. Pelleck to get the many things that were bothering her off her chest. She was certain that he was helping her keep her sanity. He listened attentively and gave advice to cope with her increasing problems, some of which she followed.

When she mentioned Lance's nightmares and bed wetting, and that she had allowed Lance to sleep with her, she left out the more intimate relationship she had with him. His advice was that she put Lance back in his own bed, but she ignored this for the time being.

Jennifer no longer thought of Ralph's absence around the house as unfortunate. She enjoyed the break from him, relief from the mental abuse and the beatings. She no longer became depressed over the thought of a separation or divorce. If that ever happened, it would actually be a blessing for both she and Lance.

On Lance's tenth birthday, she and Coleen had a party for him. Ralph didn't come or even acknowledge he knew about it. It was a solemn occasion in which Lance ate some cake and ice cream while sitting on the floor by himself and they sang happy birthday to him. He then proceeded to tear the presents apart and break the new toys that he got. They had invited some of the kids from around the neighborhood and from his school, but no one showed up.

He ended his ninth year with a part time, son-of-a-bitch for a father, a mother who was about to come apart at the seams, and a dog that was scared to death of the boy who was supposed to happily grow up with him. While Coleen was there to help the family crisis, she had not really been able to change the direction in which Lance's life was going. However, she knew that something would have to be done before Lance went off the deep end.

In his tenth year, his father was gone from his life permanently. It was a mixed blessing. In the years to come, he wouldn't have a male role model to look to, but the role model he had to this point had more of a negative influence on him than anything else. Before long, Ralph left Elaine, too, and was never heard from again.

Chapter 19

Psychological Intervention

Stu arranged for Lance to have some medical tests. While Jennifer was of the opinion that it was a routine check-up, a number of tests were performed that they wouldn't have normally done.

Rather than fight with Lance about a doctor's visit, Coleen said, "Let's go for a ride."

Thinking it was one of their usual outings, he offered no resistance. However, when they parked the car in town, he knew they were up to no good and refused to leave the vehicle.

"Come on, Lance," Coleen said. "We'll go get some ice cream after seeing the doctor." While this seemed to work, they could tell he wasn't happy about it.

Blood was taken, but it was primarily for DNA and other chemical tests, as well as an examination of chromosomal structure.

Although it was difficult to immediately determine if aberrant behavior was in some way connected to a specific genetic disposition, Stu and Coleen at least wanted some sort of a record to relate their studies to. It was during that examination that they found very low levels of cholesterol and serotonin, chemicals that in low abundance were often associated with aggressive behavior and criminal activity.

Lance was also exposed to sessions of MRI, but he had to be tranquilized and strapped in, and he still managed to move enough throughout the procedure to complicate the results. They had hoped to reveal some unusual hot spots, especially in the frontal lobes and inner limbic regions of the brain that were causing the brain to function abnormally.

He was also exposed to a rigorous psychological exam, but he seemed to get through it without any serious complications. What all the test results meant to Stu and Coleen was that he had the chemical make-up and anti-social characteristics of a social misfit but was already masking many of his aberrant behaviors at the early age of eleven.

Coleen's comments to Stu were, "I'm amazed at the results of the psychological test, but I'm convinced it's not a true picture of what Lance is all about. He's a very complex person. I believe Lance is actually learning to act normal. He will say the things that he thinks we want to hear. It's all part of a big game to him."

"I couldn't agree with you more, Coleen." Stu had thought this all along. "I believe we have a potential monster on our hands. While it may be possible to offer him medication to change his chemical make-up, I sincerely believe it's just a matter of time before he begins to do things that we really don't want to happen.

"Contrary to my earlier approach and the desires of the team, I am now convinced that you are right. Our job should be to attempt to straighten this kid out." Stu's philosophy toward the experiment was undergoing some significant changes, causing him to believe that they should help Lance in any way they can, in spite of the experiment and its rules.

Coleen smiled.

Stu said, "The team has repeatedly expressed its opinion that they don't want us to interfere with the experiment, but knowing what we do about Lance, wouldn't it be a challenge to attempt to change him for the better? It would be one of the greatest psychological experiments of all times.

"I'm not sure we should do it on our own or go before the team to get permission. What do you think, Coleen?"

Coleen was shaking her head affirmatively as Stu was talking. "Yes, I'd be willing to approach the committee with a proposal to get Lance back on the right track. Whatever happens, something really must be done to change Lance's direction. Otherwise, he may, at some point, go off the deep end. I'm glad you're finally changing your mind about what you think our role is in this experiment."

Stu replied, "Well, I've always been loyal to the rules set forth by the director, but Lance's behavior is now getting out of hand. If we don't do something about it, it will be too late. He's becoming what I describe as a perfect psychopath in which he successfully hides his inner psyche from anyone who has contact with him. I'm beginning to wonder if the team had ever considered something like this happening to their experimental subject."

Stu and Coleen began to share a new excitement over the possibility of changing Lance. The more they thought of the potential in developing a new technique to deal with someone like him, the more excited they became.

Stu let the team members know that he and Coleen wanted some time during the next meeting to discuss something of utmost importance. While they waited, they researched the possibilities of making psychological changes, and they reviewed the chemical, DNA, and poorly-defined MRI results. When they finally got all their notes in order, their excitement made it difficult for them to wait for the next meeting to come.

When the time finally arrived for their presentation, Stu and Coleen had outlined the experiment they wanted to carry out, but first they had to explain why they wanted to do it. Stu was a little apprehensive because what they had planned very much was a form of interference in the original plan, no matter how it was perceived, and both he and Coleen knew that this was not an issue to screw around with without proper documentation.

While the director was, of course, not there, their presentation was videotaped, and he viewed it through a conference-room camera and later planned to study it at his leisure. Since they had never met him, his absence didn't interfere with what Stu wanted to say. However, both Stu and Coleen thought it would have been nice to finally meet him and get his input.

When given his time, Stu presented a summary of their findings. He built a holographic-like picture of Lance that the team could envision in their minds, bringing up Lance's paternal abuse, his chemical inconsistencies, his intolerance toward adults and his peers, dwelling particularly on his sadistic treatment of pets, his nightmares, and his bed wetting.

Stu remarked that, "As you know, these are the signs of a severely emotionally disturbed individual, a psychopath, and there may be more that we don't know about. Although we chose to put Dr. Coleen Malvey in touch with Lance so we could observe his behavior more closely, there are many times when Lance is by himself and away from our cameras. And his thoughts are his alone. Also, the cameras help tremendously, but there's no way we can get into his head and see exactly what he's thinking.

"Lance is becoming more adept at dealing with individuals who attempt to observe and correct him. He is learning to perfect his behavior, and he often lies in order to blend in with what we think is acceptable in a modern society. Even at this early age, he is becoming a master of disguise.

"There are many things we can predict are going on in Lance's brain, but he won't expose himself to us as he should. He's covering up his deepest thoughts, but you can be sure they are very much in line with other characteristics that lead us to believe he will become a serious threat to society as he gets older, unless we do something about it."

As Stu was finishing his presentation, a phone rang at one end of the conference-room table, and the call was immediately switched to a speaker-phone. On the other end of the line was the director, Steven Morrison, and he had some questions.

"Yes, Dr. Morrison, do you have a comment?"

"Yes, I do, Stu. I understand your concern for Lance's future, but he also may work these things out as he gets older. As you know, many children do. How much of a threat do you feel he could be?"

Stu detected that Dr. Morrison, representing the most influential vote of the team, was already on the verge of rejecting their proposal if he didn't elaborate further.

"Well, Dr. Morrison," he said, "as you already know, these characteristics that are demonstrated by Lance are ones we see in a criminal mind. If Lance doesn't receive any direction in his early life, he could very well end up in this category. I'm not saying he will, but it is very possible. In my opinion, ending up a criminal is highly probable, and both Dr. Malvey and I do not think you and the rest of the team would want this to happen."

Dr. Morrison said, "Yes, you're right, but you haven't convinced us that this is definitely going to happen, and, as you know, we are strictly against interfering with the life of our subject."

"Believe me, Dr. Morrison, Coleen and I realize this, and we have spoken together at length about it, but we both agree that something must be done. This is something we must consider very carefully. Many emotionally disturbed criminals that have been caught and imprisoned had one or more of these characteristics. Lance demonstrates all of them.

"We feel that by knowing this, we may be able to work with Lance and redirect his thinking so he becomes a normal individual, or at least closer than he would be without our direction. If we can do this, it will be one of the greatest breakthroughs to come out of psychology in years, maybe ever, and it will be a giant step toward dealing with such individuals in the future. It will bring a lot of positive attention to you and the Fertility Clinic, to say the least."

There was quiet on the other end of the speaker-phone. In what felt like an eternity, Stu began to think that he may have said the right things because Dr. Morrison was possibly showing signs of being particularly attentive to his comments. Anything that would make him or the Fertility Clinic look good was something to consider. Stu decided to ride this wave and take advantage of its force, even if he had to step out of bounds.

He said, "Actually, it really wouldn't interfere with the initial experiment. In many ways, the experiment that was initially designed is over. The company made the cross. An individual resulted from it. We know the cross worked, if that was the company's goal, and we know what we got from it.

"We, as I believe we'll all agree, have created a monster. Let's see if we can manipulate what we have created. It's a great opportunity to help society, to take an individual like this and make him a better person. I'm just sorry we couldn't have dealt with Lance's problems before they reached this stage. It would have been simpler to help him if he was younger.

"Please don't take me wrong. I'm not blaming anyone in the Fertility Clinic for what's happened to Lance. Much of what happened to him may have nothing to do with his genetic make-up. In fact, we are certain that many of his problems are related to his father's influence throughout his formative years. However, I may add, I sincerely believe both his genetics and what we may call post traumatic stress disorder are working on Lance to make him what he is becoming.

"We recently looked into his and Jennifer's medical records that dealt with their life before they had Lance, and we even looked into Ralph's genealogical background. What we found was that Ralph was also abused as a child, and he had abused Jennifer on several occasions prior to having Lance. Based simply on that criteria, it's no wonder Lance is screwed up.

"I think we all would agree that we know a lot about what the things are that most likely caused Lance to be what he is. The point I am emphasizing here, however, is not how his problems originated but how we can turn them around and end up with a reasonably well-adjusted individual. I think we owe that to him."

Coleen was surprised to hear Stu go out on a limb and actually indicate that except for the success of the cross itself, the experiment was up to now a mistake in terms of attempting to create an individual that was socially adjusted. She waited to see how the director and the other team members would react to this. If they took it wrong, both she and Stu could be looking for new jobs.

Chapter 20

Knowing His Secrets

Stu was afraid that the director may decide he was openly criticizing what the team had done, in spite of how he presented his information. To him, Stu was hoping the director would not view what he and Coleen were proposing as a scientific approach.

As they waited for the director's comments, Stu's thoughts immediately blended into other considerations. While he had the right to speak his mind, any qualms he had about the validity of their experiment should have been brought it up in a one-on-one process for discussion with the director himself, not in front of everyone involved in the experiment.

Stu was facing an impossible situation. In the first place, as far as he knew, no one had ever talked to the director in a one-to-one conversation. He had never shown himself. He felt fortunate that he had his brief conversation with the speaker-phone. At least he now knew the director existed.

Secondly, if he ever got an audience with him and if he had brought it up in the manner suggested by the director, he was certain that the director would either have told him to present his material at the meeting or forget about it all together, probably the latter. In a way, he prided himself for choosing the only way of presenting such a proposal that would have a chance of being accepted.

Dr. Morrison ended his silence by directing his comments to everyone, but he was speaking primarily to Stu and Coleen. "I do see an opportunity here. I congratulate you on your research. This shows that you care, and I respect that."

This surprised both Stu and Coleen. They never expected he would give even a modicum of credit to their proposal.

"However," he said, "I don't think we should settle this matter so quickly. It's too serious a proposal to treat lightly.

"I would like to have you write up a report, covering the pros and cons of doing what you propose, somewhat like you did here, but in more detail. We'll pass it out to everyone on the team, and a vote will be taken at our next meeting. But be certain of this. If the majority of the team feels we should allow you to run this additional experiment, we'll give you the go ahead. If the vote is otherwise, you will not have the opportunity to bring it up again. How does this sit with everyone?"

In a way, the director was accomplishing two things in his approach to Stu's proposal. He was giving the appearance of being democratic about accepting or rejecting the projected research plan, but he was also biding for time. He obviously wanted to feel his way through the thoughts of each team member and make sure they weren't going to vote for the proposal just because of their moral obligations. This was an experiment, and it was going to remain an experiment, no matter what the outcome.

A sudden noise of chatter and acknowledging shakes of heads around the room indicated to everyone that this would be an acceptable approach to the problem.

Stu looked around and commented, "It appears that everyone is in favor of looking into this approach, Dr. Morrison."

"Okay, then," he said. "We'll see you at the next meeting."

Stu and Coleen now had to get busy on the report, and they agreed it had better be a good one. They didn't quite understand what the director meant when he said, "If the vote is otherwise, you will not have the opportunity to bring it up again." *What would he do if it was?*

While Stu and Coleen were doing their research, the director was apparently doing his. He made his rounds with telephone calls, talking to everyone and explaining how this was not something to toy with. In short, he did everything he could to instill negative thoughts about accepting Stu's proposal without making it appear that he was attempting to influence the vote. To counteract the director's attempt to instill negative thoughts in the team members, Stu and Coleen sent out a report that was very convincing.

At the next meeting, the director was again present through the speaker-phone, but arranged through another member of the team to take a silent vote on Stu and Coleen's proposal. He was surprised to find that the majority of the team felt it was important to allow their psychologists to go ahead with their plan. His vote to not interfere with Lance's current direction carried very little weight, and Stu and Coleen were thrilled with the outcome. Stu thanked everyone and guaranteed them that he and Coleen would do everything in their power to make a good citizen out of Lance.

Their first move in that direction was to set up more psychological meetings with Lance, using Dr. Pelleck as the examining psychiatrist. Stu didn't have to explain these extra meetings to Jennifer. She knew that Lance needed some help, and Dr. Pelleck was already familiar with the problems she was having. However, she was extremely happy that they were going to do something about his behavior, as well.

She wanted her son back. She really didn't comprehend the seriousness of Lance's behavior. She just knew that he was a bad kid and wasn't showing the love toward her that she needed so badly.

When confronted with some of the things he'd done, Lance surprisingly admitted that he had some problems, but he claimed that he didn't know how to go about changing. He also admitted having nightmares that woke him on occasion. Beyond this, Lance wouldn't share any details of his life.

Lance was offering up information about himself to Dr. Pelleck, knowing that by doing it, they would perceive his behavior as a positive expression toward wanting to change and be a better person.

In spite of his holding back certain information, Stu and Coleen fell for Lance's ploy and considered his attitude as a positive sign. Lance had never confessed to having problems before. Maybe he now understood that people were here to help, and he was ready to take them up on it. Or was he just learning to manipulate people and was now beginning to play a life-long game to dominate those around him?

His dreams of holding certain people hostage, killing them, and mutilating their bodies never rose to the surface. These were his secret personal thoughts, and they would remain his alone. He was too young to consider adding sexual fantasies to the process. That would come later.

Dr. Pelleck asked Lance specifically about certain events that had occurred in his past, starting with his cat, Jiggers. Lance expressed a degree of surprise at this line of questioning because he didn't know they were aware of that incident. He asked, "How do you know about that?"

While Dr. Pelleck didn't feel he owed an explanation to Lance for anything, he wanted to gain Lance's trust, so he offered him an explanation, although it wasn't totally true. "Your mother told us about it."

Lance appeared to accept that explanation, although it was clear that he was mulling it over in his mind until he said, "Jiggers was always scratching me and trying to bite me. He bit me really hard. I wasn't even doing anything to him. He just came over and bit me."

"But why did you hit Jiggers so hard?" Hard wasn't really the right word for what Lance did to Jiggers, but Dr. Pelleck didn't want to go into details.

Lance said, "I didn't want him to hurt me anymore," and he left it at that.

Dr. Pelleck had to be careful about what questions he asked. Stu and Coleen had witnessed so much from their hidden cameras that had to do with Lance's private life, Lance would surely know they were spying if he asked him about any of those events.

Dr. Pelleck attempted to work around them, asking Lance, "Did you do anything like that to any other animals?"

Lance was silent for a minute or so, obviously reflecting on the question and how he was going to answer it. He wondered if they knew about all the other things that were supposed to be hidden from everyone but him.

He finally said, "No." He decided to answer the question but offer no additional information. He wanted to see what they knew about the things he believed were secret.

Dr. Pelleck knew he was lying because Stu and Coleen had witnessed him doing horrible things to Jiggers, the toads, and lizards, not to mention all the times he hit, kicked, cut and otherwise tortured Penny and other neighborhood animals. Then there was the time he found a baby bird in the back yard and proceeded to rip its head off. Jennifer didn't know about that one either.

Also, no one was supposed to know about the time he caught a neighbor's cat and hung it over a clothesline by its neck and watched its thrashing until it stopped breathing, or the dog he ran a spear through and left it suspended until he stopped moving. These were things they would never know.

Chapter 21

A Session With a Psychopath

Dr. Pelleck, still on this subject, asked, "Did you ever want to hurt other animals?"

"No."

"Why not?"

"Because they never hurt me."

Observing the session behind the mirror with Coleen, Stu wondered if any of what he said could be true. He, like everyone else, realized there were things about Lance they would never know because they couldn't read his aberrant thoughts, and he was certain that no one would ever get close enough to understand his psyche, gain his trust, and hear about what he was really thinking.

On the other hand, there was a slight chance he could be telling a partial truth. Lance had not been exposed to much of the world around him. As far as he knew, Lance had lived in a solitary world, mostly confined to his house and yard. Maybe he didn't think beyond the confines of his yard, and there may still be a chance to instill in him some sort of love for animals or at least some remorse for the ones he had done in. He and Coleen would have to work this out.

After continuing to question Lance about events they already knew had occurred, Lance denied having any connection with them, whatsoever. He answered their questions if he thought his mother or Coleen were around when the events had occurred, but he seemed to understand whether they should or should not know about certain of his activities.

In the terminal minutes of their meeting, Dr. Pelleck said, "You know, Lance, we want to help you. Do you understand this?"

"Yes," he said, not really believing they had even the slightest concern for his welfare.

"We'd like to eliminate your nightmares, and we don't want things to hurt you. We want you to be a happy boy. If you ever need to talk to us about anything, just tell your mother or Coleen, and we'll try to help you with your problems."

Lance said, "Okay," and that was the end of their conversation. He left with his mother who had been sitting in the waiting area.

Stu and Coleen came from behind the mirror they were observing through and gave Dr. Pelleck a suspicious glance.

Coleen said, "That was quite an interesting session. Did we learn anything from it other than that he was lying most of the time?" She had predicted before the meeting that Lance would deny anything out of the ordinary, unless he thought they knew about it from talking with his mother.

Dr. Pelleck told Stu and Coleen, "I'll have to study my notes before I can comment. I'll have the report typed and on your desk in a couple of days."

As she and Stu were rehashing the session, she asked, "Do you think he suspects me as an accomplice to digging out his little secrets?"

Stu responded with, "No, I don't think he does, but he's a very sly boy. He catches on fast. He doesn't say anything unless he thinks about it first. He won't tell us any details about his nightmares or the sadistic things he does. And when he does speak about them, he lies completely. He's not going to incriminate himself on anything.

"I'd watch him very closely when you spend time with him, Coleen. I wouldn't probe too much or give him any indication that you know about certain things. You may be able to determine if he suspects you in any way, but be careful how you go about it."

When Coleen went to the house the following Monday morning, she asked Jennifer, "How did Lance do at the doctor's office?"

Jennifer said, "He did fine as far as I know."

All the while they talked, Lance pretended to be playing with one of his toy trucks, the only one that had survived complete destruction, but Coleen knew he was listening closely to what they were saying. In her opinion, he was waiting for her to reveal her true nature.

During Coleen's time with Lance, he never said a word about his time with Dr. Pelleck, but she sensed that he knew something wasn't right. Instead of shying away from Coleen, he seemed to draw closer to her. That made her a little aprehensive.

On one of their outings, Coleen returned to the zoo with Lance. She explained, "All the animals are living on the earth together, just like all the people, and we should love them. Don't you agree?"

"Yes," he said, trying hard to make her believe he was sincere.

To Lance, they were in a cage, locked away just like he was, and they couldn't get out. They were better off dead. Yet, he responded affirmatively to Coleen's line of statements because he knew that was what she wanted to hear him say.

He began to suspect that she was part of the spying group that wanted him to change. This was too much of a coincidence to be talking about love and how we should all get along, right after having long sessions with Dr. Pelleck. He wasn't buying it. Besides, in spite of what he had told them, he didn't think he had the problems they spoke of.

Medication was administered to Lance to help with his chemical imbalances, and when they requested that he take the pills they had given to him, he offered no objections. They didn't know that he held them in his mouth without swallowing as long as he had to and spit them out at his first opportunity.

Lance was a little angel for about a week after the session with Dr. Pelleck and the follow-up outing with Coleen. They wondered if they were beginning to make some headway with him or if he just had learned a little more about playing the game.

He was also nice to his mother. She remarked to Coleen about how much difference there was in Lance. Maybe there was hope for him after all. If he improved that much after one session and new medication, who knew how he would be after six months or a year?

Jennifer asked Coleen, "How well do you know Dr. Pelleck?"

Coleen lied and said, I know him from just the time or two that I had been asked questions about Lance." Lance was back to playing with his truck.

Jennifer said, "He seems to be a nice man. I talked with him for quite a while about Lance and our lives together, as well as about Lance's father, and he was quite understanding about it all. He must be quite knowledgeable about his field."

"I guess so. I've heard that he is very well respected and that he enjoys working with children." Coleen didn't want to overdo the sales pitch, but she knew that Lance was listening, and she wanted to let him know that both she and Dr. Pelleck really did want to help him.

She wanted Jennifer to understand that, as well. Lance continued playing with his truck, not ever glancing in their direction, but his playing was well within earshot of their conversation.

As time passed, Lance seemed to get better with each session, although Stu and Coleen could see that Lance had not really changed when he was alone. He still broke his toys. He still pulled the heads off his action figures. He still tortured Penny whenever he had the chance. He was doing it less in the presence of others, though, while becoming even more secretive about his behavior and thoughts.

The minute he got back from one of his sessions with Dr. Pelleck, he appeared to seek Penny out to take out his inner feelings of frustration on her, and it wasn't a pretty picture. He had a plastic toy baseball bat in his hand when he went looking for her. When he found her cowering beneath a rocking chair, he rocked it on her tail, and when she yelped and ran from beneath it, he clobbered her as hard as he could.

Coleen wondered if they should slack off on the sessions with Lance and rely more on the chemicals to do their job. It appeared to her that the number of people working with Lance represented an irritant to him. All their questions and attempts to change him were causing him some degree of frustration, and when he had ended a session, he was at a point of wanting to take his frustrations out on anything in his way.

During a casual conversation with Stu, Coleen asked, "Do you think we're doing any good with Lance? He has been a better child on the surface, and Jennifer is a lot happier with him, but are we really making any head way?"

Stu didn't answer her question right away. He had to think about it. After the pause, he said, "To be honest, I don't know. Yes, he does appear to be a nicer boy on the surface, but these temper demonstrations he has when he leaves the sessions with Dr. Pelleck make me wonder. Maybe we should back off a little and see what happens."

The next time Coleen took Lance to the zoo, he was unusually quiet. She took him to a petting area and attempted once again to get him involved with the love of animals, but Lance just stood and gazed at them, except when he attempted to pull a chicken's tail feathers out and stomp the foot of another.

Coleen later remarked to Stu that it appeared at times that Lance was afraid of some of the animals but boldly approached others. She said, "Maybe he's afraid of those he can't control."

While it appeared to Stu and Coleen that they had partially harnessed some of the devil in him, he was still having the nightmares. His nightmares were actually coming more often, and they were more bizarre, but they weren't influencing his behavior the same way that they had before.

Lance was actually beginning to enjoy some of them now, and he wasn't awakening and screaming like he used to. Nevertheless, a few of them still haunted him, and when they played in his dreams, they were enough to scare anyone.

He was now calculating how to manage his dreams, many of which were repeats of ones that he had earlier. Sometimes his dreams were uncontrollable while others were well within his grasp. He was still in a learning stage, but with time he knew he would have everything in his control. He still had problems with making sense of his dreams, many of which he would kill the person he didn't like.

Most of his victims were people he knew, like his father and mother, Dr. Pelleck, or Coleen, but many of them were people he hadn't even met. To him, they were just people, people who somehow represented a threat to him, either in real life or in his dreams, and that could have been almost anyone.

He often wondered what it would be like to follow through in real life with the things that were in his dreams? As he repeatedly mulled the thoughts over in his mind, he sometimes shuddered at the bazaar images he had, and, at other times, he became excited about the possibilities.

What was he to do? He couldn't find peace in his thoughts, and all the people around him that were hypothetically there to help him were actually interfering with what he really wanted to do.

Chapter 22

Playing with Peaches

It was fortunate that Lance looked young for his age, because when he was eleven and entered the fourth grade, he was already two grades behind. He had started late for kindergarten and had to stay in the first grade for two years. This embarrassed him a little, but it made him work a little harder so it wouldn't happen again.

He probably would have done better in school if he had friends to do homework with or at least study with on occasion, but he had no desire to spend time with his peers. He was a loner and lacked the same interests as the other students. They preferred talking about girls, cars, video games, the latest movies, music, parties, and TV.

Lance didn't watch much TV, and he certainly wasn't interested in parties where crowds of people congregated to talk about the same things they discussed in the school halls. What was the point of that? He wasn't interested in it at school, and he certainly wasn't interested in mingling with crowds of people.

He felt that most talking was non-essential anyway. He hated it when kids went on and on about something or other they knew very little about, often showing off about things that made little sense. He also had no interest in cars and video games. To him, these were a waste of time.

There was some music that turned him on, mostly on the hard rock end of the scale where he could submerge himself in over-powering sounds that blasted away the demons within his brain, and he did like looking at the girls. He fantasized about them at times and fondled himself in the process. He often wondered how it would feel to put his thing, as he referred to it, next to one.

Yes, he liked them, and one day he would consummate his fantasies. But he didn't like talking about them. That was a very private matter, locked away in the deep recesses of his brain.

It wasn't that he didn't want to talk with any of the girls. He had trouble with conversational skills, and most of the girls that he wanted to know thought he was weird. He didn't know how to approach them or what to talk about, even what to say if they spoke to him. So he stayed in his little closed-off world and just glanced at and fantasized about them when he could.

He had many thoughts about them. They were serious, mature thoughts for a boy his age, but they were thoughts that only he could have and maybe one day experience. Most of all, they were thoughts he could share with no one.

Because of his strange behavior, he was often kidded by his peers. This infuriated him, although he kept it to himself. The things he wanted to do to those who mocked and belittled him were unspeakable.

In his chronic nightmarish dreams of his early eleventh year, he was awakened after being chased by them. Over and over, he was running, running until he could run no more, finally getting caught but never knowing what happened after that. The same dream repeated itself over and over. Sometimes it seemed to be an all-night chase. Sometimes he would wake up screaming and lay there wondering if he could escape the constant harassment he had to endure. When he finally returned to sleep, the same dream would again haunt him.

Every morning when he awoke to the prodding of his mother, he realized that he must have eventually fallen into a deep, dreamless sleep. And then he would discover that he was wet again, the pungent urine odor strong in his nostrils.

Once again, his mother would say, "Lance, when are you going to stop wetting the bed? I'm getting tired of getting peed on in the middle of the night and then having to wash the sheets every day."

He got through fourth grade alright. He didn't pay particular attention to the teachers, but he somehow learned enough of the material that he passed. His main daily activities were still looking out the window and day dreaming.

His report card had comments about his lack of attention in class, his obsession with fondling himself, and his shortage of social skills. Jennifer had to visit with his teachers twice during the year for corrective measures, although neither of the incidences was serious enough for suspension.

He was glad when the school year ended. He was tired of looking in books. It was time to think of other things, to play and ride his bike, not that he would really go anywhere.

When he played, he played alone, and he thought a lot. He thought more about the dreams he had and wondered why he was having them. Sometimes he wasn't certain they were dreams. Some of the dreams repeated themselves so often, he was beginning to almost believe they were real, and he would plot ways of changing his dreams to either escape the chase or turn and be the chaser.

When the summer came, Jennifer had coerced Coleen into going on a trip with them, "just to get away. A change of scenery." They spent the week in the Florida panhandle, soaking up the abundant sun, inhaling the fresh Gulf air, and enjoying nature.

At first, Lance didn't like the idea. He would rather remain in his quiet surroundings so he could ponder his demonic thoughts. He didn't need a change. He already had one when school let out.

But there was no escaping his mother's determination this time. She knew the trip would be good for him. "We are going. My decision is final."

Their cabin was rustic, built years before of lumber that came from trees which occupied the very site upon which the cabin stood. They reminded Jennifer of what a cabin must have been like when early settlers forged their way through primeval New World forests and built their homes with their bare hands, simple tools, and the sweat of their brow. They were nothing special to look at, but a person could see that a lot of love and hard work had gone into their making.

Each cabin was arranged with one large room, exposed log rafters, the living area divided into poorly defined sections by log posts to provide a kitchen-bedroom-living room combination. The bathroom was separate, and it had a functional toilet.

Lance was glad the bathroom was separate. This was a very private place for him. At home, he spent many hours there in the bath tub, soaking in the warm water, kind of like being back in the womb. He felt safe there, and he didn't like to be disturbed when he was in this sanctuary.

He often played with floating toys in the water, and sometimes he played with his genitals. Sometimes he just laid there and fell asleep until he was suddenly awakened by the pounding of his mother's fists on the door and yelling to him to, "Get out of there." She almost always followed up with, "What are you doing in there all that time, and why do you lock the door. You're going to drown in there one day."

All the utensils were there in the cabin to cook with: sets of forks, knives, and spoons, a couple of spatulas, several large cooking spoons of different sizes, and an assortment of pots, pans, dishes, cups, and other devices that people used to cook and eat with. Jennifer noticed that they were well worn and discolored from the years of use.

She had packed enough food in a cooler to get them through the week. It was a good way to escape from the hustle and bustle of city life and enjoy time without the usual stress.

When they arrived, they got out of the car, stretching and sniffing the warm, fresh air and feeling the gentle breeze. Jennifer already felt refreshed.

She stretched her arms out again and took a deep breath of warm, pine-scented air. Coleen had already started moving things into the cabin, and Lance began to survey his new environment.

Suddenly, he liked it here. He could play where the warm wind blew through the trees, making a kind of therapeutic swishing sound. He could look under things to see what kind of critters he could find.

A couple of dogs roamed the area, one of which had a very enjoyable temperament. They apparently spent much of their time begging from cabin to cabin, kind of like the hobos sometimes did back in the early nineteen hundreds. Jennifer and Lance enticed the most friendly one to come over and get some leftover snacks from their first supper in the cabin. Once the dog had eaten, they knew they had a new friend that would come to see them whenever he smelled something cooking.

Jennifer learned from the area caretaker, Mr. Roberts, that the dog's name was Peaches because of her color. She was a friendly golden retriever, with soft, long fur. "She likes to be petted a lot," he said.

Her rear end almost shook her off her feet when she wagged her tail under the influence of petting and food offerings. It didn't even matter if she was actually getting anything or not. Just the thought of getting something sent her body into gyrations.

Lance took to Peaches unlike he had done to any other animal. She had that kind of influence over everyone. He had never been so friendly to Penny or Jiggers, except possibly when Penny was first introduced to him. But this was different. Penny was a house dog. He and Peaches had an almost unlimited area of the outdoors to roam and play in.

When he played with Peaches, it seemed to Jennifer that he may be missing the closeness he had when they first got Penny for him. He seemed to be happy to play and romp with her all around the area outside the cabin.

She yelled to him on one occasion, "Lance, be careful with Peaches. Don't be too rough with her, and get ready for supper. We're going to put it out."

Lance said, "Okay, momma. I'm coming." He threw the stick he was holding, and Peaches ran to get it, and while she was chasing it, Lance left and went to the cabin.

Jennifer said, "Wash your hands, Lance. You've probably got a million germs off of Peaches."

Lance did what his mother told him to do, and they all sat down to eat. Jennifer smiled at Coleen and wondered if she was thinking about the same thing that was on her mind. She had been impressed with Lance's behavior ever since they got here. It made her think that they were going to do this again, often, if possible, and she wondered why she hadn't thought of it before.

When they finished, Jennifer and Coleen picked the dishes up and began washing them, and Lance went out again to play with Peaches. As he was leaving the cabin, Jennifer said, "Lance, be careful outside. Don't go off. It'll be time for bed soon."

Lance could see the other dog on occasion. Patches was its name, apparently named that because of the dark black spots on its otherwise white fur. He wasn't sure who named it, but the name fit. *Probably Mr. Roberts.*

It wasn't as friendly as Peaches by a long shot. It begged for food just as Peaches did, but it most often wouldn't come to the food until the person offering it went inside. Most of the people who watched Patches thought the dog must have been abused at one time.

Chapter 23

Lance is Lost

Lance was usually out early every day, looking for Peaches, hoping she would come around to play. He called her, "Here, Peaches, where are you?" Peaches, like Patches, had her priorities straight. It was eat first and play later, so Lance had to wait until she made her rounds.

When Jennifer and Coleen watched him playing, it was almost like looking at a new Lance. He appeared happy and interested in life. He looked like any other kid that was having a good time.

Nevertheless, he still wet his bed, and when his mother and Coleen weren't looking, he still fondled himself as much as he could. He still had nightmares, although Jennifer claimed to Coleen that they appeared to be less unsettling.

Jennifer wondered if all this would change if they could lead a simpler life, away from all the pressures that were obviously taking their toll on Lance. But that was just an impossible dream. Lance had to go to school, and he needed to learn social skills. The country setting and slower pace would be too isolating.

Lance did everything he could to entice Patches to join him and Peaches in their romping, but she never got passed the point of getting just out of reach, putting her head down and sniffing the playing pair. Then she would turn and go off. She did the same when offered food. She sometimes got close but kept that wild look in her eyes so she could react at any sign of danger. She continued to sniff, and when you weren't looking, she darted in, grabbed the food, and was gone.

As the week progressed, Lance went out as usual after breakfast to play in the area around the cabin, acknowledging the words of caution from his mother to be careful. Jennifer and Coleen did the dishes, Coleen looked out and saw Lance playing with Peaches, throwing the stick, as usual, and they sat down to a cup of coffee and some conversation.

Jennifer and Coleen were getting closer to one another than ever, and spending this time together was good for Jennifer. She had no other close friends. Most of the women in her neighborhood shied away from her, not because they didn't like her but because they didn't care for Lance and didn't want their kids playing with him. Jennifer always thought this was cruel, but that's how people were.

Jennifer said, "I appreciate what you've done for Lance, Coleen. I know it's been hard for you, and I want to thank you."

"Don't mention it, Jennifer. Both you and Lance needed someone, and you both mean a lot to me. I'm just glad I can be there for you. I hope I've done some good."

"Oh, I think you have. I don't know what I would have done without you. I think I was going out of my mind. Without you and Dr. Pelleck, I might have . . ." Jennifer was looking at Coleen, wanting to say something else, but not knowing just how to put it.

Finally, she asked, "Coleen, do you think Lance is getting any better? It seems to me he is. When I look at him here, he seems to be just like any other child. Even at home and at school, he seems to be a better person. I know there are still some problems, but it does seem that he's made some progress."

Coleen thought about it and said, "I think things are progressing a little better. Lance has had a rough life with the physical and mental abuse he got from his father. You were the only stabilizing force in his life. Whatever you do, never blame yourself for what has happened to Lance."

Jennifer smiled, and tears formed in her eyes. She needed to hear this. She was so self-condemning, it was sometimes difficult to live with herself. But what Coleen said to her made sense. Yes, it was

Ralph that caused this situation, and, yes, she was there for Lance when he needed her, even though Ralph couldn't have cared less. She didn't always know what to do when Lance did the things he did, but somehow they got through it and now things were better.

Coleen said, "I don't want you to think Lance is out of the woods yet." She was beginning to sound like the psychologist that she was, so she decided once again to tone it down a bit. "I think Dr. Pelleck would say that you should continue telling Lance you love him and also continue believing that somehow we're all going to get through this together."

As their conversation continued, they talked at length about all sorts of life's meandering qualities, sometimes reminiscing about Lance's past. Jennifer realized that in spite of Lance's present condition, there had been many good times with him.

Her most precious moments were when he first arrived. She could still form a picture of his tiny, gyrating arms and legs and hear his baby sounds. They had come a long way since that time, and the road had been quite bumpy on occasion.

In her mind, Jennifer again thanked God for Coleen. She wondered how she had gotten so lucky. She followed her thoughts by verbally thanking Coleen again for her help and then, as if in shock, looked toward the window and said, "I wonder what Lance is doing. I haven't heard him lately."

They both got up from the table and looked out the window. Lance was nowhere in the front yard. They went around the house and looked out the other windows. Still nothing. Finally, they both went to the front door and stepped out onto the porch.

Jennifer called, "Lance. Lance, where are you, honey?" Still no response. "I wonder where he could have gone. I hope he's okay."

"I don't know, Jennifer. He was just here a short time ago. He was playing with Peaches when I saw him last. Do you think he may have gone off looking for Patches? I know he wanted to make friends with her, too."

They went into the yard, and Jennifer said, "Oh, dear God. Please let him be alright." Pointing to her left, she said, "Let's try to find him. You go that way, and I'll go over here."

Each of them went off, calling for Lance, going to each of the dozen or so cabins to ask if anyone had seen Lance. Nothing.

The cabin next to them was vacant, and the door was open, so Coleen went in and called for Lance. It looked as though someone had gone inside because some of the drawers were open, so she looked around closely, thinking that Lance may be hiding behind or under a bed. She didn't know why he'd do something like that, but you never know. Still nothing. Their searching continued for well over an hour.

When they had exhausted the possibilities in the cabined area, they began frantically looking for Mr. Roberts or a ranger for help. By this time, both Jennifer and Coleen were getting progressively worried. This was no place to go off and explore when you're eleven years old. Anything could happen.

When they couldn't find Mr. Roberts, they headed back towards their cabin, thinking that they might find Lance back where they saw him last. As they drew closer to the cabin, this time to use the phone inside to call 911, Jennifer saw Lance standing there, a dazed look on his face, tears running down his cheeks, and soaking wet.

He was looking in her direction and had his arms out as if to say, "Here I am momma, here I am, come hold me."

Even with his pathetic appearance, she released a sigh of relief. She ran to him and hugged him. "Lance, where were you? How did you get all wet? We were worried to death about you."

He said, "I don't know, momma. I was playing with Peaches, and we ran off after Patches. Then I didn't know where I was after a while. Peaches was a bad dog, momma. She let me get lost. Then I fell in the water. It wasn't deep, though. I started walking, and then I saw the cabins. I don't know where the dogs are."

For a boy that didn't talk much, this was a definite change. He was rattling off sentences as fast as he could, with very few pauses. Jennifer assumed he was just scared and knew that she and Coleen were afraid for him.

Coleen had heard what he said. She, too, was relieved that he had come back. For a while, she wondered if he had run off on purpose, but that obviously wasn't the case. She had been right, thinking that his disappearance had something to do with Patches.

"Let's get him inside, Jennifer, and give him a hot bath. He'll catch a cold if we don't get him out of those wet clothes."

After the warm bath, Jennifer gave Lance some pudding she had in her ice chest, along with some hot chocolate. They all sat at the table and talked about how fast the week had gone and how much they wished they could stay longer.

Jennifer said, "Wouldn't it be nice if we could live in a place like this all the time? No worries, no bills, no pressures, communing with nature. I think I could stand to do that for a while."

"I don't know, Jennifer," Coleen said. "You may like it for a while, but I think you'd eventually get tired of it. Personally, I would rather be closer to things."

Jennifer looked at Lance and said, "You gave us a scare today, Lance, honey. Please don't go off like that again. It's dangerous in the woods. There are all kinds of animals that can hurt you. And what would have happened if you walked in a different direction? You could still be out there. Mommy would be very upset if something happened to you."

There was the baby talk creeping into Jennifer's speech again. Coleen didn't understand why Jennifer couldn't talk to Lance in a regular voice. It was irritating at times to hear "mommy did this" or "mommy would have done that."

Coleen threw in her two cents worth of advice. "Yes, Lance, you were lucky this time. What if that water you fell in was deep? You may have drowned. Just remember this the next time you think of running off."

That was the only frightening thing that had happened during their otherwise pleasant week. They all hated to leave the rustic housing and woodland setting they learned to love in such a short while. It probably did more for them than ten sessions with a shrink.

Jennifer and Coleen talked all the way home about how they'd like to go back, but Lance was non-committal. He apparently was sad he had to leave. Seeing him in his current pensive mood, Jennifer said, "Don't worry, baby, we'll come back some time and you can play with Peaches and Patches again. Did you say goodbye to them?"

Lance didn't say anything, but Coleen said, "I didn't see either of the dogs when we left. They must have been begging at some of the other cabins. That's kind of unusual, though, because they almost always were outside, waiting for Lance every day. At least Peaches was. It's probably because everyone is in a state of flux, preparing to leave."

Chapter 24

The Demise of Peaches and Patches

Later in the day, as the three of them were on their way back to Louisiana, Mr. Roberts was walking his beat through the cabined area when he stumbled upon an animal that was partially covered by leaves. As he moved the leaves aside, he realized it was Peaches.

With tears in his eyes, he bent over to inspect his good friend. She had stiffened and was covered with blood. She also had a butcher knife protruding from one side of her chest. It looked like a knife from one of the cabins. It was going to be his job to determine which cabin was missing such a knife.

Temporarily leaving Peaches where he found her, he rushed to report to all workers what he had found. In turn, they were advised to be on the look-out for anything or anyone that looked suspicious.

As the cleaning crew prepared the cabins for the next occupants, they found a knife missing from the cabin that had been vacant during the weekend. It was a knife like the one found in Peaches.

A very depressed Mr. Roberts returned to Peaches, picked her up, and buried her near his cabin. He knew he'd miss her. Peaches was his only constant companion out here in the wilderness. As people came and went, it was only Peaches and Patches that lingered, and he looked forward to seeing them every day.

When searching for Patches, he finally saw her in the distance, on the side of a hill, not far from where he had found Peaches. When he called her, she just looked at him and ran in the opposite direction.

During his first week back at school, Lance was silent. His teachers wondered what was causing him to be that way. In some respects, they found relief in his present mood. He didn't cause any problems in class, but he was distant and day-dreamed more than ever.

He was quiet at home, as well. Jennifer said, "What's the matter, baby? You miss Peaches and Patches? We'll go back some time. But we have other things to do right now. Maybe we'll go back to the cabin next summer. Would you like that?"

Lance just shrugged his shoulders and went back to playing with his favorite truck. He moved it around, one way and then the other, not really going anywhere with it. Something was obviously on his mind, but no matter what Jennifer did, he didn't want to talk about it.

After a couple of weeks, Lance seemed to be his old self again, and their routine of seeing Coleen and Dr. Pelleck resumed. There wasn't much to talk about, though, except for their trip together. When Jennifer explained the enjoyable week they had, Dr. Pelleck remarked that it was a good sign to have Lance enjoying himself so much. He encouraged them to do it again, and Jennifer agreed that they would.

Lance finished the fourth grade with halfway decent grades, no serious mishaps for Jennifer to visit school about, and they spent the next summer mostly going to the movies and taking short trips to neighboring communities for a little sightseeing and shopping. The wilderness trip she had promised him seemed far away by now. The trips they went on weren't very exciting for Lance, but at least they were together, and Jennifer occasionally bought things for him. One day it was a nice toy. On another day, it was some candy or ice cream.

He generally took his favorite truck with him wherever he went. That was about all he had left of his toys, and it functioned like a security blanket.

All the life-like action figures had their heads pulled off or were torn to shreds. Jennifer didn't understand why he did these things, and she learned that it wasn't worth buying replacements.

Jennifer eventually arranged a trip back to the rustic cabin, but Lance didn't initially seem to be interested. When Jennifer pleaded with him and spoke of the good time they would have, he finally consented to go, but he didn't seem to enjoy it as much as he did the previous season. They couldn't find either of the dogs, and, therefore, it just wasn't the same as before.

When Jennifer saw Mr. Roberts, she asked about Peaches and Patches, and he said that someone had killed Peaches.

Jennifer said, "Now, who would do a thing like that to such a nice dog?"

Mr. Roberts said, "Some sicko, I expect. There are a lot of them around, you know."

"Well, I just don't know. I'm sorry to hear that. What about Patches?" Jennifer didn't find Mr. Roberts to be very talkative so far, but he did answer her questions.

"Patches stayed around for a while and then disappeared. Probably got killed too, although it would have been difficult to catch her. She didn't trust people very much. It probably would have been better if Peaches would have been that way."

Jennifer was curious. "What happened? Was he shot, or what?"

"No ma'am. He had a butcher knife shoved in him, and he apparently had been stabbed a bunch before that. He had holes all over him. And whoever it was took some of his teeth. It looked like they used the knife like a hatchet to chop the teeth out. Then they chopped off his right paw. Can you imagine someone doing that? I just don't understand people."

"That's terrible, Mr. Roberts. I'm so sorry."

Jennifer was hoping Lance wasn't listening to their conversation, but he was standing behind the front door when they talked, not three feet from his mother. When Jennifer said goodbye to Mr. Roberts, she went inside to find Lance sitting at the table. He was playing with his truck and looked up as she entered. She looked at him and said nothing about what Mr. Roberts had told her. She knew it would break his heart to hear about it, so why even bring it up?

* * *

Later in the summer, Jennifer and Lance were preparing for the fifth grade. They had gone shopping for a school bag, lunch pail, and the various other items she knew he would need. When they got home, she noticed that Lance went to Penny and began playing with her. His truck, the one he always played with, sat silent in the corner of the room.

She imagined that the thought of Peaches may have opened a place in his heart that needed stimulation, a place where love was trying to get out. In lieu of Peaches, he was showing some attention to Penny, and that was good.

When school started in early September, Lance went to school just like any other twelve-year-old. He didn't seem to be particularly happy about it, but he went.

He didn't especially want to see anyone, and he didn't greet anyone unless someone said something to him. He wasn't that type of child. He was still the silent type, with thoughts of his own, and he didn't want anyone to know what these thoughts were.

He was sleeping better now, and while his dreams were nightmarish in content, he didn't mind so much. Only on occasion did he wake up to the chasing, just before he was caught. There was always blood, but he often wasn't sure who's blood it was. It could be his blood for all he knew, but this didn't bother him either.

His bed wetting had not stopped, but it had subsided. This pleased Jennifer. She also wasn't suffering as before when he wet the bed because she was now back to sleeping alone. One day, when they were preparing for bed, Lance just told her he wanted to sleep by himself.

In the beginning, she missed his warm body, but knew this was his decision, and it was best for both of them. She still didn't like the chore of washing sheets, although it was no longer an every-day event, and she woke up dry.

The only thing that Lance seemed to do a lot of, which was left over from his previous behaviors, was fondling himself, and it seemed to be increasingly evident. Jennifer had consulted with Dr. Pelleck about it at an earlier time, and he had told her it was a natural behavior unless it was done to excess. What defined excess? She didn't know.

He had given her a text book explanation. "Masturbation, the fondling of one's privates for pleasure, has been found to even occur in prenatal babies but it is more common in two-year-olds or older infants. There is a tendency for it to increase further in adolescence, but still there is a point at which it was considered to be excessive." Whatever that meant was still unclear.

Testosterone and other hormones were influencing Lance's body and mind in many different ways. His long bones were growing, and his features were changing to make him almost appear like a young man. His speech was better, and he was learning to communicate a little better with those who would talk with him. Jennifer was impressed.

Most of his peers still thought of him as weird, but there were other weird students around, so he didn't stand out as being that different anymore. He even got to be quasi-friendly with a couple of his classmates, and they reciprocated by acknowledging his friendship.

He now knew it was up to him to cultivate the types of friendships he wanted, but he had to be careful, very careful. No one was to be totally trusted, no one, and there was a definite limit to what they needed to know about him. With better control of his emotions, he suspected it was going to be a good year.

Chapter 25

Attraction to Girls

The week was a busy one. Both Lance and Jennifer saw Dr. Pelleck separately and then in a joint session. Coleen had been at the house every day, and Stu came by to see if Jennifer needed anything.

Jennifer reported to Dr. Pelleck that Lance had settled down at home and was the perfect child. She said, "I never thought the day would come for Lance to be so good."

In actuality, Jennifer was looking at Lance through rose colored glasses, and he wasn't quite perfect, but he was a whole lot better, at least on the surface. He wasn't showing overt signs of wanting to harm someone or something. He had apparently cut down on his more obvious fondling behaviors, and he was showing some respect for his mother and those around him.

He was a little strange at times, and he spent most of his time alone. Only God knew what he was thinking about all that time, but when he met people, he showed that he could be quite the gentlemen. Jennifer was proud of his progress. Arriving at conclusions based on his meetings with Lance and his mother, Dr. Pelleck had written glowing reports of his progress.

He attributed Lance's change mostly to the medication he had prescribed. Jennifer determined he was religiously taking his mediation by periodically checking to see if his pills were dwindling in number. Lance, on the other hand, had limited his concern for medication to removing the pills from the pharmaceutical containers at the prescribed times and flushing them down the toilet.

Even though they had studied Lance through their TV monitors, Stu and Coleen never saw him discarding his pills, so they assumed he was taking them as prescribed. Yet, they had another opinion of him. They believed Lance was much the same as he was before, maybe even worse. They had witnessed him having temper episodes when he was alone, and they saw the way he looked at Penny.

Yet, on the surface, Lance was just what Jennifer had described him as, a gentleman. He acted pleasant around people, although he hardly ever started a conversation himself. But when someone else spoke to him, he responded in a cheerful, almost programmed way. They thought he had polished his act well enough to cover any inner feelings he might have, and he was now being accepted by the society that once only represented a frightening barrier to him.

They were convinced that what Lance feared more than anything right now was getting caught doing something that society deemed out of the ordinary. Yes, he was nice on the surface, but this was a cover up. They were certain of it.

He probably still had the recurring nightmares and deeply guarded thoughts and fantasies, even though he denied having them. He still masturbated more than anyone knew about. Stu and Coleen were aware of much of it because of their candid cameras and microphones. He still wet the bed, but there were many nights he got through without the foul stench of urine permeating through his room.

So it was through fifth, sixth, and seventh grades. Visits to the psychiatrist, Coleen's help, and the assistance Jennifer got from Stu had spoiled her, and Lance still had very little structure in his life. He was now fifteen and hadn't even taken the trash out except on a few rare occasions. There was the occasional time that he washed the dishes, but only under duress from his mother.

He never had any kind of job, like a paper route, working a few hours in a shop of some sort, or delivering pizza. He had no desire to do these things. Why should he? He had other people to do them for him, and he got an allowance.

All through these grammar school years, he spent much of his time in private. When he wasn't in school, he was usually in his room.

Jennifer tried not to pry into his private world. When she did ask questions, he became overly defensive and told her to mind her own business. This was one of the only times he talked back to her, and since she wanted to avoid any arguments, she kept quiet about his personal life.

Sessions with Dr. Pelleck went well. Stu and Coleen expected no less. Lance was now in control or almost in control of many of the events in his life. There was no way that he would ever slip up and let Dr. Pelleck or anyone else know what lurked in his brain, not on purpose, that is. He would talk about the things he wanted to discuss, and he would avoid the rest.

He continued to get good reports from Dr. Pelleck, and Jennifer was certain he was a totally different child. She still worried some, but she thought that anyone who talked in a negative way about Lance was overreacting to certain of his odd traits. Even she understood that he was strange at times, but when you got right down to it, who wasn't? "Everybody's got their unusual habits," she would say.

With his acquired good disposition, he got as far as he did in school with increasingly better comments on his report card than he had the years before, and even his teachers felt he had a chance to do something of a positive nature in the world. He was adjusting to society's demands, and soon he would be graduating and going to high school. They had done the best they could to train him. It was now up to him to finish his present school and get ready for a new life.

He met Sheryl Collins in the eighth grade. She was tall, beautiful, and had extremely well developed breasts. Besides perfect skin and pleasant looks, this was one thing that turned him on. Most of the girls in his classes were poorly built compared to Sheryl, and many had skin problems. To him, she looked like a well endowed model, like one of those women that got hired by bra companies for their advertisements, possibly even better. He began to salivate and feel a twitching in his genitals every time he thought of her.

The problem was that Sheryl wouldn't give him the time of day. In their home room, she sat about four seats in front of him and to his right. He planned it that way. He would watch her, fantasize about stroking her long, light brown hair, and undressing her in his mind whenever he desired, all the while fondling himself through the hole in his right pocket.

In his mind, he caressed her smooth arms and long, shapely legs, pressed his body next to hers, and tasted her skin. Sometimes he closed his eyes and day-dreamed about what else he wanted to do with her. One afternoon, in his dreams, he bit her on her soft, smooth shoulder and licked the blood as it oozed from the wound. He had her in his control, and she let him do whatever he wanted.

It was on a Tuesday, in home room, that Sheryl turned around in her seat and looked at him, after she had a feeling that she was being watched. When she saw him staring, she said, "What are you looking at, creep?"

Needless to say, this hurt Lance, and he spent the rest of the day in a silent, pensive mood, away from other students. He was sure she was telling her friends about him, but he quickly forgave her. He thought he was in love.

He also knew that she could love him if she would give him half a chance. He wanted more than ever to show her how he felt. He just had trouble expressing himself.

Sheryl hung around with a number of other students who seemed to like the same things she liked. Lance never knew all the things they would do and talk about because he wasn't part of their little clique. When he said or did anything around them in an attempt to get their approval, it always came out wrong, and they shunned and made derogatory remarks about him. Nevertheless, he knew he loved her, in spite of what she did to hurt him, and he couldn't understand why she didn't see that.

Roger Dunn, one of the boys in her circle, was attracted to her, and Lance noticed that she had begun paying an unusual amount of attention to him. Lance didn't like it one bit. He glanced at them whenever he could and eventually learned to hate Roger more than anyone he knew.

Upon following Roger at one of the rare times he wasn't watching Sheryl, he learned that he was on the football team. After his daily practice sessions, he went to Sheryl's house. While on the surface he knew they had some kind of thing going, he was certain it wasn't simply to do homework together.

He occasionally hid behind the bushes at her apartment and attempted to look through her window. He had never seen Sheryl and Roger together inside her room, but later, after Roger had left, he did witness Sheryl undressing, and he masturbated while watching.

Occasionally, she sat in front of the mirror and ran her hands slowly over her breasts, caressing them and sending cold chills up his spine. This was precisely what he wanted to do to her, if only she would let him. Sheryl never knew, but Lance was there with her on many occasions, sharing some of her most intimate moments.

One evening, he was rustling around in the bushes, trying to get a better view, and a neighbor spotted him. When she yelled to him, he ran, never looking back. He believed that Sheryl had never found out about the incident. If she had, she probably would have approached him about it. For a time, he didn't return, but he missed his beauty queen and had to masturbate with the image of her in his mind.

As he followed Roger to the locker room after school one day, Roger had just finished changing into his uniform and departed for practice. Lance entered the locker room, dumped a bag of feces in his locker, making sure it got on everything. He wanted to stay around and watch, but he didn't dare. He was pretty sure Roger wouldn't go to Sheryl's house that evening because his clothes would be rank with the smell of feces.

The next day at school, he heard comments from students he didn't even know about what had been found in Roger's locker. There were never any comments about him being the culprit. Strike one for Lance.

Chapter 26

Learning a Lesson

He also put broken glass in his lunch a couple of weeks later, and Roger cut his lip on one of the pieces before he learned what was going on. Who knew where the other pieces had gone. Lance had hoped it would cut his insides to shreds, and he would bleed all over the floor, dying in the process.

He even experienced the torture in one of his dreams, with Roger wide-eyed and lacking color in his skin, standing zombie-like in a pool of his own blood. Roger reported the sandwich incident to one of the teachers, and Lance decided they would be watching for unusual behavior from then on, so he decided to cool it for a while.

In spite of Sheryl's indifference to him, Lance wanted to show her how much he cared before the school term ended. He bought her a box of chocolates for Valentine's Day and gave it to her with a card. On it, he wrote, "Roses are Red, Violets are Blue, Give Me a Chance Because I Love YOU." He stood by her, waiting for her to look inside, certain that the gift would make a difference in their relationship.

When Sheryl took it from him, staring at him in disbelief, she opened the envelope, read the card and started to laugh. Then she said, "You've got to be kidding." She never said thanks, kiss my ass, or anything else. She threw the card down and walked away with the chocolates, laughing to herself. The hurt he felt cut deep into his heart, and the sound of her laugh began to haunt him. Not one to give up easily, his naiveté drove him even further toward seeking her acceptance.

As Lance rode his bike past her apartment later in the day, she and all of her friends were sitting on her porch, eating the candies he had given her. When he stopped and looked at them from a distance, hoping they would wave him over, they whispered something and all laughed while they watched him ride away in haste.

That hurt him more than anything else she had done. It was over, he thought. This was the first time he had ever shown signs of liking a girl, and it turned out to be a catastrophe. He swore he'd never do that again, especially with her, and he never went back to her house.

This didn't keep him from masturbating while fashioning a picture of her in his mind. In a way, he hated and desired her at the same time.

One night in a dream, he approached her completely in the nude, and she was in the nude, as well, standing there, with a seductive look on her face. Her eyes, her light green, beautiful eyes were inviting him to come near. Her breasts stood out, beckoning for his caress. He got closer and closer, and when he got close enough to feel her hot, sweet breath on his face, she looked straight in his eyes and spit on him.

He pulled a knife from his pocket and plunged it into her chest, just to the side of her left breast, and he watched the horror in her eyes, the blood gushing out of the hole and running down her side, over her slender waist and feminine hips. When he grabbed her and pulled her closer, she stared unbelievingly into his eyes. He lay her gently on the floor and proceeded to make love to her.

When he was finished, her eyes had closed. He picked her up, hugged her, tasted her tender skin and let her drop to the floor, splashing the pool of blood that had drained from her body. As a parting gesture, he bent down and stroked her skin, ran his hand across her breasts and then urinated on her. He had finally had her under his control, and it felt very good, good enough to have the last laugh.

When he awoke, he was sticky with his ejaculation, and his heart was still pounding. For a moment, he had thought it was all so real, but he soon returned to a waking state, undressed, and put his underwear in the clothes hamper. He either didn't think the pungent odor would reveal to his mother what had happened or he didn't give a damn.

Secretly, he thought of Sheryl and Roger, pretending to walk up to them and slash them repeatedly with his knife. That would teach them. They'd never hurt him again. Fortunately for them, his thoughts never became a reality, in spite of his wanting them to. With his own preservation in mind, he realized that to act out his innermost desires would result in his being caught, condemning him to a life of misery, and he couldn't fathom that.

* * *

Lance didn't want to attend high school. He heard of all the cruel things they did to freshmen, and he dreaded the first day. As it turned out, it wasn't so bad, and he survived unscathed. He apparently wasn't one of their targets.

Most of the pranks they did to freshmen were silly. He heard of some of the seniors making a person talk to the wall, salute the water fountain, or wear funny hats or signs that said *Kick Me*, nothing to really get up tight about. Once in a while, he had heard that they required students to do worse things, and he had hoped it wouldn't happen to him.

On the last day of the first week, just about when he began to feel safe, a group of senior boys cornered him. They had apparently watched him during the week and chose him for one of their ridiculous pranks. He couldn't help but think that he had almost made it through the first terrible week, and he was dreading what they had in mind.

They made him strip to his underwear and enter one of his classrooms. It was a room with desks arranged parallel to one another, with an aisle running down the center. His seat was near the center of the room, to the left of the aisle. He really didn't want to do this, but how was he going to escape the prank with a bunch of seniors on his back.

He got to class late, and as he walked slowly down the aisle and toward his seat, eyes in a daze and pointed at the floor, everyone turned and stared. They subsequently burst out laughing and pointing to the ridiculous scene. The teacher reeled around from the whiteboard and looked at him standing there, now wide-eyed and with the sign of fear in his expression. Lance was so scared, he peed all over himself and commenced to stand in the puddle while everyone continued making fun of him. It was one of the most embarrassing moments of his life.

The teacher ran to him, grabbed his arm and shuttled him out of the room. As they stood in the hall, Lance was still wild eyed and shaking with fear. Under normal circumstances, she would have taken him directly to the principal's office, but she could see this was not his idea.

She said, "Lance, what is the meaning of this?"

All Lance could say in a low, whispering voice was, "They made me do it. I didn't want to."

When she asked who 'They' were, he spouted off a few names and began to cry. When asked where his clothes were, he said he didn't know. With assistance from the janitorial staff and part of the maintenance crew, they found them hidden behind one of the toilets in one of the boy's bath rooms. He was sent home, and he remained there for several days on his own volition. He had told his mother he didn't feel well.

The boys that had done it to him had been given detention for the rest of the week and were told that if they ever did something like that again, they would be expelled. They now could thank Lance for their punishment, and they were determined to get revenge for their pain. The last laugh was going to be theirs.

A couple of days later, as Lance was riding his bike home from school, he rounded the corner, and standing before him were the boys that caused him so much embarrassment. When he stopped, they approached him from different angles, encircling him, apparently after having waited a while for his arrival.

Johny Debbins, the ring leader of the group, approached him and said, "Hey, creep, why did you tell on us?"

Lance said, "Because you shouldn't have done what you did." Although Lance was scared, he managed to stand there and give an appearance of being tougher than he really was. And he didn't pee on himself.

Johny pushed Lance, but Lance didn't retaliate. He pushed him again, and shortly afterward, a number of the boys were pushing him around their circle, and he fell.

Johny said, "Get up you coward and fight."

Lance just sat there in the dirt, his eyes becoming wider with the challenge. He didn't want to fight, and he didn't like the control they had over him. He just wanted to be left alone. They shouldn't have asked him to take his clothes off and walk into his class room in the first place, and now they were embarrassing him all over again.

Nevertheless, sitting on the ground wasn't causing them to give up their relentless struggle to make him fight, and if he got up, he was certain Johny and the others would attack him. He envisioned them as a pack of wolves rushing in on their prey, snarling and tearing at the animal they had trapped.

When he didn't budge, Johny kicked him and kicked dirt in his face. He rolled over and attempted to rub the dirt from his eyes, all the while entering deeper into a night marish world, seeming all of a sudden to be oblivious to the threat at hand. He slowly arose and stood there with his hands in his pockets, and Johny punched him in the face. He fell, nose bleeding, but got up immediately, and when Johny lunged at him again, Lance pulled a knife from his pocket and swung it at him, barely missing his mid-section.

Johny backed off. Now taking a more subordinate role in his approach, he said, "What you gonna do with that, creep, kill me?"

Lance stood there, wide-eyed and holding the knife in front of him, waiting for the next lunge. He stared at Johny and said in a low, confident voice, "Maybe."

Johny could see the hate in his eyes, and he knew that his next lunge would possibly be his last. He truly believed that Lance would kill him if this altercation continued.

He backed away, hoping that Lance wouldn't follow, and others that had supported his aggression backed along with him. They also saw the terror in Lance's eyes, and they no longer wanted to have anything to do with him. They were the ones afraid now, and they knew that if they pushed him any further, he would crack and wouldn't stop until he had killed someone.

Lance was left standing in the dirt. No one stayed with him. No one asked how he was. No one seemed to care. They were all afraid. It seemed to him it was the loneliest he'd ever been. He also felt the power.

It took him a good ten minutes to move from that spot. By that time, everyone had left. When he did move, it was slow. He picked his books up, wiped his nose with his sleeve, put his knife away, and moved toward home.

Later on, he didn't remember anything between the time he was standing in the dirt until he was sitting in his room, staring at the floor. He didn't remember opening the door or hearing his mother say hello. And he didn't know how long he was sitting there. All of a sudden, he was just there.

Before he arose from the chair, he reflected on a mental reenactment of what had happened in the street. Initially, he was sorry Johny hadn't come after him one more time. He would have run him through, and that would be the last of him. He would have cut him open, spilled his guts onto the sidewalk, and laughed. That would teach them all. Then he thought about the consequences, and he realized how lucky he was that it hadn't happened.

He didn't mind killing someone. In fact, he probably would have enjoyed it. It was being caught that bothered him, and this would have put an end to him. He realized he would have to work on this, control of his emotions better.

It wasn't like he didn't benefit from that event. From that day forward, Lance was not bothered by anyone. He had new strength. They did talk about him, whisper little things about him when they thought he wasn't listening. He knew what was going on. They could say what they wanted, but he was certain they would be careful not to upset him again.

Chapter 27

Learning to Kill and Liking It

Before he finished high school, he had taken whatever biology courses he could get. He liked biology. It was a subject he could lose himself in and shut out the negative world, and it was a subject that allowed him to stand out above his peers. Along with some topics of lesser interest, students had a chance to dissect frogs and a few samples of higher animals. He spent extra hours in the laboratory, examining his specimens and those of other students and picking out the various organs.

Whenever they got live frogs in, it was Lance who pithed them. He loved it. He learned to single pith by running a dissecting needle into their cranial cavity through the opening of the back of the skull and scrambling their brain by wiggling the needle from side to side. Most of the time, he would double pith them by running the needle into the brain through the skull and then running it back down the spinal column to destroy the nervous tissue there.

Once the frog was pithed, he could lay it down in a dissecting tray, open the body cavity, and watch the heart beating. This was fascinating to him, and his ability to pith made him somewhat of a classroom celebrity. He pithed most of the frogs in the classroom, while many of the other students refused to even look when he did it. They didn't even like to handle the frogs to begin with.

Biology was just about the only class he got a good grade in. He hated history and math. He liked geography a little, but he deplored physics, chemistry, and English.

It was during biology class that he was introduced to snakes. From the first time he had seen one, he had thought they were fascinating. When Larry Hagen, a herpetology graduate student at Tulane University, noticed Lance's sincere interest in snakes, he took him on a tour through the university collection and asked if he would like to go collecting some time. Lance replied with an enthusiastic, "Yes."

Larry took Lance to one of his favorite spots near Bridge City on a weekend, and they caught fifteen or twenty snakes, several frogs, a turtle, and a few salamanders. Among the snakes were a few water snakes, representing about three different species, a black racer, a speckled king snake, a common hognose snake, and a number of ribbon snakes. It was one of the highlights of Lance's student life.

He thanked Larry for a good time and basked in the glory of seeing some of the specimens they had caught in the biology classroom, with his name typewritten on the aquarium side. When the other kids asked him about the trip, he went into detail about how he and Larry were almost bitten several times in the process. He could see and feel their simultaneous envy and terror.

"How can you touch one of those things?" one student asked.

Lance said, "It's not so hard. I like it. You just have to be careful when you pick them up. If they bite you, so what?"

He was actually looking for more credit than he really deserved. Larry had caught most of the snakes, and Lance was obviously nervous when he caught his. Larry told him how to do it, but he ended up needing help with transferring them to his bag. His heart pumped harder during the catches, and he realized he had a new thrill to take him through the summer.

When the following summer came, between graduating from high school and entering college, Lance went snake hunting by himself on several occasions. He told his mother he was just going out to look at plants and animals.

She encouraged him to do it. He was now taking an interest in something academic, and she thought this was good. She never learned about the snake collecting or what he did with them.

Even though he was still a little afraid of them, he caught them by putting a stick on their neck and picking them up with one hand just behind their head. Larry had taught him how to hold them with the thumb and bird finger on each side of the neck and the index finger on top of their head. He practiced this until he got it right.

While investigating the various rumors he had read about snakes, he had heard that they didn't die until the sun went down. As far as he was concerned, this needed some experimentation. He caught a water snake, held it down to a board and cut its head off with a knife. The snake's body began to contort, wiggle, and jump, red blood squirting out of the headless end, its head simultaneously lying still on the board with its tongue flicking out as if nothing had happened.

Lance watched it, and sure enough the snake continued to wiggle for a long time. As he waited, the wiggling became progressively slower, and it eventually ceased and left the snake motionless on the blood-laden board. Likewise, the snake's forked tongue became slower and slower until it lay down on the board next to the silent head, its lidless eyes still staring at its surroundings. The experiment was a total success. The snake didn't wait for the sun to go down. It was motionless within an hour or two.

Being afraid of them bothered him tremendously, so he made an attempt, another scientific experiment, to get over his fear by putting a bunch of non-poisonous snakes in a wooden box and dangling his hand in front of them.

When he initially did it, he waited nervously for the first strike. He closed his eyes and wiggled his fist in front of them until they struck.

When the first bite was over, he wondered what all the fuss was about. It didn't hurt at all. In fact, after the first few bites, he actually had begun to enjoy it. By the end of the day, his hand looked as though it had been run through a meat grinder. He never minded, though, and the blood had turned him on.

He rather enjoyed the attention he got when he showed his classmates his mutilated skin and all the scabbed-over tooth marks. Again, he was the center of attention and, in his mind, a hero.

He never did this with poisonous snakes. He didn't want to die or even chance that possibility. He just wanted to have some fun and get some attention from his peers. This was attention that was different from what he experienced in earlier years when his peers made fun of him.

Once he reached the point of being bitten a few times in the wild, he never feared them again, and when he entered college, his snake-collecting days had terminated as rapidly as they had commenced. He now wanted a new game.

* * *

He entered college as a biology major, and Jennifer was proud. Unlike many other students that entered college and floundered around in their selection of a major, Lance seemed to know precisely what he wanted to do.

To her, his going to college was nothing short of a miracle. Who would have thought that her son, the son that gave her so much trouble when he was younger, would enter college, and with some direction. She now was certain that her love for him and the hard work of everyone connected with the Fertility Clinic had helped change her bad little boy into a pleasant young man with a future.

To learn more about his subject and be near a source of animals, he even took a part time job as a biology laboratory technician, spending much of his time in the animal room, taking care of and preparing animals to be used in classrooms and research. Although most of the live specimens were white rats and mice, there were occasional other animals, as well.

Some of the ones that he was familiar with in high school were also used in these classes. He learned primarily about their care, but he took pleasure in preparing them for classroom examination.

On occasion, he had to etherize white rats, and once they were dead, he opened their body cavities to expose their internal organs.

He loved the colors inside, the pinks and grays of the lungs, muscles, and intestines, the browns of the liver and kidneys, and the iridescent silvers of the nerves, tendons, and ligaments. Then there was the blood, a beautiful red. To him, it was like a multicolored contemporary painting or a lit up sky on New Year's eve.

When ether wasn't available, he used chloroform. Actually, he preferred the latter, because ether slowly put them to sleep, but chloroform made them nervous, and it took longer to put them down. It excited him to see them climb and scratch the sides of the jar in a futile attempt to escape their certain death.

Since ether and chloroform were relatively slow-acting chemicals, their use in killing quickly became less exciting to him. It was for that reason that he decided to develop a faster method. After all, that's what biology was all about to him, experimentation. He had learned that in high school.

During one of his laboratory preparation periods, he picked up one of his rats by the tail as he had always done, but this time he swung it around quickly and whacked its head on the metal door sill. It worked like a charm. The rat was quickly immobilized except for some thrashing about and violent shaking during its last few breaths.

Once it was over, Lance experienced a feeling of inner peace, almost as though he had discovered something of great importance. Since he had to spend time wiping the blood off the wall, he decided to use the edge of the table to do his future bashing.

With time, he learned to like the killing. It no longer bothered him to smack them down with force, scrambling their brains in the process, and the students that studied their body parts never really knew how they had become immobile. He killed lots of them. With that and the pithing, he enjoyed his job very much. The rest of his job description was relatively boring, but the live animals made it all worth it.

Chapter 28

Learning About Girls

Lance had spent the first two semesters of college in a dorm room. He enjoyed the freedom he got from not seeing his mother on a daily basis. Being his first time away from home, he also began to understand what it was like to experience a life where others wouldn't interfere with his free time.

He experienced this freedom at the disappointment of the Fertility Clinic. They had lost their main system of surveillance, and it was going to be more difficult understanding precisely what Lance was doing with his time.

Lance quickly learned that there was a definite down side to college. He didn't especially enjoy all the classes he had to take. He felt many of them were boring and useless, but in order to experience this new life, he had to do what he had to do, and he hung in there with the rest of the students without failing anything.

As was customary, he made no friends. His extracurricular activities amounted to staying in his room, looking at girlie magazines, and performing his favorite sex act on himself during intermissions from studying. On rare occasions, he occupied some of his time going to campus movies. Wherever he went, he watched the people around him.

Watching was one of the activities he enjoyed most. When he went to class, he watched the girls in his room. It was the same when he went to eat, visited the library, and walked around campus. And when the evening came, he watched the girls go to their dorms, and he began to have bazaar thoughts about them and what he could do with them.

At the end of his first two semesters, he left his dorm for the summer break. His job in the animal lab was taken over by a student that just wanted summer employment, so he knew he'd get it back when the fall semester started, if that's what he desired.

The summer was spent back at his mother's house. Personnel at the Fertility Clinic were happy again, and Jennifer enjoyed having him home the first couple of weeks. In spite of the hardships she had suffered during his early years, she missed him terribly.

He was a different person now, still very private but more grown up. His grades at college weren't particularly good, but, as he had said, he passed, and this pleased his mother. His best grades were in his major.

The only thing she wished would improve was the closeness between them. Yes, he was her son, and he was living in the same house, but somehow he seemed even more distant than he had ever been.

The bed wetting was now something lost in their past. Jennifer knew that Lance was glad this was over, and she certainly was. No more urine smells. No more washing day, after day, after day. Yet, she thought she'd take that all back to be closer to him, and she was feeling a little remorse for yelling at him about it during the past.

After all, it wasn't really his fault. He was a victim of severe paternal abuse, and, as Dr. Pelleck had suspected, some chemical imbalances. While everyone was of the opinion that he was taking his prescribed medication, he had long stopped, and, in his mind, he was apparently doing alright without it. Yet, he continued to get pills and remove them from their containers at the prescribed time, only to flush them away, knowing that someone would periodically check to determine if he was doing as they suggested.

What puzzled Jennifer was that after the first two weeks at home, Lance became even more private than usual. He spent far too much time in his room. He brought no one home, and he didn't seem to have a girl friend.

Jennifer worried about this. Not only was he distant with her, he was the same with everyone, and contrary to his beliefs, she felt he needed someone his own age to talk to, to spend his idle time with. Even she knew that being alone all the time wasn't healthy.

She hadn't seen him reading much, although there were signs of an impending genius around his room. He had a number of books on his desk, mostly on animal and human anatomy. There were also pocket books of mystery, horror, and non-fictional accounts of American homicides. She wondered if he was becoming interested in medicine or one of the forensic sciences.

He never shared with her anything about his desires and goals, and when she asked about them, he didn't comment. Whatever he had in mind, she wasn't aware of it, but she was impressed with the book titles and was glad he was showing signs of reading. With the apparent attention he was giving to his studies, it was a direct turnabout from his earlier years.

He had certain rules about life that she had to abide by. She dared not go into his room when the door was closed. She wouldn't even knock unless she had to tell him she was putting the food on the table. He made it very clear that he needed his private time to read and think and that no one was to disturb him when his door was closed.

She found this out the hard way. She had always respected his privacy to a point, but when she wanted to talk on one occasion, she went to his room, knocked her usual three times and began to open the door. Before she had a chance to put one foot into his room, Lance yelled as loud as he could, "Close the door!"

She jumped at the sudden outburst, closed the door immediately and stood there, staring at it, waiting for an explanation. It finally came when Lance opened the door and said, "Don't ever come barging in on me like that. I was in the middle of something very important. I'll be out in just a little while."

She had no clue about what he was thinking so hard about, but she never opened the door again without his permission. She also never even approached the door unless she had something very important to talk to him about. Even then, if he didn't respond to her knocks, she went away and brought it up at a later time.

In spite of the impression Jennifer got from the scattered books, the reading material that Lance got most of his use from were the same magazines of girls in the nude that he spent so much time with when he was in the dorm. These were his secret books, ones generally hidden in his closet. He read and reread the confessions of horny writers like those who fantasized about meeting some young woman who was beyond-belief beautiful and gave him the best head he ever had in the bushes of a local park.

He always read these passages with his dick in his hand, stroking with the thought of experiencing the same fantasy he was reading about. He wondered why he never met someone like that. It always happened to the other guy, but it never stopped him from hoping that someday it would happen to him.

Jennifer guessed that something like that was going on. She heard his occasional grunts and groans and heard the rattling sound of his metal bed banging on the floor when he was at the peak of his activity, but she never brought it up. She remembered what Dr. Pelleck had told her about excess and wondered how much of his private time he spent in that activity.

When Lance finally left the house, she entered his room once or twice and was overwhelmed by the pungent odor of seminal fluid. She could also see the stains on the bed sheets. What she found, though, was only a small part of what his private sex life was about. Before he left, he had put all the magazines away.

Even though they lived in the same house, she didn't see him much. When he finally left the bedroom, he went directly to the bathroom and spent another hour or two there before he would come out to eat. Immediately after eating, he left the house, and usually didn't tell his mother where he was going. Basically, she was his maid.

Most of his time away from the house was in the evening, after supper. Without giving Jennifer any form of explanation for his activities, he would walk to wherever he wanted to go, ride his bike, or catch the bus. He would stay out all hours of the night, and

Jennifer would be sound asleep in a chair near the front door when he returned home.

Upon his return, Jennifer would say, "Lance where have you been? Why can't you tell me where you were, and don't you think it would be nice if you told me when you were going to come home? I worry about you, baby."

"I just went out to be with some friends, momma," he'd say. "It's nothing special. Just some people I know from school. We don't do anything that you need to worry about, so get off my back." The terminal part of his statement generally had a belligerent tone to it, signifying his displeasure with her invasive questions.

Jennifer wondered who these friends were. She had never seen or met them, and why didn't he bring them around? There house wasn't a million-dollar show place, but it wasn't anything to scoff about either.

Jennifer said, "Why don't you bring your friends over some day? I could fix you something nice, and you could all watch television."

By that time, Lance was already half way to his room. Without an answer to Jennifer's question, he quickly made the last few steps, went into his room, and slammed the door. That would be the last she saw of him until the next day.

What Lance actually liked to do in the evenings was go down to the college and watch the coed summer students return to their dorms. There were no friends to spend time with. When it got dark, he would sneak into the bushes, pull out his small pair of binoculars and search the windows for coeds walking around in their birthday suits. Then he would masturbate while watching them.

As a break, he went down to a local campus restaurant and had a root beer float or chocolate malt, only to return to the dorms and do it all over again. He repeated this nightly until all or most of the lights were out. When there wasn't anything left to look at, he walked the campus sidewalks, hoping to find a girl that would talk to him, but by that time, just about everyone was already in bed, and he returned home.

In his own strange way, he felt the need to talk to someone, but that was impossible to do unless he approached them earlier in the evening when they were coming home from the library or from another dorm. Students participating in other activities were generally in groups.

He sometimes went to the library and pretended to look through books just to see who was there. When the library closed, he would follow some of the girls home, tailing them just close enough to see where they went and determine if they were ever alone.

He repeatedly mulled certain possibilities over in his head. How was he going to approach them? When would he do it? Where would be a safe place? What if she didn't like him? He didn't want to make a mistake, and he didn't want to appear stupid.

Chapter 29

A Close Call

Through a selection process, he watched one girl more than any of the others. She was at the library almost every night, and she usually stayed until it closed. She generally left with a friend, but they parted before she got to her dorm. He heard her friend say, "Goodnight Cathy," on several occasions when they parted, and there was a short distance that she covered by herself. That would be where he would approach her.

The thing that caught his eye most about Cathy was her smooth, almost blemish-free skin, and in addition to her outstanding skin quality, she was otherwise absolutely beautiful. While outwardly calm, her appearance and the thought of running his hands over her and tasting her soft skin drove him wild.

He attempted to get her attention in the library a couple of times. He sat close to her, pretending to read a book. Once in a while, he would look up and stare at her. When she looked his way, he would smile, hoping that she would smile back. She did at first, but she quit smiling when she realized it was too convenient that he should be there where she was studying almost every night. In all honesty, he gave her the creeps.

One evening, he waited in the bushes at her dorm, knowing that she would be coming along at any time. When she told her friend good night and approached her dorm, Lance stepped out and nervously said, "Hi Cathy. C . . ., coming from the library?"

She was startled and stopped walking the instant he greeted her. She said, "What do you want?"

"I j . . ., just want to talk to you." It was obvious to her that Lance was nervous.

"What about? Who are you anyway?"

Lance said, "I . . ., I'm the guy from the library. I've been watching you, and I just want to talk." By this time, the initial stuttering had somewhat subsided, but he was still nervous.

Cathy, obviously scared at this point, said, "Please go away. I don't really know you, and you're creeping me out. I was wondering why you were looking at me so much in the library. Now I know. Are you stalking me or something?"

Lance moved closer to her and asked if he could carry her books to her dorm, and Cathy responded with a definite, "No. Please leave me alone. I never encouraged you to come here, and I want you to leave." At that point, Lance grabbed her arm, and insisted that she come with him. He pulled her toward the bushes, and she began to scream for help. Lance panicked, released his grip on her and ran behind the dorm. Cathy ran into the building and told the dorm manager about the incident. She, in turn, called the campus police, but by the time they arrived, Lance was already home and in bed.

He had run the entire way home, through areas with bushes and shrubs where he could hide from anyone that would be out that late, then down some of the side streets that were usually vacant by that time. When he got home, he was delighted to find his mother already in bed, and he ran directly to his room and softly closed the door.

Jennifer raised her head and pointed her ear toward the hall. She checked her watch and wondered what all the running through the house was about. What was happening that she didn't know about?

Since nothing had really happened on campus that night, the presence of a stalker never got in the news. However, the campus police spent the next few nights checking around the dorms to make sure no one was hiding in the bushes.

Since Lance wasn't a student at that time, and Cathy didn't actually know him, no identification of the stalker was ever made.

Following their brief meeting, Cathy made sure she either came home early from the library or had an escort on her way to the dorm. She later quit going to the library at all unless she had a term paper to write.

Lance knew that he was too bold in his approach. In spite of all his planning, he had muffed it this time, and he took far too many chances. He'd have to work on his procedure, perfect it if you will. He didn't need the cops breathing down his neck.

The next morning, at breakfast, Jennifer asked Lance why he was in such a rush when he came into the house, and Lance told her that he was jogging, that he had been jogging for quite a while. It was a way for him to keep in shape during the summer. "You know," he said, "you can study and study, and that keeps your mind in shape, but you need to get that heart going to keep the old body in shape."

Lance remained at home for a week or so. Jennifer detected he was a little nervous about something, and she noticed a scratch mark on his hand. He explained that he had gotten the scratch from a broken glass when he had visited the biology laboratory.

His main concern, though, was that he didn't want to go out on the street and accidentally run into Cathy or anyone that may be able to put the finger on him. He'd rather cool it and let the incident die down a little. After his quiet period at home, he did begin going out in the evenings, but it was usually to a spot around the corner from the main campus, a place at which he had never seen Cathy.

There was a vacant lot near the house that was overgrown with a variety of types of vegetation, including some tall, canopy-like trees. A poorly defined dirt drive went through the property to a telephone pole that stood near the back edge of the lot, well out of the way of anyone that would be passing by. The pole had metal spikes sticking out the side, providing an easy way to climb to a height above most of the vegetation.

He found he could go there in the evening and spy on an apartment that three nurses were sharing. Needless to say, he got in some good viewing there because while their apartment was mostly out of view to the public, he had a bird's eye view from ten feet in the air. He made love to his hand many times while he watched them undress.

That's how his summer went, mostly home during the day and out scouting the territory during the evenings. When he returned to class the following semester, he decided to spend his extracurricular time at home. He was still afraid of being spotted by Cathy, and he wanted to stay away from campus as much as possible. Even with being at home, though, he saw his mother very little, and that's the way he wanted it.

Jennifer's summer turned out to be a lonely one, and this continued through the next semester. What she thought would be a pleasant period in their life, a period in which she and Lance could spend a little quality time together, turned out to be a bust.

He was at a stalemate in his daily activities. No matter what he planned, he couldn't get the thought out of his head that Cathy could identify him. He was forced to return to campus whenever he had class, and it was likely that she was there, somewhere. This was something he'd have to look into. He couldn't live with himself, thinking that she could cause him some harm for something he didn't even have fun doing.

He was right about it not being fun. In fact, when he approached her that night, it actually had been an overwhelmingly painful experience. He had never approached a girl before, and he felt quite awkward. His words got twisted when he spoke, and he knew his nervousness couldn't have been more obvious if he had a flashing neon sign hanging around his neck.

Sure, he had done it in his dreams and in his repeated bouts of planning, but those always worked out. When it was time for the real thing, he couldn't handle it. He wasn't in control, and this bothered the hell out of him.

In order to keep a low profile, he decided to give his laboratory job up. He told his teachers he needed more study time. He didn't burn his bridge with the Biology Department, however, and they agreed that the job would be available to him if ever he needed it back.

He started checking the area out as soon as the semester began. There wasn't any use to plan further until he knew the coast was clear. He didn't notice any particular amount of activity around the dorms by the campus police. They were back in their routine, and that's what he had hoped for.

So it was back to the bushes for Lance, binoculars in hand, viewing the sights of the coed's dorm. He was especially careful now, taking every precaution to avoid being seen. He noticed a few new faces and some old ones. There were many beautiful things to see, and his vantage point was still as good as it had been the semester before.

When he thought it was time for Cathy to return home from the library, he moved to a spot near the front of the dorm, but she was nowhere to be found. The thought entered his mind that maybe she hadn't returned to school. Maybe the summer session was just a one-time affair to earn a few credits for a job she had. Whatever the reason, she wasn't coming home at the prescribed time, and this disappointed him.

He thought, and suddenly an explanation popped into his head. *Maybe she's changed her routine. I'll have to check, maybe go back to the library and see if she's there, and if she is, then follow her to learn where she goes.*

While he stood there, he formulated a quick version of his master plan to renew his relationship with Cathy. It wasn't just that he wanted to see her again. For reasons beyond his grasp, he had to.

At the library, he looked everywhere from a vantage point in the book stacks, but she wasn't in her regular place. He looked some more, walking through the stacks and surveying the reading tables and stalls. She had disappeared. If he knew her last name, he could look it up in the college phone book, and if he found it, he would at least know she was somewhere on campus.

After carefully searching other locations around campus and experiencing repeated waiting periods by her dorm, he reached a point at which he assumed she was no longer a student at this institution. If this was true, he was wasting his valuable time.

He had to seek out someone new, although he hated the thought of it. So much time was already wasted in the preliminaries on Cathy, and now all that was lost, as well.

He returned to the library and selected two or three new coeds that appealed to him, and he began to follow each of them for a period of two weeks. He found that they had routines, too, and this would make it easier to get them alone.

One of the girls, Shirley was her name, another campus beauty with smooth, beautiful skin, had similar habits to Cathy's. She stayed at the library most of the evening and went back to her dorm when the library was ready to close. She, too, walked with a friend and parted ways when they neared their respective dorms.

He followed her nightly until he had her routine memorized, and he waited in the bushes so he could practice a dry run once or twice before he actually approached her. He also spent time at home, behind the closed door of his bedroom, repeatedly going over his memorized dialog, and when he thought he was ready, he dressed in dark clothing and set out on his quest.

He was in the bushes much too early for Shirley to come by, but he wanted to be sure he didn't miss her. He ran his plan through his mind once more, then moved to a spot near the front of the building. As he moved forward, he came to an abrupt halt when he heard voices, one of which sounded somewhat familiar to him. He moved again to a new location closer to the sounds and peeked around the vegetation to find Cathy standing there with a male companion about her age. They were kissing as though they had known each other for some time.

Of course, he thought, *her routine has changed. She met someone she's spending time with, and her goings and comings are manipulated to fit in with her social agenda. Why didn't I see that before?*

He wondered where they had been before they came here, whether she had been seeing him for a while, or if she kissed everyone like that and he was some new toy to play with. He watched. They kissed some more, whispered a few words to one another and then parted. Her boy friend watched her return to the dorm, and then headed for his car.

Lance wanted to follow him, but he didn't have suitable transportation. He had to let him go this time. Maybe he could find out more at a later date. As he watched him leave, Shirley and her friend came strolling by. They parted, and she went inside. It was not her night to meet Lance Housler.

Chapter 27

Ron and Cathy Meet Lance

His mind was back on Cathy now, so he filed Shirley away in the recesses of his mind. If Cathy didn't work out, Shirley would be her substitute. He couldn't deal with both girls at the same time. It would complicate his plan.

He went to the bushes nightly, but no Cathy. He tried to make sense of her routine, and then it dawned on him. The night he had seen her was on a Friday. She probably spent her time during the week studying someplace else, maybe in the dorm lobby where he couldn't see her. On the weekend, at least on Friday and maybe on Saturday, she probably went out on dates, possibly with the same guy he had seen her with. This made sense to him, but he'd have to check it out.

When Friday came, he told his mother he didn't feel very well and went to bed early. He didn't think this would seem unusual. He had used this excuse to get away from her in the past. Jennifer asked if she could do anything for him, and he told her not to worry and to just let him sleep.

He turned his light out, and everything was silent. Jennifer genuinely believed he must not be feeling well because she didn't hear the usual bed-banging that went on at other times.

Lance waited, and when his mother's light clicked off, he silently arose from the bed, wearing the dark clothes he had put on just after he turned the light off. He slowly lifted the window and crawled through to the alley. He walked down the alley to the street and walked in the direction of the dorm.

As he had planned, he was soon waiting in his usual spot. It was a good night for him. There was no moon, and the night was pitch black. When he was away from the street lights, he could hardly see his hand in front of his face.

Sure enough, Cathy and the same fellow returned about ten o'clock, a little earlier than they had returned when he saw her last. They stood in front of the dorm, a little off to the side, out of the direct path of the entrance lights, and they shared a few passionate kisses.

He was close to them, so close he could hear their whispers and smell her perfume. She said, "Ron, I really enjoyed tonight. I wish it could have lasted longer, but I've got to get in before curfew ends and finish my class report."

Ron said, "I know. I enjoy every minute I'm with you. I think I'm falling in love with you, and it hurts to not be able to spend more time with you during the week." Lance detected a slur in his voice, like he may have been drinking.

"I know, Ron, but we have to think about our studies. Since I haven't been going to the library, I've fallen a little behind, and I can't afford to let my private life interfere with my studies. Please understand. I want to spend more time with you, too, but it's just difficult right now. Besides, I think you're a little drunk. You need to go sleep it off."

Lance was thinking: *Okay, enough is enough. Let's get on with the show and drop all this mushy bull shit. There are more serious things in life.*

Ron pulled Cathy close to him and kissed her, pushing his body tight against hers. She had to feel his excitement. He moved his hand to one of her breasts and gave it a slight squeeze. Knowing exactly what he had in mind, she backed off slightly and said, "What are you doing, Ron?"

He responded with, "I want you, Cathy. I haven't had you in days, and it's killing me. Holding you and kissing you isn't enough."

Cathy said, "But, Ron, this is not the place. There's no place to go, and we'll get caught."

"What about my car, Cathy? We could go there. We could park around the corner where there aren't people walking by all the time. There are no lights to bother us, and there's a little dirt drive that leads into the woods where nobody would see us."

Cathy thought for a minute and said, "Alright, Ron. We can go there for a little while, but I have to be back at eleven o'clock at the latest."

Ron walked Cathy to his car, they got in and drove off. Lance followed on foot. Ron's secret spot was just a block away. Lance hadn't realized when he mentioned the location of the lot, but he now knew it was his favorite hang-out, the one with the telephone pole at the back of the property. As Ron turned the corner, Lance could see the headlights enter the woodland area. By the time he got to the dirt drive, the lights on Ron's car had gone out, and he crept slowly and silently toward them. Ron's windows were closed, so he couldn't hear the conversation, but he did hear the sounds of moans radiating from their direction, and he saw the windows begin to fog up.

All of a sudden, Ron got out of the car, rounded the back, and stepped a little into the woods. Lance could hear the splatter of urine on the damp leaves. He was within a few feet of him, close enough to smell the foul odor of his liquid waste. It reminded him of his early days, the nightmares, and bed wetting.

He moved toward Ron slowly and carefully but stepped on a twig which fractured with a cracking sound. Ron looked around but didn't see anything, so he finished emptying his bladder.

Lance lunged at him and sunk his knife deep into his back. Holding his other hand over his mouth, he held him there, wiggling the knife a little to penetrate deeper and tear numerous blood vessels in the process. Ron attempted a slight turn to face his assailant, but Lance held on tightly and his body was already weak. He bent his head forward, ran the knife into opening at the base of Ron's skull, and moved it around, scrambling his brain.. Within seconds, his body became limp and he fell to his knees. His knowledge of pithing served him well.

Lance removed the knife and plunged it into his throat two or three times. It was overkill, but he needed more practice before he would get it perfect. He held him there for a few seconds, blood squirting out like a fountain. He dropped the body, wiped the knife clean on Ron's clothes, and went toward the car.

It was so dark there in the woods that Cathy didn't know it was Lance when he got in, and she said, "What took you so long? I was wondering if you left me."

Lance thought: He left you, alright. You'll never see him again. He moved over to her, grabbed her and planted his most passionate kiss on her lips. She tasted so sweet and smelled so good.

All of a sudden, she pushed back and said, "You're not Ron. Who are you?"

Lance said, "Who do you want me to be? I've been waiting for you ever since last summer."

When she heard his voice and thought back to her summer meeting with him, she became frantic and attempted to get out of the car. Lance grabbed her by the arm and told her to be good.

"I'm not going to hurt you. I just want to feel you close to me and taste your skin, like Ron wanted to do."

Cathy gasped and yelled, "My God, you were listening to us. What have you done? Where's Ron?"

"Let's just say that Ron won't be here to protect you. You and I are going to have a good time. I know you like it. Why can't it be me?"

"Jesus, what have you done? Let go of me. You're hurting me."

She was plenty scared by this time. Tears started to roll down her cheeks, and she thrashed about, attempting to break loose from his grip.

"I told you to be good! Now hold still!" Lance was getting pissed off, and he was losing control.

About that time, Cathy sunk her long nails on her free hand into Lance's face. She jerked away and turned to open the door. Lance flinched at the pain, lost his grip and watched her fall through the open door onto the ground. He jumped after her and caught her by the heel as she was getting up to run.

Her forceful attempt to escape pulled him along with her, but he held on. When she fell again, he pulled her over toward him. He turned her over on her back, laid on top of her and put his hand over her mouth. She could feel his erection, and she began to cry again. When he seemed to relax, she gave him a shove, turned to face away from him, and was ready to get up and escape when she felt a sharp pain in her back.

Lance had shoved the knife in to the hilt. When she seemed to lose her desire to escape, he pulled it out, turned her over and shoved it into her chest. He tore her dress, bra, and panties away as she gasped for air. He sunk his head into the depression between her beautiful breasts. He licked her and lapped at her blood, then he entered her for the first and last time.

She didn't fight any more. She was probably already dead when he ejaculated into her. It was one of his most explosive ejaculations ever, and he was almost out of breath when it was over. His heart was pounding as it never had before, and after a long recuperative pause, he began to ponder. It was over. What was he going to do?

He stroked her body and lay upon her for the last time. He got up, went back to Ron to make sure he was dead, and then he urinated on him.

His last act was to take the butt of his knife and knock out two of Cathy's teeth, her deep rooted right canine and the adjacent incisor. The pounding had broken her jaw and shattered her maxillary bone, and blood had splattered over her facial area. When he looked at her, she no longer appeared to be the beautiful coed she was moments earlier. He reached down and cut off her right pinkie finger, put his new body parts in a plastic bag, and left.

He moved through the streets toward his house, avoiding walking in the open areas. The streets were quiet by this time, so he was hoping he wouldn't run into anyone. When a car came his way, he ducked into an alley until it had passed. When he got to his house, he noticed the lights were still off.

He went down the alley to his window, slowly opened it, and climbed through. He spent the next hour undressing and showering. He shoved his blood=stained clothes into a plastic bag to be thrown away as soon as possible, and he put his small plastic bag with body parts down beside it.

He knew his mother would hear the water running, so he prepared his story. As he left the shower and dried off, he heard the knock on his door.

Jennifer said, "Lance, honey, are you awake?"

"Yes, mother. What do you want?"

"I just wanted to see if you're alright."

"Yes, I'm okay. I feel a little better. Thank you. I just woke up and decided to take a hot shower, but I'm going back to sleep. "Okay, baby. I'll see you in the morning. Goodnight."

Lance was certain his mother didn't know he had been gone. He spent the rest of the night lying in his bed, going over his evening activities and the sensations that he experienced. In certain ways, it scared him, but he knew he would do it again. The only problem was that Cathy wouldn't be there the next time. She was gone. He'd have to find someone new.

Chapter 28

The Bodies are Found

No one saw the car parked in the vacant lot. It was hidden amongst the palms and oaks, its outline camouflaged by the tall weeds and hanging clumps of Spanish moss. It wasn't until two young students, Jerry and Tocha, attempted to do the same thing that Ron and Cathy had done that the car was even noticed at all.

When they saw the car in their headlights, they were disappointed. They really wanted a secluded spot like this one, but where? Lover's Lane by Lake Pontchartrain was too visible for the privacy they wanted. Audubon park was a nice spot, but it was clear across town and you always risked the chance of being discovered by wandering police. This was ideal, and there weren't that many places like this near the campus to go to.

As they began to back out of the drive, Tocha saw something out of the corner of her eye when the headlights had scanned the bushes to their right. She didn't exactly know what it was, but she was hoping it wasn't what she thought it was.

She yelled, "Jerry, stop. I just saw something. Pull up a little."

And that's when they saw Ron laying in the grass, nestled amongst the bushy vegetation. They looked at one another, and Jerry asked, "Is that what I think it is?"

As they got out of the car, they could smell his putrid remains. They held their hands to their nose and inched a little closer, taking mini steps toward the body and stretching their necks to avoid getting too close. They stood there, motionless, not uttering a word, then Tocha simply said, "Jesus!" They scrambled back to the car, jumped in, backed out of the drive and drove off.

They weren't sure how long they had driven around, and Jerry wasn't going in any particular direction. He was just driving and thinking. They weren't sitting close to one another like they had been when they had entered the vacant lot. They were in their respective seats, sitting almost at attention and looking straight ahead. Jerry's hands were clenched like vices to the steering wheel, and Tocha was wringing her hands like you would squeeze out a water-soaked hand towel.

When he was ready to speak, Jerry said, "Tocha, I think we'd better tell somebody about this. I don't know what happened back there, but it was something bad. I've been thinking about it. If we don't tell the police, they may somehow know that we were there, and then we'd be in a lot of trouble."

"But how are they going to tell we were there, Jerry?" It sounded as though Tocha didn't want to let anyone in on why they were out so late at night in such an isolated spot.

"I don't know, Tocha, maybe from the tire tracks or our footprints. You know how all those forensic people are. You can fart in the area, and somehow they're going to know about it. We probably got blood on our shoes, and that damned luminol will find us guilty one way or another."

Tocha said, "But what about our parents? They're going to know we went there, and we'll get hell from them."

"Well, think about it, Tocha. I'd rather get it from them than get blamed for whatever happened by that car. Wouldn't you?"

"I guess so."

Neither of them wanted to believe what they had seen, but it happened, and they had to deal with it. They were in the wrong place at the wrong time.

As they thought about it, their coming upon the dead guy wasn't as bad as it could have been. It could have happened to them if they had parked there a few days earlier, and that conjured up some even more unpleasant thoughts.

Jerry and Tocha found their way to Tulane Avenue and the police station. They apprehensively approached the front desk hand-in-hand, and the desk sergeant asked if he could help them. He could tell immediately that they were both aprehensive about something.

Jerry said, "I don't know how to tell you this, but we went to park in this vacant lot on Collins Street, about five blocks from campus. When we got there . . . "

Before he had launched into his story, the sergeant asked what campus they were talking about. Jerry said, "The New Orleans University campus, out by the lakefront."

When he was sure the sergeant wasn't going to interrupt again, he continued. "When we got there, there was another car parked under the trees. When we started to leave, we saw someone lying on the ground partially behind the bushes, so we got out to see what it was.

"When we went over to it, we noticed it was some guy, and he was dead. We got the hell out of there. That's all we know."

The desk sergeant said, "Just a minute, please." He picked up the phone, quickly dialed a number and told whoever it was at the other end to "get here on the double." In a few minutes, a Lieutenant Jacobs showed up, and the desk sergeant told Jerry to tell the lieutenant what he had told him.

When Jerry looked around to see who else was listening, the lieutenant ushered them to a more private location and offered them some refreshments. When they refused, apparently wondering why the lieutenant was wasting time with hospitality when they had seen the most frightening thing of their lives, he finally asked what they had.

When Jerry repeated the entire story, the lieutenant asked them how long ago they had seen this. Jerry looked at his watch and told him about an hour ago, maybe even an hour and a half, and the lieutenant wanted to know what had taken them so long to report it. Jerry said they were scared and didn't know what to do. It was clear that they were still nervous about what they had found.

The lieutenant picked the phone up and requested assistance to investigate an apparent homicide, and in another couple of minutes, he, Tocha, the lieutenant, and his assistant, were in an unmarked car, heading for the vacant lot. When they arrived, Jerry told them where the body was found, and the lieutenant asked them to remain in the vehicle.

They did as they were told and watched as the two policemen scouted the area with flashlights. It was apparent that they were being careful not to disturb the area, and there was no need to check for a pulse because the male had been dead for at least a couple of days. Along with the stench of decomposing flesh were abundant flies and the lingering odor of uric acid.

The officer then moved toward the car. As his assistant went to the passenger side, he saw Cathy lying on her back about ten feet from the car. They noticed she had a bloody face with teeth missing and tooth marks on her shoulder and one of her breasts. She also was plenty dead and laying in a pool of dried blood, scantily clad in clothes that had been ripped to shreds.

Ants, organized in an assortment of trails and aggregations, were acquiring their protein from various parts of her body. It was obvious that she had been raped. Before they finished with the scene, they had noticed that both she and the male she was with had knife wounds, and Cathy's little finger was missing.

The lieutenant got on the radio and requested additional assistance from homicide, and they showed up within the hour. While they were waiting, Jerry asked if the lieutenant could call their parents and Cathy's dorm to let them know where they were and that they were alright.

When investigators from the homicide unit finished their preliminary work, they got the story again from Jerry and Tocha, took their names, addresses, and phone numbers, and told the sergeant to take them back to their car.

Within the next twelve hours, the vacant lot, usually starved of human occupancy, was buzzing with activity. More homicide investigators and cameramen had taken what they needed. Other specialists and the local forensic unit searched for fingerprints and other clues that could lead to the identity of the killer or killers.

Reporters showed up early in the morning to get what they needed and rushed back to their offices to insert their story of the homicide-rape in the morning news. It was destined to be the lead article on the front page of the Times-Picayune and other local newspapers.

The more investigators examined the area and discussed their findings, the more they realized they needed outside help. There were too many features associated with Cathy's body that were indicative of a killer who was programed in the way he or she carried out their business.

Lieutenant Jacobs got on the phone and called headquarters on Tulane Avenue. He requested FBI assistance and suggested they come immediately. "We've made a lot of preliminary observations, but this is something the feds should get involved with. It looks like the markings of a serial killer."

When the story came out, it shocked New Orleanians. The words 'serial killer' were not released because it was bad enough without panicking everyone. Although there were plenty of murders in New Orleans, something precisely like this had not happened before in the city, not that they knew of. Everyone was talking about it, especially those who lived near the vacant lot. Certain parts of New Orleans were known to be violent sections of the city, but the lakefront area was generally thought of as an upscale neighborhood.

Yes, there were killings in this section of town before, but they generally were associated with family squabbles or shootings involving lovers that were out of their territory.

Chapter 29

Special Agent Patricia Clayton

Special Agent Patricia Clayton was a field officer in the Behavioral Analysis Unit (BAU) for crimes against adults, a subdivision of the FBI's National Center for the Analysis of Violent Crimes (NCAVC). Their main headquarters were on Leon C. Simon Boulevard.

She had been assigned to head up the investigation of the murdered college students, but since she had been requested after much of the preliminary work had been done, she had gotten there late, sometime after all the local law enforcement officials had been in and out for various reasons.

Most of the initial forensic work and routine chores of an investigative nature had been done by local law enforcement. It was her job to make a final sweep through the crime scene to search for clues that may have been overlooked and then to coordinate the investigation.

* * *

Patricia was a long way from what she was when Lance had seen her last. After baby sitting for the Houslers at fifteen, her childhood dreams eventually came to fruition by her dedicating herself to reaching a life-long goal of becoming associated with law enforcement.

There were plenty of reasons she could be proud of herself. She had graduated from New Orleans University *magna cum laude*. She had been one of the top students in the early stages of her FBI training, and she had graduated as an FBI agent with honors.

Now at thirty-five, she had moved up in rank, through her association with the Violent Criminal Apprehension Program (VICAP), and finally became one of the top investigators in her southern division. This wasn't just a job to her. She absolutely loved what she was doing, except for the absolute horrors of what some killers were capable of. Most of all, she enjoyed seeing criminals get caught.

She was good looking besides, "one of the best looking special agents in the division," as was often said by her colleagues. While this was true, she always felt that her good looks were beside the point, maybe even belittling. It was her intelligence, loyalty to her profession, and her high degree of competence that she wanted everyone to notice.

When she arrived at the crime scene, she was appalled at what she saw. What a waste, she thought, two young non-suspecting students who were just out having a good time, and they ended up like this.

She knew that young people shouldn't be engaging in sex in a very remote area of the city, but let's be real. Most of us would have considered doing the same thing when we were that age. We were all young and in love once, and under those circumstances, seclusion is just a step away from heaven. It just happens.

When interviewed by a local news team, she was asked to comment about the couple and their choice of a secluded location.

She said, "While it is very important for us to talk to our sons and daughters about the facts of life and the dangers of visiting secluded spots to be alone, the most important down side of looking for a very remote area to do these activities in, though, is that this is precisely what many rapist and killers look for. They don't want someone who is enjoying themselves out in public with an audience of people surrounding them. They want to find a secluded place and go unnoticed when they carry out the heinous crimes they commit.

"It doesn't have to be a college campus. It doesn't even have to be two people secluded in a parked car. It can be anyone who is alone and has a predictable daily behavior. That's what's so upsetting. In many ways, such predictability is part of everyone's life."

Take hers, for instance. She lived in a nice house in the Garden District, just off St. Charles Avenue, not far from Audubon Park. She wasn't married. She left the house at a specific time every morning to go to the same place of work in the same vehicle on the same route. She left work about the same time every day, traveled the same route home, and spent most of every evening at home by herself.

She did have some unpredictable events in her life, but they were few. Occasionally, she went to the grocery, although it was the same one most of the time, ran a few errands, went to a movie, or had a date, but many of those things had their degree of predictability, as well. There's no getting around it. Most people live predictable lives.

Chapter 30

Recognizing an Old Friend

When she arrived at the scene, she asked, "Why wasn't I called earlier?"

Lieutenant Jacobs said, "We initially thought we could handle it, but when we had a chance to evaluate the killings, we realized it was way beyond our capabilities."

She was upset that the scene had been almost trashed before her arrival, with all the local investigators swarming over the area. This left her with a mess, and she could only hope that the evidence they already had collected would assist in her investigation.

A second forensic team, under Special Agent Clayton's supervision, managed to collect a few strands of hair on the front seat of the vehicle and blood samples from the two victims, as well as some blood that was smeared on the front seat of the passenger's side. These clues were in addition to what the New Orleans police had already gotten. There were also semen samples taken from Cathy's body, the bite mark pattern on her shoulder, saliva from the her body, and urine on Ron's clothing.

It would be up to the coroner's office to supply specifics about the wounds. They would also take samples of semen and blood for laboratory testing and make notations of other unusual features that were overlooked by the field crew.

While the stab wounds revealed they were made with a long, thin knife, they didn't provide any additional evidence, and the murder weapon had never been found. By far, the best evidence for characterizing the killer or killers appeared to be the blood from the seat, the saliva, and the seminal fluid.

Since the bite marks were relatively clear, it was certain that they would be of value at some point in the investigation. A thorough odontological examination revealed a slight misalignment of the second incisor on the left side. It was obvious that the killer either had straight teeth naturally or came from a family that could afford braces.

The misaligned tooth probably resulted from a fall or a hit, or maybe the person quit wearing his braces before his teeth had become completely straight. There were also surface features, such as irregularities on the distal tips of the teeth that produced variations in the wound marks.

Although everyone suspected the male victim was not responsible for the bite marks on the female victim, they had to check his teeth against the marks to be sure. Also, the DNA of the sperm sample had to be checked against his DNA, as well.

While the precise pattern of the bite marks was probably characteristic of only a few people, it really wasn't of much value to the FBI at this point because it would be extremely difficult to notice on a person unless they got everyone in the city to bite something for a comparative study. What this meant was that until they got a suspect, such a comparison wasn't going to happen.

The blood was identified as O negative. This made the killer a universal donor with the same blood type as at least forty to fifty percent of Americans. If they were Native American, the percentage would even be a little higher.

The electrophoretic band pattern in the DNA analysis of both the blood from the seat and the saliva sample matched the pattern of DNA in all the semen samples, so they were pretty sure there was only one killer-rapist involved in the double murder.

However, the DNA sample showed a variation of bands that didn't look quite right. This was puzzling enough to Special Agent Clayton to make her believe that the lab could have made a mistake.

She knew this was highly unlikely, but even though they had gotten the same results from several semen samples, she had them run it again, and the report came back identical to the others. This was a characteristic to put an asterisk by in the file because it was going to be important in the future. She was certain of it.

When the results of the investigation were sent through the VICAP database, no match came up. This, too, was a disappointment. She would have sworn that there would have been a perfect match. Such characteristics associated with a specific killer were generally well documented, and it should have pulled up a match, unless the killer was new to his profession. Use of sequences in the Variable Number Tandem Repeats (VNTR) at least gave them a DNA fingerprint to file in case they got a suspect they could probe for a DNA match.

The hair and fibers that were found on both the driver's side and the passenger side were checked by every available technique. DNA tests were carried out on the hair. Both were examined to determine features such as crimp, length, color, relative diameter, luster, apparent cross section, damage, and adhering debris. They were checked for various optical characteristics, like refractive index, birefringence, and fluorescence.

A variety of microscopes were used in their analysis, including the double microscope for comprehensive side-by-side comparisons and the scanning electron microscope. From all of this, and this was the best the FBI had, the only concrete information obtained that was of value was that the killer had dark brown hair of about five microns in diameter and was probably wearing a dark cotton shirt.

Special Agent Clayton called a special meeting when she felt the time was right, and she had local law enforcement investigators and FBI experts present their summations. When it was all over, she concluded that their investigations yielded very little about the killer's identification that would lead to an immediate arrest, but it did provide some characteristics that may be important at a later date.

She was certain of one thing, though. The person who committed this crime had either done it before or will do it again. The removal of Cathy's two teeth, as well as her finger, was a dead give-away. She was certain the killer had taken them as souvenirs.

She had the computer in VICAP running full blast to make some kind of a connection to other cases with similar MOs. At first, it was a search for college students with missing teeth and fingers, then anyone who was killed, tooth Hunters, and missing teeth and fingers, cross-linked with stabbings followed by rape, victims in parked cars, and a variety of other topics that seemed to be related to this incident. There were some common features between this and other cases, but none were outstandingly similar.

It was worth looking into the matches, but she and the profiler were counting on it being a single, brown-haired, white male killer, somewhere in his twenties, type O negative blood, who was new to his profession, because killers like this either would have matched a VICAP fingerprint or they were just beginning to develop a pattern about how they did their business. Yes, they were predictable to a degree, as well.

With no clear fingerprints to use as evidence, and nothing else that was of significance to identify the killer, it appeared that the case would have to be put on hold for the time being. It got to a point that they were spinning their wheels, and they had other cases that needed their attention.

When Special Agent Clayton was interviewed by WNOL, the local, prime-time television station, she mentioned most of what she knew about the case and stated, "We don't have any good leads."

She conveniently left out the part about a serial killer. There was no reason, at this point, to refer to the person as a serial killer. It was true that the MO indicated such a person was one, but with no matches in the files, this person was not quite at the serial killer level.

She also asked for public assistance. "If anyone knows anything about this crime, please notify the NCAVC," and she gave the number to call. She also took advantage of her TV time by explaining what such a killer would be looking for, and she once again advised people who searched for secluded places to be very careful and think twice about what they are doing.

Lance watched the interview, thinking that her name sounded familiar. Then it dawned on him. She was that baby sitter who lived near him when he was just a child. His mother told him that she had even stayed with him one time when they wanted to go out on the town.

He didn't really remember the incident, but he had a faint recollection of swinging a knife at her. Then another picture flashed through his mind. The blood, the bright red blood. The image was poor, but it was enough for him to enjoy.

Now she was investigating a crime that he had committed. He hoped she wouldn't put two and two together and come up with him as a likely suspect. But, he thought, why would she? That was a long time ago, and he was just a baby, an innocent baby. There was no reason for her to know that he and the killer he had become were the same.

Chapter 31

Enters the Fertility Clinic

Within the next couple of days, local officials had correlated their notes with missing persons reports, followed up on the car's license number, and determined the identity of the students who had been slain. Final recognition by fellow students and family members confirmed their identity. Further investigation revealed nothing of importance to enable them to determine who the killer may be.

At the supper table, Jennifer asked Lance, "Do you know the students that were killed?"

Lance said confidently, "No, I don't." He had thought about what he would say if anyone asked him about it. But again, why would they tie him to the event? The only person who could identify him was now dead.

Jennifer looked at him sorrowfully and said, "That was a horrible thing that happened to those two students over on Collins Street."

Lance agreed, "Yes, it was," and he attempted to change the subject.

Jennifer watched his puzzled expression and decided it must be upsetting him. Nevertheless, she decided to make a couple of additional comments before she dropped it. After all, Lance was reckless about how he spent his evening hours.

"I worry about things like that happening to you when you stay out half the night. It was a good thing you were home when all that was happening, or you may have been one of those that got hurt. You never know what can happen out there. Please promise me you'll be careful."

As he got up from the table, he said, "I will, mother."

He was unusually calm about the whole thing. He noticed this about himself right after the event. He hadn't felt the nervousness that he thought he would feel. He only felt the pleasure in planning it, what little actual planning there was, the absolute rush at the time it happened, and the feeling of calm once it was over.

Jennifer reflected on their lives together. Yes, she thought, Lance was a problem at times, but she had a lot to be thankful about. At least she wasn't the mother of one of the victims. She didn't know if she could cope with that.

For a while, the lakefront community was not the same as it had been before the murders. The chronic questions that everyone had to endure, the parents of students flooding into town to talk to their children, some of the students dropping out for the time being, others transferring to other campuses, like Tulane and Loyola. Everyone was on edge, everyone, that is, except for Lance.

He had covered his back, and he wasn't worried about clues unless they brought him in. There were none that could link him to the murders unless they caught him. He understood about the DNA comparisons and the finding of certain forensic evidence, but how were they going to link it to him? Once again, he thought about who knew anything about his presence, and he reminded himself that he had no connection whatsoever with the deceased, and no one had seen him when he stalked Cathy. This put a smile on his face.

The only things he had in his possession that could incriminate him were the two teeth and the finger he took for souvenirs, and they were in a place that no one could find.

Lance had paid a visit to the Biology Department where he worked during his early days as a laboratory assistant. He had gone to the carpet beetle colony that the department used to remove flesh from skeletons that were destined for the museum, and he had collected twenty adults and an equal number of larvae so he could start a colony of his own.

The beetles had been placed in a plastic bread box and stored in the crawl space of their house. In it, he placed the teeth and finger trophies he removed from his human victim, just as he had previously put teeth and paws from animals he had killed. Once they were cleaned of the flesh, he had a plan of sorts in mind for their use.

Lance spent all of his time that semester either in his classes or at home. His mother insisted he not go out in the evening unless it was at a public place, somewhere he would feel safe, and he abided by her request.

He would have done those things anyway. He knew it was in his best interest to not frequent places where the law may be watching. Jennifer was happy he didn't fight with her on this matter.

When the semester ended, Lance decided he didn't want to return to college right away. He told his mother he needed a break. Jennifer was initially upset with his decision, but she could understand it, to a degree. She thought he must still be a little scared over what had happened.

As she told a neighbor, "I don't blame him. That was a horrible thing to happen, and it made a lot of people feel uneasy about going out at night." And even though she hated to see him quit his schooling, she went along with it so he could get his head straight about it.

* * *

Stu and Coleen at the Fertility Clinic didn't know for sure that Lance had anything to do with the killing, but he had an excellent alibi. In fact, it appeared that he was nowhere near the location in which it happened.

They had seen Lance go to bed early that night. They weren't able to see or hear him leave from the room after he had turned the lights out, nor was it possible to see him sneak back through the window after his ugly deeds were done.

They also didn't see him stuff his clothes into a plastic bag at one o'clock in the morning. It had been dark the entire time. When he carried them out with his books the following day, no one thought anything about it. He later threw them in a dumpster that had an assortment of mixed refuse.

The next picture they had on the screen during that night was when he awoke and was entering the bathroom for a shower. He was completely naked and looked a little pale at the time. He spent a long time in the shower, but he had said earlier in the evening that he didn't feel well.

To many of the team members at the Fertility Clinic it appeared that Lance was almost developing into a model citizen. They were happy with his progress, and they commended their psychologists and psychiatrist for a job well done.

They knew there were still a few problems to work on, like masturbation, girlie magazines, and the non-social life he was leading. Yet, they suspected that half the population of young men in their area probably did these same things at one time or another.

Chapter 32

Lance Takes a Job
And Gets An Apartment

Lance decided to take a job over at Gromler's Meat Market in Bucktown. It was close enough that he could ride his bike to work every day, and since he didn't have a car, he didn't have much of a choice about how he got there. He wasn't about to have his mother drop him off every day. Jennifer didn't mind doing it, but he refused her help.

In some ways, she was proud of him. He was becoming more independent and assuming responsibilities for his own welfare. She thought if he was going to be out of school for a semester, he might as well be learning about the real world and earning some money, but she didn't like him peddling his way to work, especially when the traffic was at its peak.

Lance wasn't knowledgeable about meat cutting, so he spent the entire semester basically cleaning the machines and all the areas of the shop that the owner, Mr. Harry Gromler, messed up during the day. Here and there, though, he learned something of value to the meat cutting trade. He didn't know why, but he liked it, and the pay wasn't bad.

He was learning a trade and would probably make just as much money at this, maybe even more, than he would in anything else in the field of biology. And the blood didn't bother him. In many ways, he enjoyed that part of the business.

Jennifer wasn't happy when the next semester rolled around and he told her he was going to continue working at the meat market full time. She said, "Lance, baby, you have a great future ahead of you. You need to stay in college and get your degree. After that, you can go anywhere you want."

Lance didn't want to argue with her, but he wasn't going to change his mind either. After a short pause following his mother's pleading, he said, "I understand what you're saying, mother, but I have no interest in school right now, and I do have an interest in what I'm doing at the meat market. I'm learning a valuable trade that I can use anywhere, and I can finish my college at some time in the future."

Jennifer knew that this wouldn't be the case. Once someone drops out of college and gets a job that's paying halfway decent wages, it's highly unlikely they will ever return to school. But what could she do?

* * *

Jennifer and the staff at the Fertility Clinic were extremely unhappy with his next decision. Lance announced that he was going to move and get his own apartment. By this time, he had worked at the meat market for a little over a year, and he had learned much about the trade by that time. Mr. Gromler had hired a new apprentice to do most of the cleaning, and Lance was now a full time meat cutter. Along with his new position, his wages had gone up substantially.

Mr. Gromler felt good about Lance and his high degree of responsibility. He sometimes would go off and leave Lance in charge until his return, and he got good reports from his customers on Lance's attitude toward helping them.

Lance had never shown any signs of wanting to steal anything, and that was a plus in today's world of young people. Yes, he was a little strange at times, but it was his job that was important. As long as he did his job and got along with the customers, that was most important.

What Lance's leaving meant to Jennifer was that she wouldn't see him that often anymore. It was true that they didn't communicate much even with him at home, but she, at least, got to see him on a daily basis. She was already lonely, and she knew it would be worse with him gone. What was probably at the heart of her depression, though, was the fact that she was losing her baby.

What it meant to the Fertility Clinic was that they wouldn't have him under constant surveillance anymore. With him in another apartment, they wouldn't know what he was doing, unless they could somehow set up telescopes to view him through his windows or have Coleen or someone else looking in on him on occasion. All their cameras and mikes in the Housler house would become useless now.

They had gotten a taste of what it would be like when he spent those two semesters at the dorm. At that time, they got to see him only when he visited his mother, and that was generally at meal time.

By rights, the house that Jennifer was living in should have gone back to the Fertility Clinic, and Jennifer knew it was essentially on loan to her until Lance left. However, the Fertility Clinic's director wanted to continue allowing her to live there so they could observe Lance whenever he paid a visit, and there was always the possibility that he may move back in.

Living at home during that last year allowed Lance to save some money. He had the deposit for an apartment, utilities, water, and what have you.

He hadn't given his mother a dime of his earnings. He ate her food, used her water and electricity, and he didn't go anywhere. When he washed his dirty clothes, he did it at his mother's house. Every bit of the money he made was his, and he spent as little of it as possible.

Lance told his mother he would see her on occasion, and he meant it. After he left and got an apartment closer to Gromler's Meat Market, he occasionally called his mother. He also had supper at the house about once every two or three months, and when he went there, he usually brought her some meat.

Their conversations during the visits were actually much better than they'd been when he lived there. He now told her about some of the strange events that happened at work and how he and Mr. Gromler laughed at some of the customers. Lance and his mother even had a few laughs together.

Jennifer remarked to Stu about how it was nice to see him laugh. This was very unusual for him. He was generally overly serious about life, and he laughed very little. She thought that maybe their occasional meetings were good for him.

He didn't stay long, though. He'd come just in time for supper, and when it was over, he'd say, "I have to go because I have to get to the market early in the morning."

When Jennifer asked him if he had met any young ladies, he said, "No, but several nice looking ones shop at the market. In fact, I kinda like one of them, but she doesn't pay me any special attention."

"Well, give it time, Lance," Jennifer said. "Rome wasn't built in a day."

Chapter 33

Meeting Rachael

Rachael Hawkins was the young lady he spoke about. She apparently worked as a house maid/cook for an affluent elderly couple that lived in a ritzy neighborhood called Eagle's Landing, about three or four miles from Bucktown. She shopped at their market because she said she liked the meat, and they would cut it any way she wanted it. Although the price was a little higher than it was at some of the chain stores, she felt the quality and service were much better there.

Lance made comments once in a while to her about how beautiful he thought she was and about her cute dimples, but she never allowed him to follow up with a more direct approach to getting her in bed. She ran into that all the time, and she was getting better at shooting her potential suitor's attempts down.

She really didn't have any interest in Lance anyway, although she thought he may make decent money and could probably afford some of the things she wanted out of life. What she was looking for was someone a little more sophisticated, a gentleman and a scholar, so to speak. She wanted a man who was suave and debonair, someone who could sweep her off her feet.

Lance, she thought, didn't fit this picture by any stretch of the imagination. He wasn't bad looking, but he was nervous, unsure of himself, and at times, a little creepy. She knew she was a confident person and looked good, and she wanted someone who deserved her.

However, she did flirt with Lance whenever she visited the market. She enjoyed teasing most men just to see them squirm. It was part of her make-up to have control over those who wanted to use her. Lance was one of these, and she loved to torment the hell out of him.

Rachael lived in a separate building from her employers, but she was still on their property, with a narrow stone path between the two houses. Her quarters alone covered an area close to fifteen hundred square feet, and it was furnished in dark woods and oriental rugs. She couldn't complain about her surroundings.

Her employer's house was spread over five thousand square feet with five bedrooms, four baths, a more-than-adequate kitchen, living and dining room, four garage doors, a greenhouse, pool, hot tub, and semi-formal garden. They had no children and hardly ever had visitors.

She had no clue about why they needed all that space, but that was really none of her business. It was their money to do with as they pleased. When they weren't using these amenities, which was most of the time, she was welcome to utilize the entire outside area for her activities, unless they needed her.

Her employers, the Rankins, were travelers. They had made a considerable amount of money in a business and the stock market, and they were enjoying their later years. While she had to cater to their needs when they were in town, she was free to do as she pleased when they were gone. To her, it was the ideal job.

She got a good salary and a substantial sum of money to buy groceries, and the Rankins didn't care how much she spent as long as she got receipts for what she bought. The only other person around was the gardener, an older man named Rolph, who pretty much stuck with the details of his job, and he only worked on week days. Rachael hardly ever spoke to him except for wishing him a good day.

Lance learned all about her life through casual talking when she came to buy meat. He also learned that she had occasional men at her place, although she never invited him to be one of them.

Sometimes she would come in and say, "The Rankins are coming back from their trip tomorrow, so I'll need something special for their supper." At other times, she would say she wouldn't see Lance and Mr. Gromler for a while because "the Rankins were leaving town for a couple of weeks." She would take enough meat to last her and whoever she was entertaining until their return.

Over time, Lance felt he knew Rachael quite well. He would lick his lips when she entered the store, generally wearing a tight, low cut dress. Her breasts were round, firm, and appeared to be ready to jump out of her clothing at any moment. Her skin was well tanned, and she had that walk that drove him wild. He could imagine the heat generated between her shapely thighs when they rubbed together.

He could understand why someone like her didn't want to know someone like him better. He really wasn't in her class. He wasn't sophisticated, he didn't have a college degree, he wasn't a good communicator, and he wasn't particularly good looking.

His mother didn't agree with him on this latter point. She often told him that he was nice looking, but what did she know? She was his mother.

No matter what the truth was, he still didn't understand why she wouldn't even give him a chance. He should be allowed that, at least. He wasn't some kind of monster, although the women he was attracted to generally treated him like he was, and it frustrated him.

When she came to the market, he would do everything he could to get to know her better. He knew he was nervous in her presence, but he felt she should overlook that. What was it that turned her off, he wondered? Maybe it was him or maybe it was the white apron stained with blood that didn't appeal to her.

Whatever the reason, she never said things like, "I'd like to see you some time," or, "Why don't you come over this weekend, and I'll show you what you can do with some of your meat."

His meat. That was a joke. She didn't realize that his meat was standing at attention whenever she entered his market. He wondered what she'd do if she knew that. Would it turn her on or drive her away? He was afraid to find out.

One day, she came in and was in a particularly flirty mood. He sensed that she may be somewhat vulnerable to his advance, so he mustered the courage to ask her out, just "to eat and have some fun." She laughed and gave some excuse about having a busy weekend.

The next time she came in, she made the mistake of saying that her weekend was relatively dull, that the Rankins had come back and she had to hang around just to be there in case they wanted something.

Lance asked, "Are you confined there twenty-four hours a day?"

Rachael responded with, "No. My evenings are mine to do what I want."

This really pissed him off. She apparently had forgotten that he'd asked her out. Maybe she didn't even accept it as a valid invitation when he asked her. Whatever the reason, he'd been rejected, and it hurt.

Lance occasionally got a chance to leave the meat market for a delivery. Rachael was apparently too busy one day to go, and she called to see if Mr. Gromler could send over some ground meat and a half dozen of his finest porter house steaks.

Mr. Gromler yelled across the shop, "Hey, Lance. I have an order we have to fill immediately, and I want you to take the package over to Miss Hawkins's house."

Lance was nervously anticipating his meeting with her. He wondered if she had sent for the meat just to have him deliver it. His mind was running over with thoughts of what he would do if that were the case.

He was amazed at the spread she had. She let him in, and he remarked at how beautiful the house was. Rachael said, "If you think this is beautiful, you should see the house the Rankins live in." As soon as she said it, she thought it may have been a mistake.

"Can I see it?" he said. When he saw her expression, he realized he was stepping out of bounds.

Rachael, a little puzzled at his question, replied, "I can't take you to the house right now. They're not here, but maybe if you come to deliver some meat on a day that they're here, I'll have you deliver it to their house, and you can see what it's like." She was hoping the topic would never come up again.

Lance made a few awkward statements about the house and asked if she liked her job. As she searched for money to pay for the meat, she told him it was a living, although she didn't have the freedoms she needed while they were in town.

She didn't want to let him know what she really thought, that she enjoyed the hell out of her job, that it was perfect for her, and that she made more money at it than any other job she ever had.

She told Lance, "Mr. Rankin is sometimes a son-of-a-bitch, and he comes on to me once in a while when he thinks Mrs. Rankin isn't looking."

Lance said, "I can understand that because you are so beautiful."

Although nervous from his comment, Rachael forced a smile and said, "I guess you'd better be going." She was getting annoyed at his poor attempts to come on to her.

Lance knew that his time here was nearly over, so he took one last chance to invite her to engage in a romantic outing with him. "Is there any way I could convince you to go out with me? Maybe you'd like me if you could see who I really am." He was making a pass but a very awkward one.

But what did he have to lose. The Rankins were away and there wasn't anyone around. He had other thoughts about the two of them, as well.

When she ignored his comment, he asked a question that was totally out of context. "Where did you say the Rankins' house was?"

She squinted her eyes and looked right at Lance. When he persisted, she pointed out the window at the house. He noticed her hand was shaking a little. He leaned over to look out the window and almost touched her. He could smell her sweetness and wanted to grab her right then and there.

She backed away slightly and stood there, staring at him, while he looked out the window. He saw that lights were on in the house. He realized that her statement about them being away was just another lie, an excuse not to take him up there.

So she wasn't alone after all. This made a difference for what he had in mind. Also, Mr. Gromler knew he was delivering meat to her, and he knew he was here. All of a sudden, his advances toward Rachael didn't make a whole lot of sense to him, and he backed off.

"Well, Rachael," he said, "If you need anything, anything at all, give me a call, and I'll be right over."

Rachael assured him she would keep that in mind. As she closed the door, she released a sigh of relief. For some reason, she was getting extremely bad vibes near the end of his visit, and it was making her nervous. *Thank God he left.*

She began thinking about their short time together a little more and felt a little ashamed at her reaction to him. As she analyzed his behavior and thought about it some more, she wondered what her problem was. She concluded in her mind that the come-on wasn't as bad as it had seemed. *After all, he's just a lonely guy,* she thought, *and he wants me. I can understand that.*

Lance couldn't wait any longer. He masturbated in the meat wagon before he left the property, thinking the whole while of what it could have been like with Rachael. That hour-glass figure, those luscious boobs, those shapely legs, and her light blue eyes. And, most importantly, her smooth skin. Don't forget her lovely skin. He couldn't think of anything that would be more heavenly.

On one of her visits to the meat market, he gave her a package of ground meat into which he had ejaculated. If he couldn't have her, at least he was going to give her a piece of him. She smiled her usual smile and went home, delighted that he hadn't made his usual pass at her. Later, she told him the Rankins really enjoyed the meat, that it was some of the best they'd had. When Lance asked her how she liked it, she said she hadn't tried it.

This was a disappointment for him and a slap in the face from her. He envisioned her eating it and salivating at its exceptional quality. She would be enjoying him without ever knowing the truth, and this would mean that he had some control over her in spite of her dominant attitude. Yet, it would be just a minor step in his plan to see her intimately.

Chapter 34

Lance Visits Rachael's House

On the surface, Lance appeared just like everyone else who was struggling through a working life and not having much to show for it. Occasionally, when he had Mr. Gromler's truck, he would make a pass by Rachael's house. This would have been another predictable habit of his if only he had his own vehicle. He refused to buy one, though, because as far as he was concerned, it was just something else that people could use to identify him by. Besides, he didn't want to make payments on a vehicle or insurance.

He never saw her much on these outings, but he kept hoping that he would. He knew that she spent most of her day time either in her apartment, in her employer's house, or in the back yard, swimming in the pool or lounging in the hot tub. Yet, he had hopes of catching a glimpse of her in the front garden once in a while.

His obsession with her resulted in changes to his routine. He no longer visited his mother as he had done before. She hadn't seen or heard from him in about six months, and this upset her.

In certain ways, though, her life was much better without him. She had her own personal activities to keep her busy, and without Lance, she could do as she pleased. It wasn't easy for her at first, but she was growing accustomed to being alone, and she was finally beginning to experience a life that pleased her.

She had been seeing Ernest Neilow, a gentleman she had met through a mutual friend, and she had him over quite often for super.

If Lance had been there, however, she probably wouldn't have had Mr. Neilow over at all.

In many ways, this man was all the things that Ralph wasn't. He seemed to care for her, and he didn't have a violent bone in his body. She couldn't help but think that both her life and Lance's would have been a lot different if she would have married Ernest instead of Ralph. She wondered why she couldn't have found someone like him earlier.

She nevertheless missed Lance and worried about him, like mothers generally do. She asked Stu if he would have someone check in on him occasionally, just to see if he needed anything.

Stu said, "Of course, Jennifer. I'll do what I can." He and the Fertility Clinic were, in fact, looking for an excuse to see him anyway so they could set up some kind of a surveillance system at his place. If they could somehow gain access to the apartment, they could work out a plan to secretly install the things they needed.

One evening, when Stu thought Lance was home, he called and asked him if he could come over and talk to him. Lance told Stu that he didn't really have anything to talk about, but Stu insisted he had some good news for him. Reluctantly, Lance told him to come over, but he couldn't imagine what sort of good news he could have.

When Stu got there, Lance was already coming out of his apartment to meet him on his front steps, and he made no attempt to invite him inside. As he exited his apartment and pulled the door closed, Stu detected a musty odor that had emanated from inside, and as he began to talk to him, he noticed a similar odor coming from Lance himself. It was a smell that reminded him of old skins or clothes that had been stored for long periods of time in a humid environment. Stu immediately suspected that the inside of Lance's apartment was not as tidy as the meat market he worked in.

Lance asked Stu what he wanted, and Stu said, "Lance, we have an offer that may appeal to you. We know you're busy and are watching your pennies, and we want to help. We're willing to send someone over to help keep your house straight and do your gardening, maybe even run errands for you. How does that sound?"

Lance looked at Stu as if sizing him up, and said, "I don't need any help in my apartment, and I don't want to see my psychiatrist any longer either."

While the mention of his psychiatrist was a little out of context, what he was telling Stu was that he wanted to be free of everyone associated with his earlier days.

"Quit interfering with my life. If you want to continue helping my mother, that's fine, but I want to live my life without you or anyone else snooping around."

Stu said, "I understand how you feel, Lance, and I will respect your wishes, if that's what you really want, but the assistance I'm offering will be paid for by my company."

Lance asked, "Why would your company pay for someone to come into my house and do work for me?" He was obviously highly skeptical about Stu and anyone that would want to help him for no apparent reason.

Stu responded with, "It's an agreement we had with your parents before you were born, Lance, nothing more."

Lance came back with, "What kind of agreement was that? I've never heard of it, and I don't like the sound of it."

"Well," Stu said, "it's a long story, but I'll try to put it in a nutshell. Your mother was attempting to get pregnant at the time, and she was having difficulty. She had tried every conceivable method known at the time, but nothing worked. There was a new procedure under investigation that they needed volunteers for, and it came with a substantial financial package, including the house you lived in, money for taking care of you, your schooling, and many other things that were needed. Your mother volunteered, the procedure worked, and that's how you were born."

He didn't say anything to Lance about egg and sperm donors or about embryo transplantation. He wanted to keep it at a simpler level, and he wasn't sure about what Jennifer had told him. He didn't really need to know the details.

"Well, that's all nice and everything, but I still don't want somebody snooping around my house. I want my privacy." It appeared to

Stu that Lance rather enjoyed the information about how he came to exist in the world, but that was no reason to take his privacy away.

Stu said, "There would be no snooping around, Lance. This person would be there to help you."

Stu was impressed with Lance's scrutiny of his plan. Actually, he was right about the snooping. That's precisely what their intentions were. Other than setting up surveillance, he and the Fertility Clinic had no further plans about what they were going to do to eavesdrop on him.

There was no way they could spy by using another method. Lance had kept his blinds closed on his entire apartment, and it was impossible to see into it from the outside. On their one-time approach to look inside when Lance was at work, they even noticed that he had some type of paper covering the inside of the blinds so that they couldn't even see by looking through the cracks.

Lance, now quite irritated with their conversation, said, "Let me make it perfectly clear. I don't want and never plan to want anyone giving me help in any form. I don't need your help, so leave me alone."

Stu said no more about helping him. He apologized and told Lance if he ever changed his mind to let his mother know or give them a call, and he handed Lance his card. He wished him luck, said goodbye, and was on his way.

With his insistence on having no remaining ties to his doctors and other people that had at one time surrounded him, Lance knew that he had finally gotten the freedom he had been dreaming of for some time. He was now at liberty to do whatever he wanted.

He no longer had his mother to worry about or all those people that came to and went from her house. He never trusted them anyway. He had this feeling that someone was always watching him, and with what he wanted to do in the future, there was no way he could have any close connections with anyone.

For instance, if he found a woman who cared about him, like Rachael, he didn't want anyone hanging around, saying how nice it was. He thought about this for a while and concluded that there must be someone out there who thinks like he does, someone he could talk to. *Maybe Rachael is the one, and maybe not. Maybe she just doesn't know it yet.* There were the other things he wanted to do, as well. He didn't need help. He needed privacy.

Mr. Gromler let Lance take the meat truck home on occasion so he could get there early in the morning and open up. Lance enjoyed this. Frankly, he got tired of riding his bike, and he wished he could take the truck home every day.

Lance usually didn't take advantage of having the truck, except for his brief forays past Rachael's apartment or going out to night clubs on occasion. Nevertheless, he thought he'd use it this time to watch Rachael a little closer.

As he went past her house to see if anything was brewing, he saw Rachael in the yard with a man friend. They were talking, and it appeared that the man, tall, good build and wearing a suit, had just come from work. He knew Rachael had seen the truck as it passed. So what, he thought? He had other deliveries to make besides hers.

He also looked over at the Rankin's house as he passed and saw that their car wasn't in the drive. This didn't mean they weren't home, however. He'd have to come back later and see if there were any lights on in the house.

That evening, he arrived near the house at about 10 PM. He made one pass by the house and noticed her lights on. The Rankin's house had lights on, as well. He then parked the truck down the block, walked to her house, and entered the garden after looking around to see if any neighbors were watching.

He crept up to the house, carefully worked his way through the garden to the lit kitchen-dining room area, and peaked inside. Rachael and her man friend were sitting at the table, eating some of the meat she had picked up recently. He thought it was kind of late for a supper. Maybe her friend had to go home after their discussion in the garden, shower, and change clothes before returning.

When they had finished eating and had consumed almost an entire bottle of Valpolicella with the meal, they got up and retired to the living room. Lance had to change his vantage point, which he did without any problems. They were now sitting on the couch, talking and sipping the last of the wine when the man leaned over and kissed Rachael.

What excited Lance most was what Rachael did next. She appeared to turn into an animal in heat. She reached down and fondled the man's groin area, and he stretched out to let her do as she wished.

He grabbed her luscious breasts and fondled them while kissing her on the back of the neck. As he was working his way down her body, she unzipped his pants and withdrew his erect penis and began kissing it. Soon she had it in her mouth and was giving him pleasure that Lance could only dream about. She didn't stop until he ejaculated, and she began kissing him all over again to re-stimulate his desire to become erect.

Within fifteen or twenty minutes of hot petting and massaging the right body parts, they were at it again. This time she moved for him to give her the stimulation she desired. He put his hand into her panties and began moving his fingers on her hot button while he caressed her breasts with the other hand and kissed her on the lips.

Soon, he had her bra off and was fondling her nipples with his tongue, still manipulating her now highly moist vaginal area. Within minutes, their breathing was almost turning to gasps, and they were both sweating profusely and on the verge of climax.

She pulled them both onto the soft Oriental rug, slipped out of her panties and helped him penetrate her. As he did, he stimulated her clitoris for the last time with his finger and then pushed inward, changing to a slow, rhythmic movement in and out. She clung to his back as though she wanted to sink her fingers into him. Within seconds, they both climaxed, and Rachael screamed in ecstasy while tears rolled down her face.

This was more than Lance could take. He had his penis out early in the love making and was secretly taking part in the action that was going on. When they were in the throes of copulation, he was yanking his stem, and when they climaxed, he was right there with them. They would have heard his moans, except that their noise was greater than his.

Chapter 35

Lance Plans Another Visit

Lance didn't violate Rachael's inner privacy that evening. He had to think and plan. He didn't want any mistakes. He didn't want the incriminating meat market truck parked down the block when he visited her again, and he preferred to have the Rankins gone.

Lance looked at Rachael a little differently after that. When she came into the market, he couldn't help but envision her at her most excited moment. He wanted her to be his experience. He wanted it badly, but she wasn't going to give it to him freely. No matter what he did, no matter what he said, she was going to reject him and offer it to someone else. He was going to have to do something about this. It just wasn't fair.

Lance looked at the calendar. It was July 21st, and it was hot and humid. He didn't spend any more time outside than he had to. When he went to work in the morning, he stayed in the much cooler market unless Mr. Gromler needed to have him make a delivery. When he got off in the evening, he went right home and had a cold beer.

The only time Lance liked to be outside was in the late evening. This was fortunate for him because that's when he had other business to think about. Take Rachael, for instance. His prime time with her was in the evening, although he thought about her all the time. There wasn't a morning he awoke or an evening when he retired that he didn't think of her.

Then there was the rest of the day. Yes, he thought about her then, too. But it was only in the evening that he could do anything about it.

He counted on her periodically coming into the market so he could renew her image in his mind. He wanted her to talk when she came in so he could hear her voice and learn more about what she had been doing, and more importantly, what she was going to do. He wanted to know when she would be home and when her employers were not in town.

His times for seeing her intimately were limited to when he could use Mr. Gromler's truck. This was no more than once or twice every two weeks. He waited impatiently for the time to come, and when Mr. Gromler told him to take the truck home, his disposition changed instantly with the thought of being able to peek in on Rachael.

And he didn't miss a time. When he had the truck, he would count on being there in the late evening. He almost never was disappointed. He didn't always experience the sex scenes, but he did always see her long enough to masturbate at least once or twice. Sometimes, he saw her undress, and seeing her fine naked body was the highlight of his evening. There were other high points, as well. She wore this thin, see-through night gown that turned him on almost as much as the sex she had.

He wanted to go in and touch her, smell her, and taste her beautiful skin. He had to find a way. But he never felt safe with the truck parked down the block. He didn't want to run the risk of having someone link the truck to his activities.

What he decided to do was ride his bike to Rachael's house on a night that he didn't have the truck. It was a long way to ride, but in some ways this was good. For instance, whatever happened, he could never be linked to it if he lived clear across town.

He'd park his bike in the bushes. Better yet, he'd somehow get another bike and park it there. He'd go to his favorite window and start his spying. He'd also have to think of a way to get into the house.

He just needed the right opportunity to consummate his plan. He went over the plan nightly, working out all the angles, and finally his day came when Rachael called the market to order some meat. She told Mr. Gromler that she wouldn't be seeing him for a few days because her employers were going out of town, so she wanted to buy whatever meat she was going to personally need.

She told him to deliver it, so Mr. Gromler sent Lance with the package. When Lance got to the house, Rachael met him at the door and told him to wait there so she could get money to pay for her order. This was unexpected. He stepped inside anyway and asked Rachael if he could call Mr. Gromler to see if he wanted him to pick up anything on his way back.

When Rachael said a reluctant yes, he went to the phone and picked it up. It was a cordless phone, one you can walk all around the house with. He dialed and walked casually over to the window and flipped the lock while Rachael was on her way back with the money.

He held the phone up to his mouth and said, "Hi, Mr. Gromler, Lance here. I'm at Rachael's house right now, and I was wondering if there was anything you wanted me to pick up on my way back. What was that? Oh, okay. I'll be back in about twenty minutes. Bye." He put the phone down, turned back to Rachael and thanked her.

He didn't even know what number he had dialed, but immediately after dialing, he had pressed the off button, so the conversation was one sided. He was pleased with how it went. Now all he had to do was come back at the right time and hope that no one was there with her.

Before he left, he had asked about the Rankins, and Rachael told him they decided to stay in town. *Another lie.* If they had decided to do that, Rachael would have called the market back to change her order. No, she would be by herself for the next few nights, and he was going to take advantage of it.

By now, Rachael was almost pushing him out of the door. She shoved the money into his hand and gave him a tip for the delivery. He thanked her again and left without another word.

She was relieved and surprised. She felt uneasy about his presence inside after the last time he was there. When he stepped in anyway, she fully expected him to linger, talking about this and that so he could give her the third degree and scan her body again. He gave her the creeps.

Lance could tell she was nervous, but what did it matter. He had accomplished what he wanted to do. He, on the other hand, didn't feel the nervousness he generally experienced. For the first time being near her, he felt in control, and it made him feel good.

Chapter 36

Rachael's Demise

When he went home, he paid particular attention to see if anyone was following. He even stopped on occasion to let cars pass by that were behind him. His feeling of paranoia reminded him that Stu may have someone watching him again.

He had stolen a bike from a shopping center parking lot two weeks earlier, and he had parked it behind some bushes in a vacant lot adjacent to a row of houses two blocks from his house. If anyone was watching his house in the evening, he didn't want them to know where he was going or even that he was leaving, so he planned to sneak out.

He didn't know why he suspected someone was watching the house or that they would follow him. To this point, he never really detected anyone engaged in suspicious behavior, but he had his intuitive feelings, and they told him someone was watching.

Late that night, about ten thirty, he put his usual dark style clothes on, extinguished the lights and left his house from the rear entrance. It was late enough that most of his neighbors were either in bed or watching TV. He climbed over the fences in their yards and scaled another fence to climb over a shed that led to the lot.

From there, he started on his four-mile trip. He didn't put on a lot of speed, but he was more than casual in his peddling. He got there about eleven thirty, checked to see who was around and found no one outside. He pulled the bike into the bushes and headed for the window.

Most of Rachael's lights were off, including those by the window he was going to go through. He put on a pair of latex gloves and raised the window. As he entered, he accidentally kicked a flower pot that was on a low table by the window and was afraid Rachael would hear it. After waiting silently for a few minutes, he assumed she hadn't noticed, so he raised the window and began to work his way through the house toward the lit area.

He found Rachael alone and in the process of taking a shower. She was shampooing her hair and humming along with a tune on the radio about a phantom in the night. He removed his gloves, shoved them into his pocket, and waited, once in a while getting a glimpse of her shapely but fuzzy body through the etched glass of her shower door, until she got out and toweled off.

When she had finished, completed her grooming, and subsequently put on her assortment of lotions, she moved into the bedroom to put her nightgown on, and she saw Lance standing there with a starry-eyed look on his face. She gasped and attempted to cover her body with her hands. Lance immediately rushed over to put his hand over her mouth.

He said, "Rachael, I've waited a long time for this opportunity, and I hope you have, too. I've wanted to be with you for the longest time. I know you like me because of the way you talk to me at the market, but you've never invited me over. Why is that?"

He let his hand relax over her mouth and then lowered it to let her talk. "Now don't scream, or I'll have to do something."

Scream, she thought. She almost couldn't speak. Except for her quivering lips, her mouth was stuck. She initially didn't know what to say, and a million things were running through her mind. Finally, she said, "Lance, where did you come from? How long have you been here?"

"I just got here, Rachael. Don't you want me to be here? You didn't answer my question," he repeated, suddenly raising his voice. "Why didn't you invite me to see you?"

"Well, I . . . " She still was having trouble coming up with a viable answer, but she knew she'd better do something, and it had better be good. "I didn't know you wanted to come over." She didn't want to piss him off because no telling what he'd do if she did.

"You should have known, Rachael. I love you. I love your body, your skin, everything about you, and I've wanted to see you like this for a long time." All the while, he was rubbing his cheek and chin over hers. "I've seen you before, from the window. I've seen you doing a lot of things, by yourself and with that man you see once in a while. I want to share the same things with you."

"You mean you've been spying on me, looking through my window?" She wasn't thinking straight again. "What are you, some kind of pervert or something?" She no sooner got the words out of her mouth before she knew she shouldn't have said that.

This pissed Lance off. He didn't like her calling him a pervert. He wanted the same things out of life that everybody else wanted, only he wasn't getting them. He grabbed her and tried to kiss her, but she turned her head and attempted to squirm away. He pulled her back, and when her balance returned, she stomped on his foot with her heel as hard as she could.

When he momentarily released his grip on her, she began to run to the kitchen door. He recovered and although he was still in pain, he caught her again just as she reached for the knob. He pulled her toward him and back-handed her across the face. As she fell to the floor, halfway dazed by the blow, he reached down and picked her up and carried her back into the bedroom.

He threw her onto the bed and jumped on top of her. She attempted to fight him off, but he was too powerful for her. Finally, as he held her arms to the bed, she stopped thrashing about and began to cry. With a tearful voice, she said, "Why are you doing this?"

Lance said to her, Don't worry. I won't hurt you."

He then took her hand and directed it between his legs and told her to rub it. She grabbed him by the balls and squeezed as hard as she could.

Lance let out a groan and followed it with a "Son-of-a-bitch." He rolled over as she was making her second attempt to escape, but he grabbed her before she got off the bed. This time, he slammed her back onto the bed and punched her on the side of the head. She lay there, again in a partial daze for a minute or two. During that period of time, he recuperated from the pain she had given him.

As she came back to her senses, she spit in Lance's face and attempted to get up. The next thing she knew, she felt a sharp object go into the side of her chest, just to the edge of her left breast. It stung upon entry, and she knew it had gone deeply inside of her. Blood immediately began to bubble out of the hole, frothed with air from her lungs.

She remained still now, her eyes wide with disbelief, and her breathing became labored. There were no more tears. Lance removed the knife and plunged it in again, this time in the front of her chest, just to the right of her sternum. Her breathing now extremely impaired, blood issued from both wound holes and from her mouth. Lance bent down, putting weight on the knife, and he kissed her bloody lips.

He had the sex he wanted with her. It was all too quick, though. He no sooner got his penis inside her when he ejaculated, and he lay on top of her for another few minutes until he could finally catch his breath. Her eyes were staring at nothing, her breathing had ceased, but she was still warm when he removed himself. He wanted more, but he was afraid to linger. He had to return home and clean up.

When he arrived in his neighborhood, he parked his stolen bike back in the vacant lot, climbed the post by the shed, went through the obstacle course of back yards to his apartment, and went in the same door he had left from. The remainder of his work that night was done in the darkness of his house. He had the plastic bag ready for his clothes and gloves, and he spent an hour in the shower, washing the night's tell-tale residue from his skin.

When he went to work the following morning, he was in a particularly good mood. He got to work early and worked harder than he usually did. He was renewed.

It wasn't until two days later that the news broke out. Rachael's employers had been trying to reach her to tell her they would be back early, but she never answered the phone. They had someone go to the house where they found Rachael on the bed. They couldn't believe the amount of blood that had spilled out onto the bed sheets.

Also, they noticed her face was bloody, there was something wrong with her teeth, and there was a semicircular abrasion on her shoulder that looked like tooth marks. Her little finger on her right hand was also missing.

When Special Agent Clayton went to the house, again at the invitation of the local police, she was sure the murder was carried out by the same person who had done the college kids. It was the same MO, the knife wounds, the tooth marks, two teeth missing from her mouth, and the severed little finger. With this murder, the killer had come entirely under her jurisdiction.

Chapter 37

Perfecting His Art

While the features that linked the killer to both this and the earlier crime were clear in Special Agent Clayton's mind, the aspects that baffled her were their differences. One had to do with a double murder, including a young man and a young woman, both of which were college students. The other involved a single woman who lived alone and had nothing to do with college.

She felt safe in assuming that the prime force behind the slayings was sex, or at least control within a sexual encounter, and the appearance of the victims was apparently important. Both women were good looking, one a few years older than the other, but looks appeared to be the only common link. Both women had been attacked sexually, and the man had been urinated upon. As she had determined earlier, it was her guess that he was murdered simply because he was in the way and irritated the killer because he was the one with the girl.

For obvious reasons, there was one thing that she was certain of. All of these people were murdered by the same person.

Forensics in this case later revealed the murderer to be a brown-haired, white male that was wearing black cotton clothing. These data fit with the earlier case. DNA from semen also matched that of the vacant lot killer. The report from the coroner's office described the murder weapon as knife-like with a long, slender blade. The removal of a couple of teeth and the little finger, as well as a bite marks on the left shoulder, were also corroborative evidence.

There were other links, as well, although they were weak. Both murders occurred within the city of New Orleans, they were within five miles of one another, and they both were on the north side of town. That meant the killer was probably living in the city and wasn't extremely mobile. Mobile serial killers would have committed similar crimes in other areas, possibly in other states, but since VICAP hadn't come up with a precise match, she was pretty sure the killer was somewhere close.

Special Agent Clayton was happy that they were acquiring some information about the killer, but she was frustrated about having to wait until someone had died before they obtained this knowledge.

But what was she supposed to do? Her hands were tied. She had no good leads on where to find this person, and none of the people they had interviewed fit the pattern. Just when they thought they were getting somewhere, none of the leads led to persons that had the proper DNA.

Her colleagues were now referring to the killer as the "Tooth Fairy." She didn't particularly like naming killers, but she had to admit, it was convenient to use such terms instead of having to describe him with full sentences. Most killers acquired a pet name, usually based on how they did their killings, and this killer had definitely left his signature.

In many ways, though, he was no different than the others she had dealt with. He, like others before him, had formed a pattern in his technique.

Once again, Special Agent Clayton had her TV interview, and she again made a pitch for assistance, but nothing came of it. They got plenty of calls, but all led to nothing of value, and there were several crank calls. It got to a point where she was going to have to wait for a third murder and hope it would provide additional clues that would help them catch the killer.

The press hadn't caught on yet that the killers in the two incidents were the same, but she knew it wouldn't be long before the link was made. She had not mentioned the link in her interview, and she was going to keep it under raps as long as she could. She didn't believe in lying to the public, but she did believe in withholding information if such information was something that could cause panic in the population.

Thoughts of murder and serial killings settled down after a while, and it appeared that the person responsible had vanished. On the other hand, Special Agent Clayton didn't like the silence. She was worried that the killer was still doing his evil deeds, but they just weren't hearing about them. She envisioned him being in a planning stage, and he no doubt would show up when he felt he was ready to do so.

She had to admit that he had been extremely sloppy in his first two killings. He had left outstanding marks of identity, and it appeared that he either didn't care that he left them or was so new at his game that he didn't know any better. It was because of his attitude toward leaving clues that they knew as much as they did about him.

She couldn't help but wonder if he was now perfecting his art and considering hiding his victims in the future? There wasn't evidence to support her thoughts. She felt it was intuitive. Since missing persons reports didn't support this hypothesis, she concluded that maybe he was now operating out of town or simply taking a breather. Some serial murderers went years without killing, but when they resumed their activities, they often made up for lost time. The lapses most probably were tied to periods of planning.

With the heat dying back, Lance was enjoying coming out of hiding again. He had spent just about all of his time at Mr. Gromler's market or at home during his long silence, and he was feeling the need to get out and take in some sun.

He got permission from Mr. Gromler to take a week off, with pay. While he knew Mr. Gromler would miss him, he couldn't really complain because he sometimes put in a lot of overtime just to get the orders out, and Mr. Gromler smiled all the way to the bank. And in addition to his making money for him, the market was always spic and span. Lance was becoming a master at getting rid of meat wastes and blood.

Actually, Mr. Gromler insisted he take some time off because he was working so hard. He was afraid Lance was going to burn out. Knowing it would be a rough week without him because he would have to do all the chores that Lance did, he counted on his return with renewed energy.

Lance spent his vacation days mostly sitting and thinking on the seawall at Lake Pontchartrain. His nights were spent in the French Quarter, walking along Bourbon Street, checking out the girlie shows, and walking along River Walk until he was so fatigued he couldn't walk any more.

In his meanderings, he noticed a few women he would like to have taken back home with him, but he was afraid he'd get caught doing it. His heavy thoughts on what he wanted to do and what he could get away with were partially responsible for his fatigue at the end of the day, and when he could walk and think no more, he took buses or hired a cab to take him home.

On one or two days, he sat on benches at Jackson Square to watch tourists milling about and checking out the artwork. He watched the young girls and pretended to be their lover. He'd walk across the street to have café au lait and beignets until he couldn't eat any more. If he had the strength, he'd finish the evening off by walking Bourbon Street again and finally going home to masturbate until his penis looked like one of the pieces of raw meat he butchered at the market.

The vacation wasn't anything to brag about, but he had no desire to leave town and go somewhere else. He wasn't into touristy things, and he didn't drink or enjoy frequenting bars or gambling. His wants and desires were more basically driven, and his mind was directed mostly toward sexual fantasies.

When the week ended, he couldn't wait to get back to his routine of working and seeing some of his female clients. He missed them terribly, and he felt more confident about his control of them on his own turf. He agreed with Mr. Gromler that a change was good, but what it did most for him was help him to clear his mind and get new ideas, ideas that he thought he may want to put into action in the future.

Mr. Gromler's business had grown since Lance began to work for him, and he gave all the credit to Lance. He felt lucky to have found him, and he couldn't think of anyone he'd rather have as an assistant. They had gone through several additional assistants, but none had stayed long. This resulted in periods with additional help, at which times the days were pretty much nine to five.

At other times, when it was just Lance and Mr. Gromler, it was always Lance that remained to clean up the market. His days became long and tedious. Sometimes, it would take him three or four hours to clean up after the regular working day. Mr. Gromler went home at his regular time, no matter what the circumstances, and he knew he could count on Lance to have the place ready to go in the morning.

Working the hours he did, it was only right to allow Lance to take the truck home after a long day. It got to where Lance was taking the truck home more often, and when he did, he sometimes put his bike just inside the market door and left it there until the following morning. Then he moved it back outside upon arriving in the morning and preparing for a new day.

When he did take his bike home, he'd park the truck behind the building, attempting to establish a routine so people that knew the market wouldn't notice if things were out of the ordinary, like moving the truck around at all hours of the night and turning lights on and off after they had closed.

When he was there late in the evening, he occasionally got a knock on the door from a customer who wanted him to sell them something or other. They learned that if the lights were on, he'd be there. Besides, they could see him through the glass because he left the blinds up while he was cleaning. So, he'd open the door, let them in and wait on them.

Mr. Gromler didn't mind. That was more money for him, and Lance's courteousness kept them coming back. So he allowed Lance to do just about anything he pleased.

The only problem was that some of the customers were learning that they could count on stopping by late in the evening, and they began to make a habit of going to the market after hours. Each time they came, Lance had to stop what he was doing and wait on them.

Since Lance had to stay until he finished his cleaning and they got what they wanted, he was working later and later and growing tired of dealing with them.

With Mr. Gromler's approval, he decided to install one of those little reverse telescopes in the main door of the shop. Mr. Gromler felt if that's what he wanted to do to be happy, go to it. He then pulled all the shades down and went about his cleaning. He also began moving the truck around back earlier in the day so no one would know it was even there.

When someone came by, he crept silently to the door and peaked through the telescope to see who it was. If it was one of his younger, more pleasant-to-look-at shoppers, he often let them in. He'd scope them out and talk to them to find out whatever he could about their personal life. Some of the younger customers later refrained from shopping after hours because he was freaking them out with his strange questions. If an older or less-than-pleasant-to-look-at shopper was standing there, he would usually ignore them.

If the ladies he ignored came back during regular hours and asked him why he didn't open when they knocked, he'd say he was in the back or in the freezer and didn't hear them. Since they couldn't see inside, he could have told them anything.

Lance wondered why he hadn't done this a long time ago. Being out of view not only cut his hours back, it gave him access back into his private world. He then could think of the things he wanted to do and plot to carry them out. With the long hours of dealing with customers, he missed his true pleasures, and he wanted to think about himself for a change.

Chapter 38

A Case of Deceit

Occasionally, he got lucky and was visited in the evenings by some of his beauties. That's what he called them when he talked to himself. This was one of the rewards he got for working late and by himself.

He could talk to them and think of being with them, loving them. Often, he would masturbate in the back of the shop as soon as they had left while he still had their image in his head.

Tonya was one of his favorites. She had replaced Rachael in his daily rituals of women to think about.

Actually, she was nothing like Rachael except for her looks. She was even prettier and a lot more pleasant to deal with. She wasn't a tease like Rachael, though, and she had a more congenial personality. It didn't make any difference what time it was when she knocked on the door. He loved it when she came to see him.

Most of the time, she came at regular hours, but when she had to work late, she sometimes came by to see if she could pick up "a little thing or two" for the evening, and Lance would always accommodate her. He preferred to see her at these times. He could concentrate on her and learn the things about her he wanted to know.

He asked a lot of personal questions after she had been coming around for a while because he wanted to know her quite well. She didn't seem to mind, being free with her answers. Sometimes she would even stay for a few minutes after the sale to talk to him.

Lance thought she may be lonely, but he couldn't understand how that was possible. She had all the right qualities to attract someone special. She was as cute as she could be, with a body that he wanted to see more than anything else. She had a smile that would grow on you, beautiful teeth, and dimples. Her skin was flawless and smooth as silk. He wondered how it would taste.

For some reason, she was attracted to people that eventually hurt her emotionally. Being as such, whatever loneliness she experienced was self inflicted, and after she had left a relationship that went bad, she'd go back for more.

Lance understood her plight, and he wondered if this was the woman for him. After all, she was sensitive and quite willing to listen to his problems, and he enjoyed listening to hers.

The more he thought about it, the more he believed they could be a perfect match for one another. But she didn't really know him. She only knew about his very open world. She didn't know about his deep-seated desires, those things that drove him to do the wild things he did. He wondered how she was going to react to him when she found out.

He'd have to be very careful about how he treated her. He didn't want to lose this one.

She was a nurse and worked odd hours. One day she went to work at the crack of dawn, and on another she'd have to be at work at noon. She also went in at eight, nine, ten and eleven, whenever they needed her. Occasionally, she'd work the night shift or pull double shifts. Her life, it seemed, was highly unpredictable.

It was a good thing she wasn't married because her odd working arrangements would have put a strain on her marital relationship. He knew she had a previous marriage and was thinking that maybe this had something to do with its dissolution. She had been doing this for years, so she was accustomed to the variation, and it often brought her extra money.

There was one feature about her he absolutely didn't like. She had a little shit-ass of a toy poodle that was her companion. He made her monotonous life more bearable. He greeted her enthusiastically on a daily basis when she returned from work. She expressed her pleasure at seeing Tonya with whines of delight and a wagging tail that almost threw her rear end out of alignment. To a degree, it reminded Lance of his early childhood days and his dog.

If she went to work early, she woke an hour earlier just so she could walk Cuddles and spend more time with her. By the time she got home from work, Cuddles would be waiting by the door, almost ready to burst, and Tonya would rush her out to do her business. In spite of sharing only odd hours with each other, the little time they spent together was quality time, and Tonya carried her whenever she could.

If Tonya worked a double shift, she arranged to get enough time off between shifts to go home, let Cuddles out, feed her, play with her a little, and then return to work. It took her about two hours to do this because she lived near the foot of Canal Street, and she worked at Charity Hospital near the Superdome which was about six or eight miles away.

She didn't have any close friends because she had recently gone through a very unpleasant divorce and moved from Chalmette to her new apartment. To her, life was often unfair. Just when she'd surround herself with people she thought she loved and trusted, things would turn bad.

It was her best friend that she had caught with her husband of three years, and she was trying to forget the unfortunate circumstances of her past. She needed a new lease on life and a friend who would listen whenever she needed them.

Once in a while, Tonya brought Cuddles to the market with her, and Lance attempted to play with her. Cuddles never seemed to like him, though, and would bark and growl as he approached. One time, she almost bit him.

The minute she snapped at him, Lance added her to his shit list. Tonya really didn't want to know what Lance was thinking of doing with Cuddles. They were not pleasant thoughts.

"I don't know why she's doing that," she said. "Maybe she knows that you butcher animals, and it's what you do with all the meat that she doesn't like. I just don't know."

She didn't know what else to say. Cuddles usually was snippy with other people upon first meeting them, but she almost always learned to accept them after a while. This wasn't the case with Lance. They never got along.

"Maybe you're right Tonya. I would imagine this market appears as a threat to Cuddles. Maybe we can work on this. He spoke as though they were a couple with a simple problem to solve.

Tonya was pleasant enough around Lance, and he attempted to date her on several occasions. She told him no each time, but she always let him down easy with what he felt was a logical excuse.

When he asked her out, she'd say something like, "I don't know, Lance. I'm having a rough time right now. I just got over that divorce, and I'm not really ready to think about going out. Maybe some other time. Let's just be friends for right now."

She didn't realize how hard this was for Lance to do. When he got thoughts of her in his silent periods, they would haunt him and control his mind to shut out other thoughts he generally had under normal circumstances. He couldn't do anything else, and masturbation was his only release to guide him through the day. Then, when he'd see her on another day, the thoughts returned. It was a vicious cycle.

Each time he brought it up, she pretty much gave the same excuse. He seemed to understand, but he was becoming skeptical. He had hoped she was being honest with him and not just putting him off. He hated to think that she may be like Rachael and the others he'd met.

After six months of keeping certain people out of the shop in the evenings and allowing certain people in, most of the market's customers learned whether they could count on getting meat in the evenings or not. In a way, Lance was training them to suit his needs.

Tonya came by on one particular occasion, wearing a beautiful dress, stockings and nice shoes instead of her usual uniform. It was obvious that she hadn't come from work and probably had been out on the town.

"You look very nice," he said, and she thanked him.

When he inquired about what the occasion was, she said, "I went to a bar with some girl friends, and I'm just getting home."

"I'm about to close. Would you like to go for some café au lait and beignets at the all-night coffee house?"

"No, Lance. I'm tired and have to go to work early in the morning. Can we make it another time?

"Yes, sure," he said, making one last attempt to get her to go, "but you're going to miss those delicious sugared donuts. I love those things. If you're ever in the mood for some, just call me, and we'll go get a few." He maintained his jovial mood on the outside, but he was inwardly frustrated with her rejections.

"I need my rest," she said. Changing the subject, she asked, "Could I get a couple of steaks before I leave?"

He fixed them for her and let her out the door, wishing her a good evening as she left.

He could hardly keep his mind on what he was supposed to do while she was there. He wanted to grab her and make love to her right there in the shop. If she would have given him any indication that she wanted him, that's precisely what he would have done. But he was afraid, afraid to lose her if he did something she didn't accept and afraid of someone else knowing that they were inside together.

The following morning, a young man came in looking for Tonya. Mr. Gromler hadn't gotten there yet.

"Hi. I'm Jim," he said. "Have you seen Tonya?"

Lance told him he hadn't seen her. "Why do you ask, Jim?"

"I've been looking for her all morning, and she wasn't at her house or any of her other usual places. She told me when I dropped her off at her house last night that she was going to come by to see if you were open. And if you weren't, she was coming by this morning to pick up the things she wanted. She's cooking a couple of steaks for us tonight. I just thought she might be here."

"I wish I could help you," Lance responded, "but I haven't seen her today."

Lance didn't tell Jim she had come to the market the previous evening. He really didn't like Jim. He looked carefully at him, studying his features and personality, wondering why Tonya was willing to spend time with him but reject his offers every time he made one. It wasn't fair.

"How long have you known Tonya?"

"We've been dating off and on for a while," Jim said. "I met her at a dance on the River Queen one night, I guess about a year ago. We haven't been dating a lot, but I see her once in a while. She goes to the dance every week, but it's sometimes with other guys. How about you? How long have you known her?"

"Oh, not that long," Lance said. "She's been coming here about a year, I guess, but we've never gone out. We're just friends." Lance actually thought they were more than friends, but he didn't want to tell Jim anything that would divulge his true feelings for Tonya.

Having found out what he wanted to know, Lance was tired of the conversation with Jim, so he curtly said, "Well, I'd better get back to work. I hope you find her. If she comes in, I'll let her know that you came by." He had no intentions of doing what he said.

"Okay," Jim said. "Thanks man. I'll catch you later," and he left.

After Jim's departure, Lance went berserk. Here was another case of deceit. He had trusted another woman and went out of his way to help her whenever she wanted it, and she had lied to him. She had manipulated him and eventually betrayed him, just when he was going to tell her more about himself. *That would have been a bad mistake.*

In his rage, he picked up a knife and went to the cooler. He pretended the hanging slabs of meat were Tonya and Jim, and he attacked two or three of them, stabbing them repeatedly until he had expended all the energy he had. He left the knife in the last slab and sunk to the floor, staring down at nothing in particular, his thoughts on hold for the time being.

When he finally came out of his trance, he arose, grabbed the knife, and returned to the front of the shop to finish cutting the meat he was working on when Jim had come in, functioning in his job as though nothing had happened. He apparently had depleted his rage and was ready to enter society again.

Chapter 39

Going to City Park With Tonya

The next time Tonya came in, it was during regular hours, and Lance asked, "How's Jim?"

She blushed and said, "I guess he's okay. Where do you know Jim from?" She was immediately nervous, knowing before he said anything else that she had been caught in a lie.

"Jim came in looking for you on the morning after you had been here," he said, "and he explained how he'd dropped you off the evening before, you know, the evening you said you were out with the girls."

Lance knew he was being a little hard on her, but, hell, she was the one who got herself in the position she was now wallowing in. He didn't mention the steak supper.

Tonya blushed again and appeared to be having trouble with a follow-up response. She finally told Lance, "I had met Jim the night before, and he had agreed to drop me off."

Another lie, he thought.

What was passing through Lance's mind at the moment was not something he could tell her, and he also couldn't tell her how much it upset him that she was lying again. She could see he was upset, though, because he quickly processed her order, took her money and didn't say another word. She wondered how much Jim had told him.

When she left, she attempted to make everything right by kidding with him and offering him a cordial, "Goodbye," but he wasn't buying it. It was a good thing for her that she came in during the day because otherwise he would have let her know exactly how he felt, and it wouldn't have been pleasant.

Lance was thinking that it was happening all over again. He wondered if everyone was like this. *Doesn't anyone have at least some degree of integrity? If so, where is it?*

The next time Tonya came, it was again during regular hours, and she tried to have a pleasant conversation with him. Initially, he hardly talked, but by the time she departed, he had cooled off a little.

He never reached the level of cordiality that he had before all the lies, but when she left, he did say a cool, "Goodbye."

About a week later, she had gotten off late and came to the shop with Cuddles, evidently thinking that her dog would help get her back in good graces with Lance.

It had become clear that it wasn't Lance that she wanted. She liked the meat at Gromler's Marjet and the service she got, and she didn't want to lose that connection. She knew she'd better tow the line or she'd have to find another butcher to cater to her needs, and this wouldn't be easy to do without going clear across town.

There was one other thing she got from Lance, possibly something of more value. As weird as he was at times, he was always willing to listen to her, and when she had a problem, she knew she could count on him to cheer her up a little. She knew her relationship with him would never involve romance, and she attempted to be as friendly as possible without encouraging him to go any further.

Lance looked through the little scope in the door, thought it over, and reluctantly let her in, but he let her wait for a few minutes before he opened it. Since she had hurt him, he was beginning to get interested in some of the other clients, and his mind wasn't on Tonya so much these days. When he masturbated, he attempted to think of the other women he liked, and Tonya had lost his favor for the time being. However, it didn't take much to gain it back.

When she entered, wearing her tight, form-fitting white uniform, white stockings and shoes, his heart began beating a little faster, and he began breathing a little heavier. She looked so sexy, he couldn't be anything but cordial to her. In reality, he could hardly contain himself.

"How are you?" he asked.

"Fine," she said. "How about you?"

"Alright." He kept staring at her, thinking thoughts about her naked body and her beautiful, smooth skin.

She was the picture of purity, almost angelic. He was thinking of making his pass now and wondered if they were safe. Only thoughts of getting caught were holding him back. What if someone saw her come in? Maybe they were watching to see what would happen, and if she never left, that would be a problem.

They talked for a while, and she could tell he was finally forgiving her for what she'd done. He was intent on listening to her every word, and they were now friends again. Lance leaned down to pet Cuddles, momentarily forgetting his standing with her, and she snapped at him. Lance said, "I can see she's still the same."

Once again, Tonya said, "I just don't understand it."

Lance was thinking: That little shit. One day, I'm going to get her ass. Not only do I get screwed by the women who come in here, but I have to put up with their fucking dogs, too.

When Lance was standing there in his trance, looking at the dog, Tonya put her hand on his arm, thinking that he was upset because Cuddles hadn't accepted him, and said, "One day we'll get you and Cuddles together. I'm sure she'll change."

Lance hardly heard a word she said about Cuddles. Her touch had charged him. It almost had felt as though her soft, slender hands were on fire. He could feel his heart pounding in his chest again. He went to put his hand on top of hers, and she drew away. He made a step toward her, thinking that this was the time for him to make his move, and a sudden knock at the door startled him.

Lance jumped back almost as if his lunge at Tonya had shocked him. He went to the door and peeked through the telescope to see Mrs. Grobin standing there. She knocked again and said, "Lance, where are you? I know you're in there because I saw you open the door for Snow White."

Lance didn't know quite what to do. He immediately felt the fear of what would have happened if he had touched Tonya and she would have screamed. He thought as fast as he could about his next reaction, and decided to let her in.

When he opened the door, he said, "Mrs. Grobin! I'm sorry. I was waiting on this lady. I'd be happy to fix something for you, but I do have some more cleaning to do, so let's make it fast."

She placed her order and gave Tonya a few snooty glances. It was obvious that she knew there was more than a sale going on here. When she got her meat, Tonya was still there, holding on to Cuddles and watching her. *Snow White, indeed,* she thought. As Mrs. Grobin left, Lance bid her a good night, and he returned to Tonya.

After a little more casual conversation between them, Tonya said, "Thanks," to Lance and left.

Lance just stood there after she departed, still shaking from the close call. He was afraid not only of being caught with Tonya but also of what he'd have to do to Mrs. Grobin if she knew. That would be too close to home. His life, then, wouldn't have that degree of security he generally experienced, and he would have to leave the world he now lived in.

He didn't see Tonya for a while after that. When he saw Mrs. Grobin, she asked where Snow White was, and he told her he hadn't seen her in a while. "I think she works odd hours, and maybe she can't get here anymore.

"I don't think you should call her that, though, Mrs. Grobin. She's a nice girl, and she's has some problems. She just wants someone to talk to. That's all there is to it." He wondered if he was convincing her or making matters worse.

The next time Tonya came in, it was in the middle of the day, and she brought Cuddles again. When Lance asked how she was, she told him okay, but he could see she was depressed about something.

When he pried, she said, "A lot has happened since I've been here." She apparently needed someone to talk to.

"What's up?"

"I broke up with Jim and have changed jobs."

Lance asked, "Where are you working now?"

Tonya said, "At a surgeon's office near Elysian Fields."

"Why the change?" he asked.

"I got tired of working random hours all the time, and I needed to begin having a life besides working.

"I'm still living in my old apartment, so I have a little further to drive to work, but that's alright. I get paid more, and the work is easier. My life is just not as fulfilling as I'd like."

Tonya had no idea what she was accomplishing by giving Lance tidbits of information. The more she said, the more information he filed away to use to his advantage.

Lance said, "Well, Tonya, why don't we go out one evening, and I'll cheer you up?"

"Okay," she said. "Where do you want to go?"

Lance was so surprised at Tonya's response he didn't know what to say. It was like a dream coming true. Finally, he enthusiastically blurted out, "What about just going for a walk, then we'll get some café au lait and beignets? We can go to City Park or walk on the seawall. You can bring Cuddles with you."

Tonya said, "Okay? I don't want to go to City Park, though. There's nothing going on there at that time of night."

That's exactly why I suggested it.

She said, "I get off at nine on Friday. Is that too late?"

Chapter 40

Tonya's Demise

Lance couldn't believe it. His mind began to make strides to irrational conclusions. Maybe Tonya was the person he could express himself to, after all.

But now he had a problem. He didn't have a car. They'd have to go in the meat market truck. This wasn't the romantic outing he wanted to experience with Tonya, but he had no choice. Besides, after considering the possibilities, he liked the idea of going in the truck for some reason. It had become part of him, and some of his fondest memories were indirectly connected to it.

"Could we go in the truck?" he asked. "I don't have a regular car."

Tonya stared at him for a minute, momentarily wondering why he didn't have a car of his own, and she said, "I guess so. We could go in my car if you want to."

"No, let's go in the truck."

Since Lance had to prepare the shop for the following day of business, he persuaded her to drive to the market and park her car behind the building at about ten. From there, they would take the truck. She reluctantly agreed.

Lance scrubbed the truck inside and out. He thought he'd gotten most of the meat smell out, and he sprayed it with air freshener before she arrived. He had not gotten permission from Mr. Gromler to use the truck, but he had the keys, and he decided to use it anyway.

When Tonya arrived at the shop, she had just showered and was wearing a cute, pale blue pastel colored blouse and matching shorts. She had just enough make-up to enhance her natural beauty, and she smelled like only an angel could smell. He was dressed about the same as he was at work, but his clothes were more toward the dark end of the color scale.

Tonya had reservations about the outing they were going on as soon as she and Cuddles got into the truck. Lance didn't open the door for her or show any of the courtesy most of her men demonstrated on their first date. He just ran around to his side while yelling, "Hop in." She overlooked it, though, thinking that it wasn't really a date, and maybe he felt so comfortable with her that he thought of her as a true friend, and she needed that.

They first visited the coffee house and had coffee and donuts over a conversation mostly about her new job. She told Lance again that it was less stressful and more money, and she liked it.

When they finished, they went for a ride in City Park. She felt a little apprehensive about this, especially since she had said to him earlier that she didn't want to go there, but nothing happened, and she relaxed. When they exited the park, Lance cut south along the road past Delgago College, turned toward I-10 and north on Canal Boulevard to Lake Pontchartrain. He parked in one of the lover's lanes, and they sat there, looking out into the moon-lit water while Cuddles sat upon Tonya's lap, looking out the window at whatever dogs look at.

Conversation, at first, was almost non-existent, except for one comment that Lance made about the causeway being the longest bridge in the world. They could see the causeway lights across the water. They each were apparently lost in deep thought about something or other. As the conversational hiatus continued, Lance got a little nervous about it and put his hand on Tonya's arm. She looked at him and wondered what he had in mind.

In a rather awkward move, Lance reached over to kiss Tonya, and she pulled away. At the same time, Cuddles jumped at him and bit him on the arm. It was quick, and she drew blood.

Lance jumped back and said, "God damned dog! What the hell's the matter with her? I wasn't going to hurt you."

Tonya said, "I'm sorry, Lance. She's just protecting me. You can't blame her for that, can you?"

"Well, I just wanted to kiss you. I don't see what's wrong with that, either."

"Let's not rush things, Lance. I'm not sure I want to get involved with someone right now. I'm just not ready. Can we go for a walk?"

Pissed off, Lance opened his door and jumped out. He let Tonya and her snapping bitch-of-a-dog get out by themselves.

As Tonya walked along the seawall with Cuddles, she looked at Lance and said, "You know, Lance, I wasn't going to come with you tonight. You've been acting strange lately, and you're scaring me a little. I think maybe we shouldn't see each other for a while."

Lance was visibly hurt, and he said, "Why not, Tonya? I've been friendly with you, haven't I? You know, it's hard for me to see you come into the market and not be able to get closer to you. I want us to be closer."

"I don't think that's going to happen, Lance. We're not meant for each other. I don't mind being your friend, but that's all there can ever be."

Lance looked at her. It felt like a knife had been plunged into his heart. He had thought earlier that this night, above all nights, was going to turn out better than the others, but he knew that what Tonya told him was final, and he wasn't willing to accept it.

Tonya said, "Let's turn around and go back to your truck, Lance. It's getting late, and I have to go in early tomorrow. Don't you have to go in early, too?"

"Yes, I do, Tonya, but I'd stay out late to be with you." Even after the rejection, Lance was still trying to let her know he cared.

Tonya didn't comment, and they both got back in the truck. She said again that she really should get home, and Lance said, "I don't appreciate how you've been treating me. I'm a human, too. I think you should reconsider what I mean to you.

"You spent all that time with that son-of-a-bitch, Jim, and all those other guys, but you wouldn't go out with me, even though I'm nice to you and help you whenever you come to the market. You should think about me a little."

Tonya was shaking, torn between knowing she had used him whenever she needed something and not wanting them to be romantically involved with him. She began to cry, and said, "What do you want from me. I never indicated to you that we were anything more than friends. Now, I'm not sure we can even be that. Please take me back to my car." Cuddles was looking at Lance and growling.

Shocked by her outburst, Lance leaned over and grabbed Tonya by the arm, pulling her closer to give her a kiss, and Cuddles bit at him again and began to bark and growl at the same time. Lance backhanded Cuddles with a powerful blow, and she sailed out of Tonya's arms and across the inside of the truck, noisily slamming into the side wall. For the time being, she seemed to be in a daze. She lay in one spot, occasionally picking her head up as though she was looking around, but she didn't move the remainder of her body or seem to recognize her surroundings.

Tonya, at first stupefied at what Lance had done, finally yelled at him, "What the hell did you do to my dog, you son-of-a-bitch?"

She went to hit him, and he caught her arm, giving her a hateful look.

As she struggled to get away, Lance slapped her across the face and said, "Look Tonya, I've been looking at you for a long time, and I want you. I can't stand to be close to you without touching you. You should know that. And as far as your dog is concerned, it's a spoiled fucking bitch that has bitten me for the last time."

As she screamed at him, he pulled her up out of her seat and attempted to pull her into the back of the truck, but she grabbed the steering wheel and held on for dear life. In the excitement, Lance was becoming more focused on what he was about to do. As he pulled, she started yelling for help, and Lance grabbed her by the hair and yanked her back onto the blanket that he had put on the floor before she arrived at the shop.

When she attempted to get up, now yelling obscenities at him, he pulled her down again and lay on top of her, her stomach facing the floor. He turned her over and began pulling at her clothes. Trying to hold his hands still, she yelled again, hoping that someone nearby would hear her and come to her rescue, but no one was around. Lance had made sure of that before he made a pass at her.

Now out of control, he hit her on the forehead with his fist. She grabbed her head and began to scream from the pain. With tears now flowing down her face, she started to scream again, and he hit her again twice, this time in the jaw and in the left eye. Both blows were thrown with all his strength.

By this time, she was unconscious, and Lance undressed her. As she lay there in just her underwear, he admired her body. He lay by her and felt her warmth. He ran his hand over her breasts and down her body to her warmest spot between her legs.

About that time, Cuddles was beginning to wake up. She was whining and attempting to walk, but she was having trouble making her feet move. It appeared that her hip had been broken or maybe her back, making her rear legs almost useless.

Lance grabbed her behind the head, squeezing her around the neck with all his might. As she struggled to get away, he twisted her head until he heard her neck crack, and he threw her lifeless body as hard as he could against the back door.

After the thunk, she lay motionless on the floor, and Lance said, "That'll teach you, you fucking bitch. You're not going to bite anybody again."

He got up, casually undressed and lay back beside Tonya. She was now coming around, and he hit her hard in her right temple, pulled his knife out and stabbed her in the chest five times. She was still again, blood pumping out the holes, and she began gasping for her last supply of air. Lance had silenced her, and now he could do whatever he wanted.

Finally having released her final breath, he rubbed his body on hers, removed her underwear, spread her legs and entered her for a period of just a few seconds until he ejaculated. During his climax, he sunk his teeth into her shoulder, holding onto her silky skin in a death grip until his body relaxed.

It all seemed to be over so quickly. He lay there for a few minutes, feeling her fleeting warmth, wanting to snuggle closer to become one with her, but it was over, and he had to leave.

As he drove away, he went in a direction opposite to the market, past New Orleans Airport by the lake and toward Little Woods. As he got to a wooded area, he found a dirt drive to pull into. He turned the truck lights off, got out, took Cuddles from the rear of the truck and pitched her body deep into the woods. He got back in the truck and sat in the dark for another few minutes. He then got up and went back to Tonya.

He sat by her, feeling her smooth skin again. He kissed her on her lips and continued kissing her entire body, stroking her as though he was stimulating her into an excited state. He climbed back upon her and made love to her cooling body, this time without any interruptions.

When he finished, he dressed and drove the truck back to the rear of the market. After waiting in silence for a few minutes, watching for any signs of activity in the neighborhood, he backed the truck up to the rear door, wrapped Tonya in the blanket, got out and opened the rear door.

As he pulled Tonya out of the truck, she made a thumping sound as she hit the cement. He then pulled her through the rear doors of the market, closed them and stood in the dark, listening and thinking, planning his next move. He turned a small light on in the back of the shop and threw Tonya's body up on the cutting table. He took her rings, bracelets and necklace that she was wearing and put them into his pocket.

For the next three hours, Lance proceeded to separate Tonya's flesh from her skin and bones, and he cut the meat into tiny pieces. To him, it was nothing more than what he did every day. *It's just a different kind of animal*, he thought. He had all the tools and the talent, and it seemed like the right thing to do. *No body, no evidence.*

He removed the little finger from her right hand and knocked her teeth out of their sockets. Two of the teeth, an incisor and a canine, he kept for his special stash, and he put the remaining teeth in another bag.

He put Tonya's skull and bones into yet another plastic bag. He did the same with the skin and innards. He ran the meat through the grinder and mixed it with beef to package as ground meat. He then wrapped it in five pound packages and put them into the freezer. He knew it would be safe there because Mr. Gromler hardly ever went into the freezer. He let Lance do the honors.

As he was finishing up with the grinder, there was a knock on the front door. He moved slowly and silently through the dark and peered through the telescope, looking directly into Mrs. Grobin's face. He stayed silent, listening to her every move, hoping she wouldn't persist. She said, "Lance, are you there? I see a light on in the back."

Lance ignored her, and she eventually went away. As she left, he watched her through the telescope until he was sure she had gone.

After tip-toeing back to the rear of the store, he picked up the plastic bags that were holding the bones and innards and put them into the truck, along with a couple of cement blocks, duck tape, and rope, and he left. His next ride was to the Mississippi River levee.

He drove to a secluded spot by an old log creosote dock, taped the bags shut, tied them to the cement blocks, put a few holes in them with his knife so water could seep inside, and dumped his packages into the water. They immediately went out of view into the opaque, brown water, and he hoped they would never be seen again. He scattered her teeth in the water, except for the two he kept, and returned to the truck.

When he got to the market, he again washed the truck out. He spent the rest of the night cleaning the market again so things would be ready to go on the next working day. He left the light on inside so people like Mrs. Grobin and Mr. Gromler would assume he inadvertently had forgotten to turn the light off when he left the market the night before.

He put his bike into the back of Tonya's car and returned to the levee. He removed his bike, put the car into gear and ran it into the river. Within a minute or two, it had disappeared. He hopped upon his bike and peddled back home.

When he arrived near his apartment, he parked his bike in the vacant lot around the block. The two men that were hired by Stu

Bridges to watch the front of his apartment didn't see him approach the house from the rear and enter through his bedroom window.

His final nightly chore was to shower and get ready for work. It was a long night, and it was going to be a very long day. He thought he'd just go home after work and get to bed early.

As he left to return to the market, the men noted that he had remained home for the entire night and had left for work at his usual time. Based on their report, Lance was apparently living the predictable life experienced by most New Orleans working people.

Chapter 41

Watching and Planning

Lance had another dry spell in which he worked hard and went straight home. When he was at the market, Mr. Gromler noticed he had been especially focused on his job, although he was answering the door less in the evenings so he could finish cleaning the market early. He didn't blame him. He wouldn't want to put in the hours that Lance spent there after the regular working day.

He did wonder, at times, why it took Lance so long to do his chores. It should take him a couple or three hours at most to clean the market. He learned from some of his customers that the light was sometimes on until one or two in the morning. He wasn't complaining, though. The shop was spic and span at the beginning of every work day. He never feared getting written up by the Department of Health.

During the early stages of having Lance in his shop, he attempted to get to know him. Lance had become dedicated to his job from the beginning, and this puzzled Mr. Gromler. He had been through a dozen or more assistants, and none of them had shown the interest in the business that Lance had. He guessed he just had an obsession with the trade. He, himself, had such an obsession when he was younger, so he couldn't find fault with Lance's choice of a profession.

Yet, he worried about Lance, thinking that he needed something in his life in addition to work. He needed to get out and enjoy life more. He needed someone to share his life with.

Initially, Mr. Gromler wanted to help. He even had made arrangements for him to date some women his age that he knew through relatives and clients, but this never worked out.

He gave up his attempts in frustration. Lance never took him up on his offers, and he would never talk about his personal life. From that time on, he decided to let Lance worry about himself.

Because of his dedication to his job, Mr. Gromler had treated Lance with respect all these years, allowing him freedoms that he had never given to any of his former employees. He had benefited much more from their relationship than Lance did, but he didn't pay Lance any more than he had to, in spite of the long hours he worked. He paid him meat cutter wages which were considered high, compared with many other jobs held by people without college degrees, even many of them that had finished four or more years at universities. To pay him more than he was currently making would have required him to part with some of his own income, and while he admitted that Lance was the reason his business was doing so well, he didn't think he could do that.

If Lance ever threatened to leave, which he hoped would never happen, he knew he might consider paying him a little more just to keep him there. He didn't know anyone who worked as hard as he did, and he knew that his life would be more difficult if he ever left. Since Lance was a valuable asset to his business, he knew he had to acknowledge his appreciation, and he was going to do this by giving Lance something that he felt was more value than money.

He really didn't understand Lance when it came to spending his money, anyway. All he had to spend it on was his apartment, and the apartment couldn't have cost him that much. Looking at it from the outside, it wasn't the best of apartments, and it wasn't in the best of neighborhoods. Of course, there were groceries, electricity, water, and other incidentals one needs to live on, but much of the money Lance made was apparently saved. "More power to him," he would say.

He knew Lance had purchased a digital camera. He kept it in the market most of the time, and he knew Lance took a picture of customers once in a while, especially if they were young and pretty.

He didn't begrudge him of that. At least, he thought, Lance was taking an interest in the fair sex, and this apparently was a kind of a hobby or sorts.

What he did to show his appreciation for all his hard work was allow Lance to keep the truck when he went home in the evenings. He could do with it as he pleased. In essence, it was Lance's vehicle, but it was listed in Mr. Gromler's name. And Lance used it to the limit. He went everywhere with it, and wherever he went, he'd scope out the ladies. From one end of New Orleans to the other, he learned where to find them.

In order to keep his identification unknown, he purchased some magnetic signs with Fred's TV Service, Unit 6, on them to cover the Harry's Meat Market information painted on the truck. He parked the truck down the road from his apartment after work and left it there until after dark. He left his apartment on foot and followed his secret passageways to the truck, drove it off to a remote area and installed the signs before his nightly visits. When he returned, he'd go through a reverse of the same procedure, walk to his apartment by an obscure route, and sneak in the back way.

When he was working, all he could think about was who he would see during his forthcoming evening. He partitioned his evening time between staying at the market to clean up and going home early and going out on the town. If he got a knock on the market door, he followed his instincts and dealt with it as he saw fit. But most of his time was now spent looking for women away from the market.

He'd check the bars, other night spots, the evening cruises up and down the Mississippi River, the parks, and the lakefront. He'd check the newspapers to find out about special events that might attract a young crowd, and he'd be there to watch who came. He knew what was happening in the city and when it was taking place.

He didn't do anything at these places but watch and plan. He'd buy one drink and nurture it the entire evening. He wasn't interested in the drink or the fact that it may anesthetize him to a point of relieving some of his stress. He just used it to blend in with other party-goers.

If someone approached him and seemed to be in a talkative mood, he would humor them for a while and then walk off to find another vantage point. He didn't tolerate whiners or any form of self pity. He was not someone who would offer advice to the lovelorn. His concentration was on the part of the crowd that would do him some good, and he didn't like to lose his concentration by listening to someone else's problems.

He memorized facts about the people he liked and the places they frequented. Once he had selected half a dozen or so ladies to watch, he narrowed his focus to just watching them, and he learned their routines. Over and over, he would watch them. He'd know when they arrived and when they left. He knew their intricate mannerisms, as well as the things they liked and disliked. Sometimes, he sat close enough to hear their conversations, although he never talked to them unless they said something first.

Occasionally, someone would be watching him and ask him what he was doing. Lance would look them in the eye and tell them he was a writer and was merely observing behavior. If they would continue to ask questions, he would excuse himself or tell them to fuck off. He wanted to learn more about his subjects, and he didn't have time to answer questions posed by pain-in-the-ass people who were not in his focus. He had to collect statistics.

He knew that if he wanted to see Suzie, for instance, he had to be at such and such a place at such and such a time, and she would invariably be there. Joan, Jeri, and Jackie all had their respective places to frequent, and he could almost count on them being there just before or after he arrived. He knew where and when they worked, and the only time he was wrong about their routine was when they had a change in their working or dating schedules.

They weren't always alone, and this was the most unpredictable part of their existence. Some of his favorites were going steady, a few were married, and others changed their escorts from week to week. It was the ones that routinely came in alone that appealed to him most. He had greater control over them, and they were more predictable.

They often came into the bars with a group of their female friends. At some point in their nightly meanderings, they usually parted with their friends and went home alone. This was when and where he would spend more time with them, situating himself near a window and looking in.

In his initial stages of night watching, he would somehow manage to meet his subjects, even if it was just to say, "Hi, my name is Joe." He didn't give his real name for fear of revealing his true identity to the wrong people.

Once he learned their names and habits, he would follow them home, and plan further before spending more time with them by scouting out the property and the neighborhood. He would return and repeat his surveillance until he had his plan well in mind.

At some point in his activities, he quit meeting them in the haunts that they frequented. In the first place, meeting and talking was difficult for him. He still didn't have the social skills he needed to pick them up like some of the men that frequented the bars. Also, he knew that with time, someone would notice it was him that was with a particular woman, and then he'd have a problem he may not be able to deal with.

It was beneficial to be more secret in his habits. He didn't need the social skills if he was an expert in other forms of behavior. Why should he learn more about picking them up, anyway. That was always an awkward time, a time in which he didn't have them in his control. He preferred to do it on his own terms, just the two of them in a private sanctuary.

Once focused, he'd spend less time at their haunts and more time at their house or apartment, hiding in the bushes and whacking his willie until his seminal glands could produce no more liquids for his pleasure. After all, this was what all the planning was for, to become intimate with the women in his fantasy club, and this was the only way he could be intimate without killing and disposing of them.

He'd keep records at home because he wanted to be sure who was where and when. If he wanted a particular woman, he'd consult his chart, and he'd be at her house that evening, again masturbating outside her window. And if his target stayed up long enough, he'd masturbate several times.

In a way, he looked at masturbation as a way of saving his targets. Without it, he was sure he would have killed more women. It served as a release, and, he thought, *who did it hurt? No one.* It only served him pleasure, and it would only hurt them if they knew he was out there releasing his tension at their expense.

And if he ever did get caught by the person he was watching, he knew what he'd do. If he was identified, he'd have to go in and silence the creature. Otherwise, he would run from the scene and escape by preplanned routes.

He was careful enough, however, that this never happened, and he knew that if and when the creature would ever see him, it was his decision, not theirs, and it would be their displeasure for having seen him.

Occasionally, he'd have the opportunity to silently slip in on one of them. When that happened, he'd perform his routine with all the earmarks of his signature, and he'd return home by his secret routes as a renewed and more settled person.

It was difficult to determine who he'd select for these behavioral forays. He didn't even know himself how to predict it. He'd just close his eyes and choose who he'd like to be with for that evening. Then, he'd go out to do his peeking, and he would sometimes end up in their bedroom.

Chapter 42

Remembering His Victims

No matter what the prize, though, he had to abide by Rule Number One: to stay alert and not put himself in a position whereby he could get caught. With that as the bottom line for his excursions, he could play the game any way he saw fit.

He'd think about the rule all the time. He had to. It was a critical part of his plan to be able to carry on.

Over time, Agent Clayton found out another characteristic that made him different from most other killers. There was no color barrier. It didn't make any difference to him whether their skin was bright white, yellowish, pink, tan, or a deep brown. It appeared that what was important was that they were pleasant to look at and their skin was smooth and soft.

The variation in the darks and lights formed a trait that represented an inconsistency in his methods. He knew that. But it provided some means of adding excitement to an otherwise boring repetition of killing, just like hair and eye color. It was always skin texture that was most important.

It was true that his victims were predominantly white, but that was because the places he frequented were visited by predominantly white women. He also had difficulty following darker women to their homes because he stood out in their neighborhoods and ran a greater risk of being caught. If he wanted to spend time with a darker woman, she had to be stopped before she got home.

Within the next five years, Lance had killed and raped thirteen additional women. Some of them he met through the market and others he just picked out randomly wherever he found them. Two additional victims were men who happened to be in the wrong place when Lance did his nocturnal butchering.

Whenever he left his house on an evening business trip, he would leave by the back way, and he would make it appear that he turned out his lights to go to bed at his usual time. He didn't want anyone associating changes in his routine with the events that took place. When he did his business from the market, he made sure no one was around. And if he met someone at night, he always waited at least two weeks or more before he did his business with them. He wanted no obvious ties.

Many of his victims had to be left in their homes or apartments because there was no way for Lance to remove them without attracting attention. These were the ones that gave Special Agent Clayton more to think about.

He adopted the technique of dissecting his victims as a standard. The flesh ended up as ground meat that he often took home for his evening meals. Some of it, he mixed with beef and sold it at the market. His customers enjoyed the high quality of meat they got there. The skeletal remains, except for the fingers and an occasional leg bone, generally ended up with most of the teeth and the innards in the Mississippi River

Occasionally, he would keep an entire skeleton to feed to his beetles. His colonies of beetles had grown, and rather than let them die, he kept them with a steady supply of remains. He was sure that the university would be envious of his colony.

He had different size containers to handle the parts he wanted to clean of flesh. Fingers and teeth went in a small plastic container. He had a special use for them. The larger bones went into larger plastic containers, and entire skeletons went into the bath tub.

He now had the finger bones and teeth of all his victims assembled in a necklace that he put on during his private evenings. Once the beetles had finished with them, he scrubbed them until they were clean and shiny. He had drilled holes in the finger bones to run a string through. He had to wrap the teeth in wire, and they were strung together, alternating teeth and bones.

He designed special primitive garments to go along with his necklace, consisting simply of skins from the heads of his victims that he wore around his waist, the various colored hairs hanging down over his legs. When he put this evening attire on, he would sometimes walk around his apartment in it. At other times, he stood in front of the mirror with a leg bone in his hand and pretended to be a caveman somewhere back in the beginning of time. He didn't understand his fascination with his attire, but he looked forward to dressing up whenever he could.

He often reminisced about each of his victims. On the back of each bone and tooth of his necklace, he had written his victim's name in India Ink so he could occasionally relive his relationship with them by going through the string in a prayer-bead-like fashion.

This was one of his favorite leisure activities when he remained at home. He would sit back, pick a tooth or finger bone to concentrate on, close his eyes, and picture his victims at the spots he saw them most. They were all nice looking, with skin of silk. He either remembered what they looked like and what they were wearing or he had pictures that he took to remind him. It was these features that he often thought about when he spent all those hours in his apartment.

He learned that his pictures meant a lot to him. He had many of them, and he would sometimes pull them out and spend hours looking at them before he would masturbate.

Sometimes he kept the camera at the market to photograph his favorite women. At other times, Mr. Gromler noticed the camera was gone, and he assumed he had taken it home to photograph something else and forgot to bring it back.

He generally thought about his victims one at a time, going over each of the bits of information he knew about them. When he finished with one, he'd choose the next of his numerous beads and conjure up their features in his mind. He'd sometimes take their picture out and think in chronological sequence through the process of meeting them or seeing them for the first time, getting to know them, and then following them to their homes. Each one had a particular significance to him.

Leigh was a young lady who worked for an insurance agency. He had met her at Lafayette Square where she was hanging out with some of her coworkers from the post office. He had gotten her name and phone number and promised to call her, but she had to wait. He finally called her and went to have café au lait with her one evening. After that, he put her on hold and never called her again. What he did do, though, was visit her at night when she was getting ready for bed, and he masturbated by her window.

It was a month later when he saw her again. This time it was in her bedroom. She had just turned her lights off, and he had crept in and hit her with a metal pipe before she could reach the light. He then plunged in his long, slender knife several times and had sex with her twice before she began to cool, biting her on the right shoulder during the process. His last act before departing was the removal of one finger and the acquisition of two teeth.

There was Rhonda, a young lady he met at St. Louis Cemetery when she was looking at the renowned gravesite of the famous voodoo queen, Marie Laveau. His knowledge of the voodooist fascinated Rhonda, and she ended up eating a po-boy sandwich with Lance at a local tavern. He got her address and telephone number but never called. Instead, he visited her quietly in the evenings and eventually hit her with the same metal pipe before they had sex. He left the same knife holes in Ronda, the same bite mark on her right shoulder, and had removed teeth and her little finger.

There was Julie, a young woman he met in Audubon Park, Gretchen, who he met on the River Queen, and Norma, who happened to see him killing a cat in City Park. Norma's misfortune was that she approached Lance and began to scold him about the hateful act he was performing, so he hit her with his fist and dragged her into the bushes for the final life-taking maneuvers and unsettling rape.

There were many others. Their names and histories were significant to him to keep their images alive in his head. He learned what he had to about them in order to do the things he did best. To Lance, they were much more than just another lay. They were each as important as the next one. They were the ones he picked from all the others to live out his fantasies with.

Only their friends and relatives were in a position to appreciate their presence on earth for the short time they had been there. They all were left with the hurt of missing them and the terror of how they died.

Through it all, no one knew about his secret life. No one even suspected it was him who was taking the lives of young, nice looking female New Orleanians. He was good, very good, at his profession. He had learned, like everyone else that was part of society, to accept the daily responsibilities that went along with living amongst the normal people of the world, and thus he appeared as one of them.

His job and his diurnal activities were normal or close enough to normal for him to be accepted by those who came in contact with him. He had given no clues about his identity or his whereabouts in the evenings, except for the DNA and signature killing behavior.

It was true that they had his correct profile. They knew precisely what the killer was like by the way he killed. They could even predict how he would do the next one. But they never knew where it would be, and they could never pin it on him. He was too smart for that.

Chapter 43

An Unknown Genetic Make-up

It had been some time since Stu or anyone else at the clinic had a close tie with Lance. They had people walk by his house on occasion and even set up an occasional watch to view his goings and comings. They never got the chance to bug his apartment or even enter it. Whatever he did in his home, he kept secret.

They found that he spent some of his evenings going to night-clubs around the city. They even had him tailed once or twice. He spent most of his evenings at home, probably recuperating from his long hours at work. When he came from work, he'd generally go inside and stay there until he had to leave for work in the morning. He hardly ever left his house to run errands. He picked up whatever groceries he needed on his way home from work.

The meat he ate, usually ground meat from the market, was, unbeknownst to them, mixed with the tender flesh of his victims. He brought it home in five pound packages which he thawed and either made hamburger patties or mixed it with a variety of products he could find at the supermarket. Other than the need for frying the meat, he didn't spend a lot of time cooking.

Stu, Coleen, and others at the clinic wondered if anyone had ever entered his home. They never saw anyone but Lance go in. He had no friends, and he never invited his mother over. It was as though he was hiding something. However, there was always the possibility that he just didn't want to talk to anyone. All Stu could remember was the musty smell he had detected emanating from his apartment on the last trip he made to talk to Lance.

They couldn't imagine what his apartment would be like inside. On the one hand, his life was organized. Activities at the meat market and everything associated with working were influenced by this organized side of him.

His other side appeared to be a little disorganized. He generally wore clothes that looked like hand-me-downs or something he bought in a second-hand store, and he sometimes went out without shaving. If his organized side was in charge of arranging his apartment, it might be quite nice. Otherwise, it would be a total mess.

They also watched Gromler's Meat Market on occasion, but it seemed Lance was developing into a first class meat cutter who had a good rapport with his boss and clients. What could they say? He no longer appeared to be a threat to society. They had successfully transformed a potential societal misfit into a person with an acceptable personality.

In spite of the apparent lack of activity they experienced on Lance's behalf, they had to continue their experiment by at least watching him at randomly selected times. That was part of the original agreement. However, their surveillance activities had been cut back over the years to the basics.

They had other clients. The Fertility Clinic had become quite popular by people who had trouble conceiving. Thus, much of their current time was spent dealing with sob stories by clients about life in general.

They learned to occupy part of their time visiting Jennifer on occasion and attempting to find out what they could about Lance through her. Since Jennifer didn't hear from him much anymore, she couldn't really tell them anything new. The rest of their time was devoted to watching him whenever the opportunity arose and building a portfolio of his life.

When Jennifer attempted to call him, she ended up talking to an answering machine, and he never returned her calls. The truth of the matter was that he was far too preoccupied with his own life, especially his evening activities, to spend time with his mother.

Jennifer had now been going with Ernest for over two years, and she was quite happy with her life. Ernest made her feel alive again. She got used to not hearing from Lance, although it bothered her that her son didn't seem to care if she was dead or alive. Even when she wanted to have him over for his birthday, he never bothered to return her call. At times, it seemed as though she never had a son.

* * *

Stu and Coleen were also reviewing their records in preparation for writing a couple of in-house scientific papers. Other than making their reports available to the director, none of the material was allowed to leave their files, and the completed paper would never leave the building. It never was submitted to regular journals for publication because the experiment was still secret and on-going, and there were a lot of questions that remained unanswered.

Not knowing where the information they had collected over the years was destined to end up, Stu made copies of them to keep in his personal file. While the reports were the property of the clinic, he had a personal connection to the work they had done and felt a need for a back-up.

To Stu and Coleen, Lance's life sometimes seemed a little too quiet. In reviewing their reports from the initial stages of their investigation, they wondered about all the characteristics he had as a developing boy, the day dreaming, the bed wetting, the sadistic treatment of animals, the setting of fires, an inability to socialize, and the desire to be alone. They weren't sure how these things could suddenly dissipate, although it appeared that they had. What could they have done right that was not evident to them?

Very little had appeared to change in his daily routine over the few years since he left his mother's house. He was still alone. He really didn't have a life except for his work and spending time at home. When he took a few days off, it seemed to drive him crazy. What he was thinking about all the time, and what he was doing at home were mysteries to everyone but himself.

By this time, Stu and Coleen had summarized their investigations of his earlier testing period. Psychologically, he was found to have developed schizophrenic tendencies at a young age. He learned to lie and stick to the stories he made up. He turned his problems inward but somehow seemed to deal with them so they didn't have a lasting influence on his overt behavior. He had early sadistic tendencies that seemed to dissipate at the age of eleven or twelve. He didn't have a social life and didn't seem to take a special interest in girls. They wondered if he was a latent homosexual. But there weren't males that he cared for either.

Socially, he went through some very tough times when he was young, especially at the hand of an abusive father, but he seemed to adjust to the social pressures of life. He handled his job very well, and he got along with his boss and clients. He apparently had found his station in life which many young people, normal or otherwise, never seem to do, and it appeared that he was happy at what he did.

His genotype was the result of some unknown cross. No one that worked on the team understood its significance. That it represented a scientific breakthrough involving a 200,000-year-old man and a living mother whose gametes had joined to produce a healthy, poorly adjusted son were facts known only by the director and his psychologists.

What this meant to Steven Morrison was that the baseline genetics of humans didn't appear to have undergone radical changes over those 200,000 years, that the basic chromosomal make-up was the same or, at least, very similar. Knowing about Lance's biological father and his mechanism of dealing with everyday problems in his primitive world had shown him that there was little change in that respect.

What had changed most over the thousands of years was the technological environment and the spreading of specific genes that led to a more intelligent population. The seeds of intelligence were there when man first began to place his bipedal steps in the perilous savannahs, but they only belonged to a few. It was up to those few individuals who possessed them to push humans ahead with their best qualities and eliminate their negative, animalistic ones.

It was a classical example of the survival-of-the-fittest phenomenon that led humans out of their animalistic world into the technological environment in which they now lived. It was simply a matter of perfecting the machine, so to speak, optimizing what had already been locked in the human genome.

While it at times appeared that humans had done just that, they still retained some undesirable qualities that allowed them to remain an animal species. These were the qualities that led them to deceive, to fight for dominance, irregardless of the consequences, and to kill.

Or, when we think about it, *did humans simply retain these features from early gene pools or did they perfect them, as well?* It was something to think about because it was these qualities that caused our species to have social misfits, the Stalins, Hitlers, Osama Bin Ladens, and Saddam Husseins, not to mention the multitude of social degenerates that roamed secretly through our populations.

They had given their all to understand the significance of Lance's DNA and had a complete picture of his chromosomal make-up. It was a little odd, but they accepted it as within the bounds of a normal human genetic make-up. They found very little to set Lance off from anyone else in the human gene pool.

He had forty-six chromosomes, just like anyone else that wasn't suffering from a cases in which chromosomal numbers doubled or tripled, and this generally led to malfunctions in both anatomy and behavior. But this wasn't Lances case. He had a single X chromosome from his mother and a Y from his father, although the Y was a little shorter than most. While they noticed this difference, they weren't sure of its significance since the Y chromosome generally was known to have few genes that influenced the development of an individual.

Yes, Lance was a walking, talking scientific phenomenon of enormous proportions, but a phenomenon that apparently may not really be understood by anyone but the director of a secret business and his partners. It was almost a crime in itself. Such overwhelming scientific success and no way to expound on it.

Whatever its importance, Lance was becoming less of a target for behavioral studies. In essence, his experiment was over, and based on what they knew, it was a success story. He had been born under mysterious circumstances and grown up with problems that many maladjusted people had, and he had adjusted. Stu and Coleen were particularly enthusiastic about the way he had turned out because it was their approach that made him a better person.

Chapter 44

Deliberating Deviant Behavior

Not far away, in a building on Tchoupitoulas Street, Genetics, Inc. had come a long way after its meager beginnings, when Hunter Bronson contemplated the genetic cross that would represent an academic brain teaser. But as far as anyone knew, he never entertained the cross as a viable project.

Based on what he had told everyone, about the time he put his thoughts away in his filing cabinet, someone had stolen the notes, and subsequently, someone in California stole the tissue that contained Adda's testicles. While they and the California organization had reported the theft to the local police department, nothing ever came of it, and their whereabouts remained a secret.

While the cross periodically resurfaced in his mind, Genetics, Inc. had almost immediately become inundated with requests to perform scientific analyses, and Hunter had to submerge himself in the world he had entered. Within the realm of a rapidly-growing Genetics, Inc., Hunter and his new employees eventually took on research and problem-solving that had anything to do with human genetics, and they subsequently prided themselves on their genetic capabilities.

They ran DNA samples, diagnosed polyploid-related abnormalities, identified genetic deviants, correlated genetic composition with specific diseases, and successfully dealt with a wide assortment of other gene-related issues. It was no shabby business from the very

215

beginning. It, in fact, had turned into a business that was unique in scope and was making Hunter, Buddy Jackson, and its sponsors a significant amount of money. In addition, it was constantly growing.

They had acquired a significant national reputation and were expanding into the international market. Hunter was amazed at their progress. From a simple idea and the right people came a company that was becoming internationally acclaimed.

He had come a long way from digging in the African savannah. He never thought he'd say it, but he didn't miss those times. And more than that, he was now making more money in a month than he would ever have made in a year in his old job, and he didn't have the Alex Stanfords to contend with.

Their expertise had led them in many directions. Since DNA had become the most powerful of twenty-first-century diagnostic tools, it was now important in assisting in the identification of a wide assortment of degenerates. With that, luminol, and ballistics information, forensic scientists were now catching the crooks that got away in previous years.

In addition to their success, they were still moving ahead on their potential. Their diagnostic unit was currently supplemental to those of local law enforcement units and the FBI. This meant that they would not generally be approached to do a homicidal DNA analysis unless there was a special need. For instance, if there were apparent inconsistencies in the findings of a diagnostic unit, they may ask Genetics, Inc. to validate their findings.

If this was their only claim to fame, they would not be bringing in the amount of money they currently enjoyed. No, they had other avenues to follow, as well. There were many people and organizations that required a DNA analysis, and this kept them busy. The fathers of unwed mothers that previously denied a paternal connection no longer had a leg to stand on. Native Americans and other ethnic cultures could depend on them to determine their roots and relationships. And there were many other people who used their expertise.

While many businesses and governmental offices were still not using their services, Hunter now knew the potential of his company. He could envision the day when companies like his would do all the analyses, leaving law enforcement to concentrate on other problems. They would then have an enormous database from which to work, and law enforcement could count on them to cross-link references to certain crimes and genetic compositions. There was no doubt about it. GenInc had a bright future.

Along with their Division of Genetics, they also had a behavioral division that was headed by psychologist, Dr. Alan Wilkins, and his assistant head, Dr. Sheryl Stippens. They researched the correlation of behavioral events with genetic data.

Up to this point in the scientific world, very little behavioral evidence had concrete genetic links. It was up to Alan and Sheryl to diagnose certain behaviors and work with the Division of Genetics to work out correlations. It was a difficult task at times because they had very little in the way of valid background information, but they were moving in a direction that one day could be extremely valuable to understanding genetic deviants.

They could even predict adding a Division of Neurology to complement the fields of genetics and behavior so that they would not only understand neurological malfunction but be able to predict and alter it. It was an exciting time to live.

When Special Agent Clayton noticed a flier on her desk about a seminar to be presented on "Deviant Human Behavior," by Dr. Alan Wilkins of Genetics, Inc., she became very interested in attending it. She always attempted to keep abreast of new approaches to understanding the deviant mind, and she had heard that Genetics, Inc. was a company that was, in the words of one of her more humorous colleagues, "pushing back the foreskin of science."

It was true that she had a busy schedule, and there were many things that required her attention, but she never knew what would come out of seminars like this and even casual conversations with the right people. It wasn't just that she wanted to go to this seminar. There was something in the back of her mind that told her she had to go.

The seminar was scheduled in the Harrison Hotel on St. Charles Avenue in downtown New Orleans. Special Agent Clayton noticed there was a sizeable crowd attending, including some of her colleagues, many local law enforcement agents, and a number of university faculty and students. Some of the behavioral faculty had evidently told their classes they would receive extra credit if they attended the seminar and wrote a report on it.

She wondered how many of the people attending the seminar had deviant behavior themselves. Rather than dwell on that thought, the hypothesis passed out of her mind almost as quickly as it had entered it and had been replaced by thoughts of who all the other people were. Were they just people, attracted to the diverse nature of some of our population's lowest forms of life?

There was no doubt that many people enjoyed hearing about deviant behavior. That's why there were so many TV shows that portrayed killers and their deepest desires and where it took them. While she could see the attraction, she knew that most of the audience that was here to learn about deviant behavior had not experienced the terror and subsequent hurt that was associated with it. If they had, they probably wouldn't be here.

For her, it was her job to know about these things, although she found it very interesting, as well. Ever since she was a child, she had wanted to learn more about the deviant mind and its ramifications. Just why this was, she had no inkling. She wondered about its cause and accepted the notion that it probably had both genetic and behavioral roots.

As she synthesized a picture in her mind of a person who demonstrated deviant behavior as an adult, she knew that such people had a number of childhood characteristics that were flags of impending criminal behavior, but many of the characteristics anastomosed with environmental and genetic traits, and it probably was a certain combination of all of these factors that led the person to become what they were. It was, in essence, the bridging of the gap in the long-debated concept of nature versus nurture.

Under some circumstances, a bed wetter, an arsonist, a saddist, and a loner may turn out to be a 'normal' member of society, while the same person may end up a criminal if he or she is abused or has other influences that helped assemble the combination of factors in the right order.

It was probable that genetic influence played a large role, as well. It was this combination that was the cause of manifesting deviant behavior. She was sure of it. Otherwise, there would be more than twenty or thirty serial killers at large at any one time in the United States alone.

Stu Bridges was also sitting in the audience, hoping to learn something that would tie together the mysteries of Lance Housler. He knew Lance had exhibited the classical signs of criminal behavior prior to becoming an adult. *Was it their program that had turned him around, did he finally realize that he was troubled and had to work it out himself to become a model citizen, or did he simply learn to hide his behavior?* Alan Wilkins could possibly be the one to help him understand the mystery.

When Alan delivered his seminar, it could have been a summary of what he and Coleen had found through the years of Lance during the clinic's existence. He listed the types of deviant behavior and then went through the characteristics that defined each type, ending with a synopsis of behaviors important in serial killings.

It fits, it really fits, Stu thought. *We may have something here. Alan's description fit Lance to a T. I must find out more.*

He introduced himself to Alan after the seminar and explained how his company was studying deviant behavior. "I can't divulge the name of our subject at this time," he said. "I'll refer to him as Mr. X. Maybe your database could give us information that has been impossible for us to obtain otherwise. If I gave you this person's DNA profile, could you check to see if any of your crimes have been associated with him?"

"I'd be happy to check it out, Stu, and I'm glad to know of your work. I didn't realize that your company existed."

"Well, it's actually a small company," Stu said, "mostly devoted to research and dealing with a small number of clients. I really wouldn't expect you to know about us."

"Could you do something for me?" Alan asked. "We're attempting to get as much data as we can collect to store in our computer so it can provide us with information of a vital nature. When you send your DNA profile, could you include whatever's available on your subject's behavior?"

After promising to send the information Alan requested, Stu thanked him and stated how important he felt their meeting was. He quickly made his way back to the clinic, called up Lance's DNA profile, and sifted through his research summaries to compose a behavioral profile of a Mr. X, without revealing the methods they used to obtain the information.

Much of what Alan said, Special Agent Clayton already knew. What caught her attention most was mention of the database owned and operated by Genetics, Inc. Up to now, she had used the FBI's database with complete confidence. It was through that database that all criminals were cross checked, and until now, it was the best one she knew of.

When the seminar and question-and-answer period were over, she went to the front of the lecture room and stood in line to talk to Dr. Wilkins. When her time came, she introduced herself as Special Agent Clayton and told him of her connection with the murders that had been occurring around New Orleans for the last seven years.

Agent Clayton said, "Dr. Wilkins, could you tell me more about your company's database system?"

"You can call me Alan, Agent Clayton. Can I call you Pat or Patricia?"

She usually kept a professional relationship with those she had business with, but she could see that Alan wanted a conversation on a more casual level. Since he had brought it up, she didn't see any harm in accommodating him.

"Just call me Pat. And before you get into the subject, would you have time to sit for a while over a cup of coffee or a light meal?"

Alan said, "Well, it's not often I get such an appealing offer from such a beautiful member of my audience. I accept. Where do you want to go?"

They went to an outside courtyard café in the French Quarter, and Alan ordered some gumbo. Pat ordered red beans and rice, and they both had a Jax beer.

Alan asked Pat precisely what she had in mind, so she elaborated on what the status of the murders was and what they had done in an attempt to identify the killer. She told him that she had been confident with their database before his seminar but that she now had doubts about its capabilities to come up with the answers she needed for this particular case.

Alan said, "Actually, Pat, our database is one of the best kept secrets in the world. We don't mean it to be a secret, but so many organizations are confident that their systems are the best, they don't give us a chance to prove ourselves. Let me tell you how good it is.

"Believe it or not, it currently has far more categories than the FBI or any other law enforcement organization could ever hope to have. It has data on every criminal that ever existed and possibly individuals who are not yet criminals, that is, people who are potential criminals.

"Most of our data are based on their genetic codes and behavioral traits from the time they're born until they are caught or die. It also includes a complete file for fingerprint analysis, the jobs these people hold, their schooling, the objects they collect, the pets they have, their likes and dislikes, intricate details of their personal life, and many other subjects that are associated with their lives. We've even gone back into their ancestral lines for genetic and behavioral characteristics and have made predictions about what each person would be like if certain crosses were made.

"The one thing we can't do is predict with certainty if a person with the proper traits is actually going to be a criminal. It's not a matter of just looking at traits. It's a combination of genetic traits and influences in the person's life that cause them to develop in one direction or another, and we're just not certain in some cases how one influences the other."

"This is unbelievable, Alan. I was thinking these same thoughts just the other day. Wouldn't it be great if we could tie all this together to definitely determine if a person was going to develop into a criminal or not? If that were possible, then maybe we could do something to change the pattern and have it turn out a different way."

"Yes, Pat. That would be nice, but it's not likely to happen any time soon. We're still dealing with a biological system, and that means diversity and complexity. It's not like math or physics where you can plug something into a formula and tell exactly what the answer is. The human mind is very complex, and even though we may know the traits and the environmental influences, there is always the unknown connection with genetics and the organization of the human mind."

"That's true, Alan," she said. "Say, I'm really enjoying talking to you, and I'd like to talk to you some more about this, but I have to meet someone to discuss a case. Do you think we could meet again sometime?"

"You bet, Pat. I'd also like to hear more about the cases you're working on. Your job sounds fascinating, too. Call me sometime, and we'll do this again, or possibly you can visit our facility."

They exchanged cards, and Pat said, "Alan, let me ask you something before I leave. Is there any chance you could run some tests on some of the material that we collected at the crime scenes? Maybe there's a chance that your system has information we don't have."

"Sure. Give me a call when you're ready, and I'll set it up for you."

Chapter 45

Pooling Data

Special Agent Clayton had new hope for catching the killers that had been so elusive all these years, especially the serial killer that had given them so much trouble. She was convinced that they would some day catch up with him, and maybe this connection with Genetics, Inc. was going to make it possible. It couldn't hurt. They had exhausted most of their other options.

She arranged to have semen and blood samples from the various crime sites sent over to Genetics, Inc., with a personal note marked "Attn: Dr. Alan Wilkins." In it, she told him what her needs were, and he had the genetics team start processing it.

When the DNA analysis had been completed, he had the computer section enter the results and other characteristics of the murders, murder victims, and traits of the killer into the database system. Within a few hours, he had the results of the search on his desk.

There were no specific matches. This was a hugh disappointment to both he and Pat. He was certain that their system would have chosen a match of some kind. He would have bet on it.

When they met over dinner, they talked at length about the situation, and Alan said, "Would it be alright if I keep a copy of this data to analyze further? I may like to try some new things, and who knows. It may reveal something that we haven't thought of."

Pat said, "Please do whatever you can with the data. I haven't had much luck with it, and anything you come up with will be of assistance. We have all this information about the killer, and yet, we're no closer to catching him now than we were when he started his killing."

As Alan looked at the data more closely, something seemed familiar. It wasn't the behavior that caught his attention. It was the DNA pattern. He almost felt like he'd seen it before. Yet, his database system hadn't come up with anything close to what he'd call a match.

The reason for its familiarity was unclear because he didn't spend that much time memorizing patterns of electrophoretic DNA bands. It had to be someone he knew well. Then it dawned on him. It had shades of Hunter's cave man, Adda! It made no sense that such a pattern would show up in contemporary times, but he was almost certain that that was where he had seen it.

In the meantime, Alan received a package from Stu and laid it upon his desk. The connection with the DNA samples was all he could think about, and Stu's information could wait. Further thought about the possibility of similar DNA bands in two distinctly different humans was too much to comprehend at this time, although it did deserve further consideration. At this time, however, he needed a break.

He checked Stu's data and was shocked to see the link he was looking for. This Mr. X that Stu Bridges had worked up a DNA profile for had features that corresponded to those of both Adda, the 200,000-year-old caveman that Hunter had found when he was doing research in Africa, and the person who Pat was interested in.

He immediately called Stu. "I really am interested in identifying this person you call Mr. X, Stu. Is this possible?"

"Why do you ask, Alan?"

"Because it partially matches some 200,000-year-old DNA the founder of our company collected from an individual he found in Africa, and it's a perfect match for an individual who is linked to the serial killings that have been occurring during the last few years.

"But this is impossible," Stu said. "We have been watching him for years and have never been able to associate him with any of the things that were occurring. As far as we know, he was either working most of the time or at home. In addition, he has almost appeared to us as a model citizen. How could he possibly be involved with these events?"

Since Lance's background information was known to only the director at the clinic, and this new information enhanced the importance of the matter, Stu felt it was necessary to have the comparisons run again.

Alan approached Hunter with the information he had and explained his conversations with Stu and Pat. When Hunter heard the story, he began to synthesize a reason for what had happened. Somehow, the person or persons who stole Adda's 200,000-year-old testicles from a cryogenic lab had obtained the sperm and made the cross.

"I must admit, the cross is intriguing, although illegal." He instructed Alan to do further investigation and make a full report to Genetics, Inc. In the meantime, he asked to run the comparisons himself.

When he came up with the same results, he decided to notify Stu personally. The computer had picked one match, and it was a perfect one. Their killer was Lance Housler, age twenty-six, brown hair, five feet, eleven-and-a-half inches tall, brown eyes, job specialty - butcher. His parents were Ralph and Jennifer Housler, mother still living, father had died in a mysterious accident.

When Stu heard the results, this time from Hunter, he sat stupefied at his desk. *But how?* he wondered. He couldn't get past the fact that they had been watching Lance for years, and he never seemed to do anything out of the ordinary. He repeated his thoughts about Lance that the behavior he exhibited in his adult life seemed to be beyond any of the problems he had when he was younger.

Coleen couldn't believe it either. She had been as close to the family as anyone, and she knew of the problems Lance had when he was young. But like Stu, she had thought Lance had adjusted to life and was doing fine.

When the director, Steven Morrison, was contacted by Stu in the usual mysterious way they had done in the beginning of their study and told him what had happened, he appeared to be in shock and deep thought. When Stu was about to ask if he was okay, he finally said, "I guess we should have suspected this when we knew he had all those childhood problems and characteristics that marked the development of an impending criminal mind. We just thought it was unusual that they all of a sudden vanished."

"Yes," Stu said. "I knew it was too good to be true. We probably should have persisted in watching him in a variety of ways, maybe gone out of our way to see what he was doing behind our back, but his apparent improvement seemed so real.

"We did the best we could. Lance somehow was aware of our surveillance and did these things in such a way that we wouldn't find out about them. You are the one who set this computer search up, right?"

Stu said, "Yes, I am." Noticing a strange hiatus in their conversation, he asked, "Are you alright, Dr. Morrison?"

"Yes, Yes, I'm okay. Look, if you'll excuse me, I have something to do. I would like to follow up on this as soon as possible."

As it turned out, the team never heard from him again. When they returned to work in the morning, they found the laboratory ransacked, and all data had been removed from the regular files. The computer's hard drive had been erased, leaving them with no information at the clinic to use for any purpose.

In a state of disbelief, Stu, Coleen, and the other team members who remained realized they had been scammed. They were suddenly out of a job and had nothing to show for it. Stu was glad he had made a copy of Lance's file, and he subsequently passed much of it on to Alan at Genetics, Inc.

Stu called Alan to explain what had happened. Alan immediately signaled for Hunter to pick up the phone, and they listened to Stu as he presented the story, leaving them to only one question: Who was Steven Morrison?

Hunter broke in at the end of Stu's confession. "Hi Stu, this is Hunter. I would like to get a copy of your files, if possible. You will be compensated for it, I promise you. Will that be possible?"

"Yes, sure, Hunter. Actually, the files are of no use to me now. I'll keep a copy, of course, but it appears they will do you more good."

"Thanks," Hunter said. "Now sit down, Stu. I would like to tell you a story, as well. I collected the body of a primitive human on Mt. Kilimanjaro a number of years back. We stored the testicles in liquid nitrogen, with the thought that we would one day use them in some way. They were stored in a cryonic laboratory in California for the time being.

"Just about the time we were starting our business, someone stole my notes and the testes, and we were never able to recover them. We filed a police report, but nothing ever came of it.

It now seems obvious that the director of your laboratory, this Steven Morrison, is the person responsible for the theft. If it wasn't for you and Special Agent Clayton, we may never have put this all together.

"Steven must have made the cross, leading to the birth of Lance, with the intention of studying him throughout his life. Do you know any more about Steven Morrison?"

"Actually, no," Stu said. "When we tried to pool our knowledge about him, he turned out to be a complete mystery. No one has ever met him. He was always a mysterious person. We suspected that he had some form of partnership with one or two other persons from certain statements he made, but we know even less about them."

"Well, I guess we'd better phone Special Agent Clayton immediately and give her the news. I'm sure she'll be relieved that we pooled our data and came up with a match. Thanks for your input, Stu."

Stu said, "Let me ask you a question before you do that, Hunter. Could you do me a favor when you give her the printout by not breathing a word about the data that explains Lance's past just yet? We don't need that coming out now. It could ruin all of us."

"You don't even need to mention it, Stu. You have been loyal to the clinic and have not been responsible for the unethical experiments set up by Morrison, and we have no intentions of divulging anything about the original experiment.

"In the meantime, I think you and I should look back in our records and see if there is anything we missed. At this point, it appears that crossing a 200,000-year-old man with a modern woman turned out to be Morrison's way of creating a monster, but I want to make sure there's nothing else that influenced Lance to be like he is."

Hunter continued, "Please notify all the other members of your team about our results. For our own information, I think we should both attempt to find out more about Lance's ancestry through the egg donor's side. Under proper direction, your company should have followed through with that a long time ago, but I'm sure it didn't seem necessary at the time, and I'm equally sure you didn't suspect Lance as the killer. Get right on it. There are questions about the egg donor's parents that we need answered. Come see us in a few days. Alan and I would like to talk to both you and Coleen.

After Hunter and Alan had run the data through the system twice more and had come up with the same results, they knew it was time to release the information, but they were still having trouble believing it was Lance all the time.

Under Hunter's direction, Alan collected their results, picked up the phone and dialed Agent Clayton's number. She wasn't in her office, so he left a message. "Pat, this is Alan. You're not going to believe this, but we got a perfect match on the killer. We know who it is. Please call immediately."

Chapter 46

Closing in On Lance Housler

When Special Agent Clayton heard the message from Alan, her heart began to pound, and as she held the phone to return his call, her hands were shaking. When Alan answered with, "Genetics, Inc., this is Dr. Wilkins. Can I help you?" she wasted no time with going through the usual cordial greeting or any casual conversation.

Struggling with breathing, she said, "Is this for real, Alan?

Alan said, "Hi Pat. Yes, it is."

"How did you do this? How do you know it's him?"

"It's a long story, Pat, and I don't want to talk about it over the phone. How about meeting me in a few minutes for coffee and donuts across from Jackson Square?"

She agreed, put the phone down and didn't hear any of the comments her agents were making to her as she rushed out of her office. Getting to their meeting spot took her about ten minutes when it usually took twenty. She couldn't contain her excitement as she repeatedly went over the thought that this may actually be real.

Thoughts entered her mind that told her there may be a mistake, and she began to become momentarily confused. *Is it really true? Does Alan really have her killer, or does he just think he has? How was he able to track him down when the initial results showed no matches whatsoever?*

When she rushed into the coffee shop and saw Alan already sitting at a table with coffee and donuts for both of them, she had that look on her face that indicated she couldn't wait to hear what he had to say. "Tell me, Alan! What did you find?"

"Calm down, Pat. Have some coffee."

"I don't want coffee! I want an answer, please!"

"Well," he said, "I started digging around, and I had the feeling that I'd seen the DNA pattern before. But I didn't know where. I started looking through material that had been in the to-do box, including information from Dr. Stu Bridges at the Fertility Clinic. Our company's data contains information on people that had the personalities that could lead to a criminal way of life but had not yet been entered into the computer. Stu's information was about a person they had been studying for quite some time because his mother had taken him to psychiatrists ever since he was a little boy."

Staring at Alan, Pat held her hand up and said, "Please, Alan. Don't keep me in suspense like this. Tell me who this person is. You can fill me in on the details later."

Alan saw Pat's need for an immediate answer in her expression. "It's a man who was born and lived all his life here in New Orleans, a man named Lance Housler."

Pat just looked at him, an expression of utter shock on her face. She stared into space, and her eyes were flickering from side to side, showing her intense concentration and attempt to make sense of what he had told her. Alan stared back at her, wondering what could be going through her mind. He could tell the wheels were spinning rapidly by her expression.

She looked up and asked, "Is this man related to Ralph and Jennifer Housler, by any chance?"

"Why, yes, he is. Ralph and Jennifer are his parents. Why? Do you know them?"

Pat said, "As a matter of fact, I do. Believe this or not, I lived just a few doors down from their house when I was growing up, and I baby-sat Lance once. Are you sure it's him?"

Before Alan answered, she reflected back on those days, telling him about the time she met Lance for the first time. "I was fifteen, and Ralph and Jennifer went to a rock concert."

Alan looked at her and said, "I can't imagine how things are coming together here." *It's a small world,* he thought. "What was he like then?"

Ignoring his question, she said, "Answer me, Alan, please, please. Are you absolutely sure it's him?"

Alan laid a folder with papers in it down on the table and said, "Yes, I am. I've checked the DNA pattern several times, and I had our CEO also check it. It's a definite match. There's no doubt about it. You can check it out, yourself. These folders have copies of the documents you need."

Alan repeated his question, "Now tell me, Pat, what was he like when you watched him?"

"Actually, he was just a baby, but I had a bad experience with him."

"What was that?"

"Well," she said, "as I was watching and playing with him, he kept looking at my mouth. For some reason, he was fascinated with my teeth, and he grabbed my teeth on a couple of occasions. I don't know what attracted him to them."

As she was talking, Alan was aware that she was tying open ends together as she spoke. It was hard to believe that his current fascination with teeth had anything to do with what was on his mind as a baby.

"Then, I made the mistake of laying a knife down not far from him, and he grabbed it, swung it at me, and cut my hand." She turned her hand over and shoved it toward Alan and said, "I still have the scar."

Alan quickly glanced down at her trembling finger, noticed the scar, and resumed his concentration on what she was saying.

"He was strong for someone his age. When he cut me, it almost appeared like he had wanted to do it, and he smiled when it was over. I called his parents up, and they took me to the hospital to get stitches. I remember his dad was an ass hole. I wonder now if I was right in thinking that he knew exactly what he was doing. This is just too weird."

Alan said, "Well, I know you want to get him as soon as possible. We have his address and his place of work. He should be at work right now. If you want to pick him up and stop all this killing, now would be a good time to do it.

When it's all over, I'd like to get a statement from you about the details of that night, as well as what else you know about him, so we can add it all to our database."

"I'll be happy to do that. Give me the information I need, and I'll get some back up to bring him in."

Alan presented her with the package of DNA results and a sheet of paper with a summary of the information on it, along with the address and phone number of the butcher shop where Lance worked. She immediately called her department to arrange for back up and thanked Alan. When she started to leave, she turned, hugged him, and rushed out of the coffee shop with tears forming in her eyes. On the way over to the market, she kept thinking of that night with Lance, wondering again if he had used the knife on purpose.

She pulled up across the street from the market and impatiently waited for back up. It was difficult to sit there and not rush in to take the man she had sought all these years. She felt an excitement she had never felt before, brought on by an adrenaline rush. *Why didn't I think of him, knowing of his behavior when he was a child and having experienced the trauma I received at his hand so long ago?*

Inside the market, both Mr. Gromler and Lance were both waiting on customers, and Lance noticed the car and what he thought was Special Agent Patricia Clayton sitting in the driver's seat. Noticing something out of the ordinary wasn't unusual for him. He was constantly on the look-out for anything that would pose a threat to him, and he had seen her face many times on the TV screen, appealing for assistance from the public and any other source that could help.

Without an explanation, he quickly turned and went directly to the freezer. When he came out, he had a zippered hand bag with him, and he immediately went out the back door.

Mr. Gromler stared at him, wondering where he was going in such a hurry, and he apologized to Lance's customer for the wait. He finished dealing with his own customer and then took care of Lance's.

By that time, Special Agent Clayton was approaching the entrance to the shop with two other FBI agents. She sent others around to the rear of the building, and as she entered the market, Mr. Gromler said, "Can I help you?"

She showed him her badge as she introduced herself and the agent with her and told him she was looking for Lance Housler. Mr. Gromler said, "He was here just a few minutes ago, and for some reason, he went out the back door right in the middle of a sale."

The words were hardly out of his mouth when she and the other agent headed for the back door. They met the other two agents as they exited the building and realized Lance had already departed.

Immediately, she sent three agents to search the neighborhood, reentered the market through the rear door, and asked Mr. Gromler if he had a vehicle. She already knew he did.

"Yes, our truck is parked out back."

"Could you show it to me, sir?"

As they all went back out, Mr. Gromler asked, "What is this all about?"

Special Agent Clayton didn't comment. As they stepped outside, he said that the truck was gone, and he further commented that this was very unusual. Lance had never done this before.

Special Agent Clayton got on the phone and ordered another unit to Lance's house. She had ordered one before they had left to come to the market, but she wanted to be sure they had adequate coverage in case he had a weapon. With Mr. Gromler's help, she described the truck he was driving, and she requested that an immediate APB be put out for him and the truck anywhere in the city but especially in the area between the shop and his apartment. "We can't let this one get away."

A helicopter was dispatched to the area, looking for a "Gromler's Meat Market truck." Special Agent Clayton was experiencing nausea, pacing back and forth in the shop, mentally retracing her steps in preparation for Lance's capture. There was something wrong with the picture she formed in her mind.

"We'll be back, Mr. Gromler. I need to talk to you some more. If you see or hear from Lance, please either tell one of our agents or call us immediately at this number." She quickly pulled out her card and handed it to him. "In the meantime, I'm leaving Agent Aldridge with you. He'll explain what this is all about."

She noticed her hands were shaking terribly, and sweat was pouring out of her skin. A panicked feeling was growing rapidly in her body, telling her that what was happening to her at this very moment was something she had wanted to avoid throughout her career. She felt claustrophobic, that she needed to get out of the shop immediately and be on her way. She was already feeling the guilt of missing her big chance to nab the person who had caused her so much grief. *Why haven't I heard from someone, telling me they have spotted the truck? It shouldn't be that hard to recognize. Where the hell can he be? He just left, for God's sake.*

As they left, Mr. Gromler had a puzzled look on his face. He watched them pull away before he asked, "What the hell is going on?"

Agent Aldridge asked, "How well do you know Mr. Housler?"

Mr. Gromler said, "Well, he's been working for me for about six years, and he's been a very good worker. Actually, he's the best worker I ever had. He's a little strange at times, but he's never let me down. Why do you ask?"

At first, Agent Aldridge remained silent, not wanting to divulge any information on the suspect that should remain secret. That's what he would normally do. It wasn't his place to explain their business to anyone. Yet, Special Agent Clayton had said the details would be revealed to him, and he felt Mr. Gromler deserved an explanation, some explanation that would explain their sudden intrusion and the seriousness of their timely quest.

"Mr. Housler is a suspect in the killings that have been occurring over the last few years. We were told that his DNA and the DNA we got from his victims were a perfect match, so the evidence against him is very convincing."

"This can't be true." Mr. Gromler apparently was now in deep thought. "He's been a great asset to me, and for the most part, he's been pleasant to our customers. I can't believe he would do something like that."

"Well, believe it, Mr. Gromler. Sometimes a killer can be right under your nose, and you wouldn't know it. Through life, they learn how to act and cover up their secret fantasies. They almost always get caught, but the smarter ones do their business for years before they are identified.

"Let me stress, though, that you shouldn't say anything to anybody about this, no one. I and some other agents will be staying here under cover until we are told to do otherwise. It is my opinion that you'll never see Lance again, but if he does come back for some reason, or if he calls, we would like to know about it. We'll also have someone here at night, in case he comes back at that time."

Mr. Gromler said, "Well, you can stay if you like, but I'm going to close up and go home. I don't feel so good, and I can't stay here. This is too much for me to think about."

"That's all well and good, Mr. Gromler, but we'd like to talk with you again, so please stay in town. Could you give me your home number so we can call you when we have the chance?"

Agent Aldridge already had a considerable amount of information about Mr. Gromler, including his home phone number. It was their routine to obtain information about those they had dealings with prior to confronting them. From the time Special Agent Clayton had found out who the killer was and her approach to the meat market, headquarters had gotten to know a lot about Mr. Gromler and his business.

They had determined he was a legitimate businessman who had the unfortunate karma of meeting and dealing with the likes of a person such as Lance Housler. And like most people who knew something about Lance, Mr. Gromler had no clue about Lance's true nature, that he was a psychopath of huge proportions. The concept he now had of the man he put so much trust in made him feel sick.

Mr. Gromler gave Agent Aldridge his home phone number, along with his address and a key to the shop. He turned the sign on the entrance door to read "Closed" and left. On his way to his car, one of his customers approached the market. Mr. Gromler told her he had closed because of an emergency, and when she asked what was wrong, he said he couldn't say at this time.

Chapter 47

Perusing Lance's Apartment

All the way home, Mr. Gromler thought about Lance. How could he not think of him, and only him? He was now in shock. Things didn't make a lot of sense.

It was so unreal to him. His mind battled with his previous notion of Lance and the person he was told Lance really is. *Lance, a killer? Impossible.*

Negative thoughts entered his mind. He began thinking about Lance's unusual behavior and the way he acted with all the younger female clients they had. He thought about the many nights Lance had worked in the market to all hours and his desire to keep the shades down so no one could see inside. Suddenly, the possibility that Lance was doing what they said he'd done seemed more plausible.

By the time he got home, he had started thinking about what all this was going to do to him and his business. First, he no longer had Lance to do all the chores involved with cleaning the market which meant he was going to have to do them. Secondly, when the word got out about Lance, he probably was going to lose most or maybe all of his customers, and this would ruin him. In addition, he no longer had a truck.

Assuming how the FBI and their forensic units probably worked, he was certain they would come in and go through his market with a fine-toothed comb. He had seen how they worked on TV. This meant he would have to close for that period of time, and he wouldn't have any income because of it. He might lose some of his meat, maybe all of it, in the process, and he'd have to take those losses. He thanked God for the meat that was frozen. At least that would be saved, but there was no way that this was going to be anything but bad for him.

* * *

Special Agent Clayton and her assistants arrived at Lance's apartment shortly after they had left the market. She was hoping they'd catch him at his apartment if he decided to go home, but there was no sign of him. She made another call to alert her department and local law enforcement officials that he was still on the streets somewhere and had to be caught. Her sinking feeling was increasing. *Someone should have caught him by now.*

Meanwhile, a truck with TV repair signs, Unit 6, on its sides was on its way out of town, traveling west on Airline Highway, crossing into Jefferson Parish, and headed for the Huey P. Long Bridge.

Once he crossed the river, he headed west past Willswoods and his old snake collecting area and then west. He had already passed several police cars that seemed to be patrolling and looking for someone. He was glad he had gotten away when he did.

While his driving upon leaving Gromler's Meat Market had been rapid and erratic, he subsequently assumed a more reticent composure, knowing that if he had remained in his initial panicked mood, they would easily notice him on the streets. He had to drive as though he was on a routine mission.

He hated to leave all of his possessions behind, and he knew he'd never be able to replace what he had lost. He had worked hard over the years to acquire his possessions, and they meant everything to him. They were his toys, his memories of so many personal encounters with his targets. *How could this have happened to me?*

In spite of his losses, he knew he was better off leaving them behind and putting on the miles he needed to escape. He understood that had he gone back to his apartment, he would now be sitting in the back of a squad car headed for jail. He had done the only thing he could do to escape his captors. In a way, he suddenly felt proud of the way he had made his escape, acting purely on instinct.

* * *

As Special Agent Clayton entered Lance's apartment with several other FBI agents and local law enforcement personnel, they were surprised to find the living room, even in the dark, neatly organized and clean. Yet, there was a musty odor that she couldn't place. Since it was dark with the blinds drawn, they had to turn the lights on in order to see the details of the room.

The pictures that hung on the walls, maybe fifty in all, were, to say the least, very strange. They portrayed models from companies that sold skin-care products, some with cut-outs of just part of a model's face to show her exceptional complexion.

Lance's taste in furniture wasn't anything special. It appeared to be the type of furniture you'd find in a second hand or pre-owned discount store. There were nicks and scratches on the wooden surfaces, and the upholstered chairs and couch had a couple of tears in them.

Special Agent Clayton imagined this room to be a place that Lance had initially designed to entertain his subjects before he slaughtered them. She also imagined that the room never got to be used for the purpose for which it had been designed, that Lance probably had killed his victims before they ever got here.

The living room was partitioned from the remainder of the house by a long curtain that covered closed double doors. As she pushed the curtain aside and opened the doors, she immediately smelled a more putrid odor that wasn't apparent when they had entered the apartment.

It appeared that the entire house, like the living room, was dark inside, and as was the case in the living room, Lance had the blinds pulled down and closed. As she flipped the light switch, she and her colleagues entered a long hallway that led to the kitchen, and when they entered the room, they all stood, staring with open mouths.

The kitchen was a mess. There was trash all over the floor, and the sink was piled high with soiled pots, pans, plastic drinking glasses, cups, plastic silverware, and scattered paper. It seemed as though Lance's neat side only existed through his living room, but when he passed through the curtained doors, he underwent a radical change.

There were no plates, plastic or ceramic. Lance had apparently eaten off of pieces of meat-market paper, some torn sections of which were crumpled up and strewn around the room. Flies alternated between the piles to be sure they scattered their eggs around the different sources of food. A closer look revealed maggots of various sizes crawling amongst the samples. A large roll of fresh paper was to one side of the sink.

The room was equipped with both a refrigerator and an upright freezer. While there was very little in the refrigerator in the way of accessory condiments, its freezer section was full of packages of ground meat. More of the same filled the separate freezer.

In a way, Special Agent Clayton was disappointed with the refrigerator. She expected to find human parts, souvenirs collected by the killer to represent his victims.

As they entered the bathroom, they were shocked to find the tub filled with assorted human remains that were being fed upon by a large colony of carpet beetles. In Special Agent Clayton's estimation, there were remains at that spot alone of at least three or four of Lance's victims.

There were some long bones, apparently from the legs and arms of some of his victims, in the bathroom sink that Lance must have been scrubbing to remove the stains left by the beetles. A bottle of peroxide, probably to further whiten the bones, was on the floor, adjacent to the sink. Piled on the floor were other skeletal remains that the beetles had completed their feeding upon. It appeared that Lance had put them there to clean once he got done with the ones in the sink.

The shower was relatively clean, except for large patches of black mold that occupied the darker corners, and there were signs that Lance had used it for his daily showers. The soap and shampoo were in their proper places, and a worn wash cloth and towel hung on the towel rack.

The dining room table, which was a fold-up table like people use at flea markets, had been covered with meat-wrapping paper, and atop the paper was an almost completed skeleton, the clean bones laying disconnected but in their proper positions for later assemblage. That was apparently the next step in the process that had begun in Lance's bathroom.

The walls of Lance's bedroom were covered with photographs of all types. Some were identified as customers photographed in the meat market. Others were taken at various places around the city, but they, too, were young women. While some of the pictures were full-body shots of them standing by the glass meat-display area or walking down the street, others were close-ups of their skin.

In a separately-organized section on one of the walls were pictures that Lance had taken of his victims after he had finished raping them. There were shots of their faces, bodies, and legs, and more close-ups of their skin.

He had apparently taken the pictures before he took their teeth and fingers. He evidently wanted to be reminded of their beauty, not the grim process of destroying their features and terminating their lives.

The room reeked of seminal fluid, and there were indications of seminal fluid stains on everything, including the pictures on the walls.

As she looked the room over, she had no doubt that this was where he repeatedly seduced the souls of his victims through their photographs. It was a room where he had his most intimate thoughts, and many of his plans to set up his victims were probably consummated here, as well.

As they entered the second bedroom, she knew immediately that this was another room where Lance spent a lot of his time. There was a make-shift male manikin near the shuttered window that was dressed in a loin cloth made of human scalps adorned with the variously-colored hair that hung from them, another bleak reminder of some of Lance's victims. A human leg bone was taped to the manikin's hand and a necklace of small bones and teeth had been placed around its neck. Additional leg bones were piled upon the floor, representing a cache of replacement weapons.

Over to one side of the room, a tripod supported a camera that took instant pictures. It had wide-angle and telephoto capabilities, evidently the camera that Lance used to get the full-bodied shots and close-ups of the women on the walls of his bedroom.

On a desk adjacent to the manikin were photographs of Lance, dressed in his caveman attire, including his loin cloth of human hair and his bone and tooth necklace. He apparently had assumed various stances to make himself look as though he was a wild man approaching a potential victim. In some of the pictures, he held the bone down along his leg, and in others, he held the bone up as though he was going to hit something. His facial expressions were like snarls, his teeth showing, giving him a threatening appearance. There were no signs of feelings of compassion for the people he had killed.

Clothes were piled up in a corner of the room. It appeared that he hadn't washed clothes in a while because the pile was high, and there were very few clean samples in the bedroom drawers.

* * *

Special Agent Clayton knew the forensic team was going to have a field day here, and it would take them a while to do what they had to do. Before they went into Lance's apartment, she had requested that her agents not touch anything. They were simply to write down a general description of what they found. The forensic team would do the rest.

Chapter 48

Finding the Source of Bad Genes

By this time, Lance was already headed toward western Louisiana. He had gotten through the patrol cars and was on his way to somewhere. Where this somewhere was, he wasn't really sure. As he continued to head in a westerly direction, he stuck to the smaller highways, afraid he might get stopped by the highway patrol if he used I-10. His speed on them was slower, but the environment was more picturesque.

He had been lucky so far. Even though the truck color was what the law was searching for, the TV signs had evidently fooled them to this point. But he knew he was risking being caught in the truck, even if he was driving carefully and obeying the law, so when he got to Shreveport, he left the truck in a shopping center parking lot, took his zippered bag, and was on his way by foot.

He went to a giant supermarket that had a wide variety of merchandise and purchased a small suitcase on rollers. In another section of the store, he bought sandwiches, a few cans of beans, a can opener, plastic eating utensils, some toilet paper, soft drinks, a pair of pants, and a T-shirt. He then headed toward the nearest railway yard to wait until he could recognize a freight train that was headed west.

Late that evening, he found one that was just starting to leave. Catching up with it, he entered an open car, and sat down by the sliding door. When he was certain it was continuing west, he went to the front of the car, changed into his new clothes, dumped the old ones on the side of the tracks, and lay down for a much needed sleep.

* * *

Photographers had now come to get pictures of Lance's apartment before the forensic specialists started their work. Special Agent Clayton was directing the shoot to make sure they got everything without disturbing the scene. They would return for specifics once the forensic team had decided on special shots. She wanted a complete record of this man, not only for her files but for the database at Genetics, Inc.

She wanted this to be part of their record. After all, it was Alan who identified the killer, and it was probably databases like the one at Genetics, Inc. that were going to hold more data about the criminal mind than any other database in the world.

It was difficult for her to believe that Lance had not been caught by this time. She reminisced about putting the alert out as soon as she had found who the killer was, and the police had all the information they needed to spot him. She reasoned that since the police had not yet found him, it was likely that Lance was hiding somewhere in the city, and he may have hidden the truck somewhere, as well. She made sure that all local law enforcement was on the alert to continue looking for him. He had to show up at some time.

* * *

As Alan received reports on Lance's ancestral characteristics from Stu and his own geneticists, he was especially interested in the egg donor's line. About three days later, he got a detailed report, entitled "Genealogical History of Amy Fascio Canada," Lance's biological mother. He dropped the remainder of the reports he had been reading and began concentrating on this new one.

Detailed information had been collected about her mother, but very little on the first few pages indicated a problem from her maternal side. When he got to a discussion of Amy's grandfather, he realized he'd struck pay dirt.

Amy had said her grandfather died when she was a little girl, but this was not the case. Her mother had lied about what had really happened. He had been arrested on several occasions for abuse to both his spouse and his children. He was also arrested but never convicted on two counts of rape. It was after this that he left home, and he wasn't heard from again. There was a later report of another rape, and he had subsequently been killed in a shoot-out in Texas.

Upon finishing the report, Alan immediately called Hunter. "Hunter, I think you'll be very interested in the report I just received. It's about Lance's genealogy."

"Yes, I would, Alan. Could you get it to me right away?"

"I'll be right up."

Once he read the report, Hunter understood where the bad genes had come from. It wasn't Lance's biological father, Adda, and the 200,000-year-old genes at all. Adda had actually contributed the only good qualities that Lance possessed. Lance's outward, more violent expression of his genetic make-up was apparently dominated by the complement set of genes from his grandfather on his biological mother's side. Thus, Lance had genes for both good and bad qualities which were typically expressed by humans.

This fact alone was not all that unusual. *All people possess good and bad*, he thought. *It was how they chose to express these two sides in their lives that made the difference.* And yet, the choice was not really always theirs. It was more complex than that.

An expression of their genes often involved their early life, their post-natal formative years, and how they were treated. Once the pattern of a personality is set, there wasn't much a person could do about it. This outward expression in Lance, developed in his early years, is what made him what he was. Had he not been maltreated by his father in early life, Lance may have turned out entirely different.

As it was, he expressed this diverse genetic inheritance early in life by learning to live in a very confusing, traumatic modern world, simultaneously committing little evil crimes in seclusion throughout his young years. They had become more complex and violent with the years.

Thoughts of how things could have been reentered his mind. If things had been different, Lance may have worked his problems out after the things he had done during his childhood. Other children sometimes did the same things without producing lasting flaws in their later personalities. For Lance, this, he suspected, would have required the presence of a happy childhood in a pleasant environment.

Everyone involved with Lance now knew that he never received this. It was true that he had the paradoxical dual qualities of becoming a decent citizen and the potential for developing a criminal mind, but the clincher was that he faced torturous treatment from an abusive father. In addition, it wasn't just a simple case of abuse. Lance had to endure abuse day after day, the beatings and confinement in their dark bedroom closet, and it set him on the road to finally do what they now knew he had done. What he had become was actually not his fault.

Understanding this, Hunter was upset by the fact that although Lance was pure evil, it was his parents, particularly his father, who had made him a psychopath, and the person who had made him would never be prosecuted. Life, as the Houslers had one determined, was often not fair.

Hunter said, "Alan, I also think you should get with Stu Bridges and let him know what you've found. While you're at it, tell him this: Based on his experience with the criminal mind and what he knows about Lance, we may have a position for him here at Genetics, Inc. We can use someone like him. And ask about his second in command, Coleen I think it is. Maybe we can use her, too."

"I'll get right on it, Hunter."

* * *

Following a long discussion with Alan and finally understanding the almost unbelievable genetic cross that was made, Stu realized that he had been right. They almost certainly could have helped him if they had known more and would have had the freedom to work with Lance from the beginning. The problem was that they were limited by the rules established by the director and only knew what they had genetically determined on his father's side and what they had witnessed through their secret cameras. It appeared that Dr. Morrison had set up the entire scheme to discover the workings of a psychopathic mind. But who was this Morrison person and what was his link in this complicated picture of a experiment that went very wrong?

He hated to admit it, but with all their surveillance, they really didn't know much about the background or true nature of their subject. He had outsmarted them all.

* * *

It was Stu who had to tell Jennifer what had happened. When she first heard what he had to say, she couldn't believe it. The son that she bore and had given everything up to have, the son that she at one time had thought would bring she and Ralph closer together, the son that had caused the pain she had to endure before and after he was born, was now dealing her a final blow. She may as well have been one of his victims. She was devastated.

She began having nightmares of her own, and if it wouldn't have been for Ernest, her current better half, she may have attempted to end her life. She went through deep episodes of depression, long periods of crying, and finally hate. The hate was directed not at Lance but at Ralph for doing what he did and then leaving them to wallow in never-ending strife.

Chapter 49

Contemplating Lance's Existence

While Special Agent Clayton and other FBI officials scrambled for reasons to explain Lance's escape, he had already switched trains three times and was still heading west. He wasn't in a hurry. He was well out of immediate danger and perfectly confident that he was safe from those who searched for him.

The trip he was now on was his opportunity to spend time contemplating his chaotic past and uncertain future. Everything had happened so fast at the end that his mind had since remained filled with numerous unordered thoughts, thoughts that clouded his ability to reason. Even his decision to head west was purely intuitive.

Whenever the train he was riding on came to its destination, he got off to get a bite to eat and use whatever restroom facilities were available. Since he wasn't in complete control of his traveling accommodations, he decided to buy several sandwiches and bottled drinks at each stop to tide him over, and he hopped another train going west.

He couldn't shower, and he didn't want to shave. He wanted to conceal his identity in any way possible and get as far away from his roots as he could to start a new life in a new place.

He wouldn't be able to follow his trade as a butcher. They would be looking for that. He'd have to find a new occupation. Whatever it would be, he would have to put a hold on what he really enjoyed until he became familiar with his surroundings. Whatever he chose, he needed to avoid falling into the same trap that had forced him out of New Orleans.

Pondering the most recent events in his life, he wondered how they had become aware that he was the one. It was impossible to know unless someone had been watching him for a very long time.

The only mistakes he knew he'd made were to allow someone to take and examine his DNA.

For years, he rightly suspected people had him under surveillance. This was the main reason he became careful about hiding his activities. The only possibility for them to have additional information that would implicate him in the crimes was if they could get hold of his medical records.

He suspected that there was a conspiracy of sorts, composed of several people who were spying on him. Looking back through his life, he could think of a few.

There was Coleen, a woman who spent a lot of time with them over the years. He suspected her long ago, especially when she attempted to change his ways. It was also obvious that she had some connection with his psychiatrist. She even sounded like a psychiatrist at times.

Stu was another key suspect. He spent a lot of time at the house for no apparent reason. Being leery of him for years, he became certain of his involvement when he attempted to get someone into his apartment to "help him clean and work in the garden." Did Stu think he was stupid, or what?

Finally, there was Dr. Pelleck himself, a person who tried everything he could to trick him into revealing his true personality. He was a spy of the first order, and he was sure that Coleen and Stu had something to do with Dr. Pelleck's prying questions.

How were they familiar with some of the things they knew about him, unless they were all working together? And when it got right down to whom he could trust, he didn't think he would even put his mother in that category. She, of all people, may have arranged it all.

Now determined to never allow anyone to get close to him again, he was going to be especially careful in the coming years. With a new identity, he would be ready to start all over again. No one knew him where he was going, wherever that may be, and he didn't want to know them. He would find his niche and plan his activities until they were flawless.

* * *

In their now-defunct New Orleans office, Stu and Coleen were in the process of making sense of Lance's life. With mixed feelings about what they had done, they were certain they never would have signed on to the project, had they known its true nature.

Stu, Coleen, and other employees at the clinic had spent half a generation with the experiment, and had very little to show for it, except for the legitimate activities they had been engaged in. They had helped enumerable people with their fertility problems, and this made them feel a tinge of decency.

Also, they had succeeded in recording the detailed behavior of a serial killer throughout his entire life. This was the first time in history this had ever been done. And while this information didn't help them in their endeavor to make a model citizen out of their subject, it was going to ultimately assist in the identification of similar psychopaths. Genetics Inc. would see to it.

Lance's life had been documented from his genetic predecessors on both his biological mother's and father's sides to the culmination of his heinous activities in his hometown, and this was bound to be of value in understanding future cases. Along with records from Special Agent Clayton about the identity of the victims and the details of the killings, it would be the most complete record of a person of that nature in history.

In their final discussion at the clinic, Stu and Coleen contemplated their new life at Genetics, Inc. and hoped what they had learned would, in some way, help right the wrongs they were witness to over the years.

* * *

At Genetics, Inc., near the Crescent City's riverfront, Hunter rejoiced in the fact that Adda's influence upon Lance was honorable, that there appeared to be no particular problems in the genetic cross that the mysterious director of the fertility clinic had made in terms of joining distantly related traits.

The cross had worked, and that was initially one of his biggest concerns when he was initially contemplating such an unnatural fertilization procedure. He remembered back when he evaluated the cross's potential and finally rejected it because of its unethical nature.

Yet, his inquisitive scientific nature told him that he was in some ways glad the experiment had been conducted. It had revealed the answers to many questions about the differences between early people and their contemporary counterparts, and it had provided information that could never have otherwise been gotten on a unique personality in serial-killer history. He thought about the consequences he would have to face had he carried out the experiment, and he wondered about the identification of the man who had the guts, no, the desperation to see it through.

It was unfortunate that the genetic make-up of Lance's biological mother and grandfather had complicated the issue, but it was, in some ways, fortunate that they would never have to report it. Before the cross and the rise of Lance Housler, skeptics would have insisted that the resultant offspring was destined for failure because of Adda's primitive contribution to the cross.

* * *

Special Agent Clayton was still optimistic that they would eventually catch Lance. She never gave up hope, even though he had eluded them at a time when they had him almost in the palm of their hand.

Lance's picture had been sent to every major crime unit throughout the United States, and he became an honored member of the top ten fugitives on the FBI's list. She wondered where he was now. She wouldn't be surprised if he would lie low for a while. Suspecting that things would be too unfamiliar to him to start his killings again, she reluctantly predicted that they would have to wait for his next move. Where and when that would be was anyone's guess.

Chapter 50

The Final Reality

In his dark and lonely apartment just north of the French Quarter, Hunter Bronson's longtime adversary, Alex Stanford, contemplated the problems of ethics, morality, and regret for taking on a new identity and setting his Fertility Clinic project and genetic cross into motion. The force behind his idea had arisen as a means of establishing a world-wide reputation in the field of science and as measure of revenge for being discredited by Hunter in front of the entire scientific community. Without that, his life on this planet was not worth living.

It was in the dark corners of the French Quarter, that he began to meet people who he suspected would be interested in a proposal of a very lucrative nature. Beginning with Foster Lawton, an investigator with a highly unscrupulous reputation, he talked at length about both the Fertility Clinic and a monumental scientific cross that would provide large amounts of money and respect from the scientific community.

Through Foster, he met Barry Burnstein, an equally unscrupulous lawyer, and a variety of shady people with excessive amounts of crooked money. As an attorney that had been involved in several mob-related cases, Barry was familiar with the ins and outs of problems concerning ethics and morality better than anyone else he knew of. In addition, he had made a good living at what he did.

"What's in it for me, guys?" he had said when first confronted with the initial proposal. "Come on, why would I spend my valuable time on something that won't fatten my wallet? I've been through all that altruistic crap, and I'm over it."

At that stage of the process, neither Alex nor Foster had money to invest in the business. They needed Barry and the people he knew to make it all work.

It was up to Foster to convince Barry that the business would eventually bring in substantial amounts of money. To accomplish this, Foster commenced by laying out the details of the genetic cross to him, pointing out the importance of the research and how it had never been done before. Barry became mildly interested.

"In addition to the cross," Foster said, "we'll have a well-established fertility clinic to assist other couples with fertility problems, which, by the way, is needed by many people. This is where the real money will come in. It's a win-win situation, and it will be the three of us raking in the major part of the money. We can't lose."

The part about the clinic having regular clientele and Foster's last statement was what caught Barry's fancy. He really didn't give a shit about a scientific experiment. It was the money he wanted. Alex left it up to Foster to work with Barry on how to get the monetary support they needed to commence their operation. He was a scientist, by god, and knew nothing about obtaining money for a project of that nature.

"I can't deny it. The project does intrigue me," Barry said. "I'll tell you what I'll do. I'll tentatively join with you to accomplish this task of yours, but I'll have to have a better proposal than the one you have presented to me so I can see where the money's coming from. If the proposal is sound, the three of us will carry this thing out. When you develop your final plan, get back with me.

When Barry was convinced the business had the potential to generate a substantial amount of money, he let it be known that he was in. His final statement though was that the best source of money to get the business started was the mob. "I've dealt with the mob before, and we can get whatever we need from them to start this business. While the interest will be a little higher than other sources, we'll be able to pay it all off in a short amount of time and still make a considerable amount for ourselves. After that, it's all clear profit."

This was the way it had all begun. With their devious scheming, Foster and Barry planned every detail of how they would carry out the business. The only responsibility Alex had was to sign a few documents made up by Barry, showing the mob that they would return the money they were borrowing, along with the interest that was required.

While they kept Alex's primary genetic project and his identify hidden from Fertility Clinic personnel, they set up the clinic with their main impetus on generating an impressive income for the three of them. Whether they helped a few people with their reproductive problems in the interim were not their concern.

Alex hated to admit it, but the experiment to use ancient sperm to fertilize a contemporary female had been a well-thought-out one. Yes, it had initially been designed by Hunter, but, in his opinion, he didn't have the guts to follow it through. In his crazed mental state, Alex imagined the project as yielding positive results, leading him to fame and fortune, in spite of what Hunter had done to him. If it worked, his name would go down as a leader in history and biology texts around the world.

While the experiment had been successful in certain respects, it had created a situation that could never be revealed. There was no way he could use it at this point to reestablish his reputation or even discredit Hunter. If anything, it put him in a position that further shattered his reputation, and Hunter would once again come out smelling like a rose.

Nevertheless, he knew that the money they had hoped to make was there, and his share would have been an ample amount for him to live off of for the rest of his life, possibly in a tropical paradise where the cost of living was much lower than what he was accustomed to. *Screw Hunter and screw paleontology,* he thought.

However, once the truth was out about Lance and the business responsible for his creation, he had no choice but to immediately leave New Orleans and get as far away from Hunter and the law as possible, leaving him to rely solely on the money accumulated in his Swiss account from the business established by Foster and Barry.

When he made calls to his two partners, neither answered their phone. When he visited their offices, he realized they had both departed. Upon attempting to withdraw his share of the stash, he learned that they had beat him to it, absconding with over six million dollars, and to his knowledge, they were nowhere to be found. He had been scammed.

As a final blow to his ego and well-being, he couldn't report it to the police, and a considerable amount of money was still owed to the mob for their initial loan, all established by his partners under his name. He now had to face his demise.

It was a sad day, indeed. With his energy ebbing at zero, his depression at an all-time high, and no money to pay his debts, there was no way to escape his impending doom. He picked up the gun that was the only instrument to give him peace, put it to his head, and pulled the trigger.

The End